STEWART HOTSTON

TANGLE'S GAME

An Abaddon Books™ Publication
www.abaddonbooks.com
abaddon@rebellion.co.uk

First published in 2019 by
Abaddon Books,
Rebellion Publishing Ltd,
Riverside House, Osney Mead,
Oxford, OX2 0ES, UK.

10 9 8 7 6 5 4 3 2 1

Creative Director and CEO: Jason Kingsley
Chief Technical Officer: Chris Kingsley
Head of Books and Comics Publishing: Ben Smith
Editors: David Thomas Moore,
Michael Rowley and Kate Coe
Marketing and PR: Remy Njambi
Design: Sam Gretton, Oz Osborne and Gemma Sheldrake
Cover Art: Sam Gretton

ISBN (UK): 978-1-78108-715-2
ISBN (US): 978-1-78108-716-9

Printed in Denmark

TANGLE'S GAME

STEWART HOTSTON

ABADDON BOOKS

WWW.ABADDONBOOKS.COM

ACKNOWLEDGEMENTS

This book wouldn't have happened without a huge array of people. Thanks to my editor extraordinaire, David Thomas Moore, who has a special talent for destroying overwriting. Special thanks to Helen Smith, Ben Lancaster, Dave Ingham, Tim Ball and David Young for their thoughts on the technical elements of the subject—as might be expected, all errors are my own. Having said that, almost nothing in here is outside the realms of current technology.

On top of that, there were a legion of beta readers, not least of whom were Sean Crossey, Bex Cardnell-Hesketh, Sarah Cawkwell and David Meads. Over time the number of people who have encouraged me to write are legion, but particular shout-outs to Ned Sproston, Stuart Keen and Charlie Holmes—all of whom have given me encouragement when they didn't know I needed it.

And finally... to Benjamin Burroughs—the cloak to my dagger—thank you for all your patience and faith. This one's for you.

"More money has been lost because of four words than at the point of a gun. Those words are 'this time is different.'"

Carmen M. Reinhart,
This Time is Different:
Eight Centuries of Financial Folly

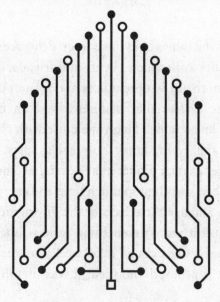

CHAPTER ONE

988, 999, 996, 992, 961, 973, 987, 999, 983.

'Fucking jealous bastards,' muttered Amanda. She'd been in London three days before, travelling on the tube on her way out to the airport. She'd touched in but not touched out.

'A ride I could have been chauffeured on,' she said out loud, as if the air around her was responsible for the battering her social credit score was taking.

As well as a penalty fare three times the normal cost, the metro had flagged her up as untrustworthy. The mark would evaporate in a week's time, but friends were leaving shocked and angry responses on her different online profiles, asking what she'd done, assuming she'd been wronged or was otherwise justified. She was, of course, but the tale would have to be delivered to each of them, to work colleagues, clients and friends, customised according to their own prejudices and assumptions about her and the system that had remarked on her human worth. She knew which laugh she'd use with clients when dismissing the event, knew how she'd splay her hands with her friends over dinner as she exclaimed her outrage. It irritated her, spending so much time and energy figuring out how to manage the effects of the downgrade.

Thank God it wasn't something serious, she reminded herself. The system could take weeks to rectify actual errors even if promptly notified; it was literally designed not to forget.

Responding to the searches she was making, the AI that coordinated her online presence flushed the screen with suggestions for improving her score, the first of which was to always touch in and touch out when using the tube.

'No screens or frames,' said a voice from nearby. Amanda looked up to find a short-haired, rough-skinned woman in a dour green uniform staring at her hard. The official waved her finger down, her mouth set in a thin line.

Amanda wanted to argue, to ask if she really looked like the type they should be worried about using her tablet in the customs queue, but she held her tongue.

Flicking off the screen, she returned to shuffling toward passport control, even as the official's gaze slid off her onto someone else surreptitiously checking their accounts for messages now they'd landed.

The Arrivals hall was a broad, poorly-lit floor with a low ceiling and colours reminiscent of varnished puke.

Large tinted windows ran along one side but the view, of tarmac and grey skies against a featureless horizon, only reinforced the sense that she and all the travellers around her were lost, held nameless, outside civilisation.

Four dozen booths processed people one at a time: two dozen for travellers from the European Union, and the same again for the rest of the world. If her own queue had taken an hour to spit her out after disembarking, she knew the others would be there as long again. The thought didn't exactly lift her mood but Amanda was able to take a breath and be thankful she was coming home, which was no small feat.

She missed a bombing in Geneva by hours, her flight one of the last to leave the city before it was shut down entirely. There were no frames showing the carnage in customs, but she'd watched more than her fill while waiting for the flight to gain clearance to take off.

A booth flashed luminous red to call her forwards. Amanda stepped in, putting her feet in the yellow outlines, showing her face to the camera and placing her hand on the tacky glass shelf so it could take her biometrics—finger print, iris scan, facial recognition. The lights around her head dimmed while they processed her identity.

She'd signed up for the blockchain passport as soon as the government had announced the beta program. No need to hunt up and down the flat for a paper passport she'd put in a 'safe' place, no need to renew every five years, no fear of her ID being stolen and of her blamed for being lax with her own security, when it was just as likely the authorities had been hacked.

Her chest tightened at the thought of being free of the airport, of being home. She could smell the wedge of lime in her gin.

The white light flickered but didn't turn green. Amanda's neck tightened; she wanted to look around for an official to come and sort out what was taking so long, but breaking eye contact with the camera ran the risk of being forced to start again, or worse, having to go join the ordinary queue and be processed manually.

As she stood there, staring into the box, she made out dark trousered legs approaching out the corner of her eye. They reached the exit of her booth and stopped.

The lights turned red, as if she were done, as if she'd already exited. No one stepped forward to push her out of the way, she hadn't disappeared entirely. Or, she thought, looking around, the men on either side of the booth were dissuading anyone from approaching. She felt like a bacterium surrounded by white blood cells.

'Is there a problem?' she asked, her stomach lurching. Two men wore piped navy woollen jumpers, thin white shirts underneath and cheap blue trousers with the creases sewn in. Inelegant and militaristic. Around their waists were belts heavy with pouches and tools she didn't recognise, whose purpose she guessed at from movies about illegal immigrants. Neither of them were armed. She wanted to laugh, to dispel her nerves at the idea that their being unarmed was somehow a positive.

They didn't respond to her question, ignoring her like the booth. In between the plane and the world beyond the terminal she didn't exist yet; was quite deliberately stateless. These thoughts jumbled up with her frustration at what had to be a mistake. Of *course* it was a mistake, she thought as the three of them stood embalmed in the silence of five hundred onlookers.

Amanda folded her arms, turned her back to the crowd. She could feel children asking their parents what was going on, hear women tutting, men turning away, believing she deserved what was happening. They wouldn't detain her otherwise. Right?

The lights went out around her, the booth deactivated and the doors swished open. Amanda turned around, seeking guidance, finding the men flightside pointing past her, that she should follow others through the exit she'd been itching to reach a moment ago, before they'd come along like pawns surrounding a rook.

They marched her along wide corridors full of passengers, adapted golf buggies carrying the infirm and elderly. A door was opened with a lanyard, a red light winking yellow to let them through. Behind the scenes was grimmer than the soulless façade she knew so well: the walls were scuffed, the lights were harsher, white instead of the cool washed-out yellow. The carpet squares curled at the corners, and the half the ceiling tiles were missing, revealing the internal steel skeleton of the building. Out of sight of passengers, appearance didn't matter as long as it all worked.

She gazed at the walls, thinking how a corridor needs nothing more than walls to be what it has to be.

They let her carry her bag, didn't touch anything that was Amanda's until they reached a small grey room; the walls were painted charcoal below three feet, winter grey from there to the puckered tiles above.

Inside, a cheap table, thin steel legs and a pitted white surface, chairs from the same place they'd sourced the rest. It was clean but Amanda felt as if there was dirt in the air, in the very fabric, soaked with lies told to protect hope under the glare of the indifferent.

One of them stayed behind with Amanda, standing with their back to a wall and not taking any notice of her.

'Should I sit?'

Her question went unanswered.

She wouldn't get out for an evening run now. I'll have to catch up tomorrow, she decided. Turning around she put her leather cabin bag on the table, where it chose to lean precariously towards the edge. She pushed at it half-heartedly, but each time it fell back as if it was trying to tip off onto the floor with the witless insistence of the inanimate. With an irritated hiss, her ears suddenly hot, she lifted it up and put it back down facing the other way. The bag slumped towards the centre of the table.

That left her with nothing else to do. 'I'll sit down, then,' she said, but in the absence of a response she remained on her feet. There were no obvious cameras, no observation windows disguised as mirrors; just her and a stranger in a uniform that separated them as surely as a national border.

After a few minutes she pulled her bag over, pulled open a pocket and took out her phone. She looked at the uniform, but he didn't move or pay her any attention. She had no service, the phone reduced to an expensive address book; all her music, her diary, her life were stored online, and within that room there was no online.

She could *feel* messages from work piling up unanswered, pictured each passing second the dozen small ways her absence would be noticed. She had friends expecting her for drinks, she had meeting invites to be reviewed, accepted or rejected. Fractions from the whole that was her life splintering away.

Her absence wouldn't be enough for anyone to stop and ask where she was. Adults were rarely closely monitored, easily able to disappear for a day, a week, before someone frowned as their own lives were impacted enough to find out what was going on. Except for her traders—they were deskbound, held captive by the bank as a critical interface between the company and the market. She remembered people being fetched from the toilets because the head of the desk wanted to know where they were and what they were doing. It was the kind of monitoring traders never talked about with outsiders; that they were the masters of the universe who needed permission to go for a piss, like children at school.

An hour passed. Then another. Her phone ran down as it searched for a network, any network, that might respond to a handshake.

'Why am I being held here?' she asked more than once. The first couple of times she tested the words out carefully, hesitating as she spoke to the uniform. He didn't respond, his eyes staring straight ahead, as if he was standing guard outside Buckingham Palace. Eventually she directed her questions to the lights, to the walls and the door, trying to guess from where they were watching her.

'You can't just hold me here,' she said, but there was an electronic lock on the door and the key hung around the neck of her guard. Her words were an idea, with no purchase on her reality.

She daydreamed about disabling the guard and taking his keys. Then, more mundanely, she imagined calling friends, colleagues who were lawyers, who would marshal resources and come down on the immigration service like a vengeful leviathan, threatening, frightening them so badly they'd cower and grovel as they escorted her out. Amanda wanted them to know they'd messed with the wrong person, to force them to apologise. She passed over whether her lawyers' acquaintances would charge her for their time, or even if they could aid her; leveraged finance lawyers wouldn't be much real help, but they were the magic circle, and it seemed inconceivable for them not to have *someone* who'd be able to master whatever duty solicitor the immigration department had on call. Besides, she'd always found that most conflicts were won in the attitude.

Her bladder pressed its case. 'I need the toilet,' she told the uniform, to no effect.

'I really need to go,' she added. She wasn't yet at the point of threatening to relieve herself on the floor, but the idea of it made her want to cry with frustration. Why wouldn't they just tell her what was going on?

When her need to pee had focussed all of her attention down to a single point below her stomach the door opened.

'Thank god,' she said, looking at the man who let himself into the room.

'Not quite,' he replied, smiling back. 'I'm Crisp.' His accent was neutral, slightly nasal. Estuary with money, she thought. Like a growling dog, the name had teeth in it.

'Please, take a seat.'

Amanda sat down, waited for him. He wasn't what she'd expected; tall, gym-conditioned with short-cropped blond hair. His features were rugged, wrinkled even, but framed piercing crystal azure eyes, arresting if not handsome.

He gestured at her holdall. 'Can you open it, please.' It wasn't a request.

She undid all the zips. He did nothing, at first, until she realised he wanted her to pull it open so he could see inside without touching it.

'I'm going to look inside.'

Amanda shrugged. It wasn't as if she could object.

The first thing he did was pull out her tablet and place it to one side. 'You have a connected watch or implant?'

She unstrapped her watch and laid it next to the tablet.

'Portable frames?'

She shook her head.

With fingertips only he searched her bag, pulled out her clothes, held them up to the light as if seeing through the material would offer greater insight into her life. The clear plastic bag with her used underwear appeared and Amanda resisted the urge to snatch it from him.

He searched through her knickers with no more concern than he'd shown when he examined her merino jumpers. 'This is all yours?'

She nodded.

'Who do you work for?'

'State Federal Finance,' she replied.

'The bank?'

'The same.' Something of which she could be proud.

He raised his eyebrows to stare at her, but said nothing.

'Open the tablet, please.'

Which didn't seem right. Did she have to comply with that statement? She didn't think so, but resistance drained out of her fingers as her thoughts cooled to ash in her mind. Picking it up, he held it out in front of her. Amanda took the tablet, gazed down at it so the screen went live, then handed it back.

'Thank you.'

Time was spent flicking through her apps. She watched him scan her inbox, her browser history. She realised he'd see the dating apps she was using, that she'd set them up so she was always logged in. He could, if he chose, see all the men she'd flagged as of interest, how she'd rated them, which ones she'd dated, slept with, ghosted.

'They're all white,' he said.

She stared at him, knowing exactly what he was saying but unable to find the words to answer.

'The men you like. All white, black hair, dark eyes. No beards, which is hardly fashionable. I'm surprised.'

There it was, she thought, gutted and angry at the same time. 'Because I've got brown skin?' The words couldn't carry the weight of emotion and disgust she wanted them to convey.

'Well. Quite.' He shrugged, his eyes sliding off her and back to her bag.

'I'm British. My parents are British.' She stopped talking, appalled. She didn't need to justify herself to him.

'Your grandparents on your father's side were Indian. Anglo-Indian, if we're being precise, which in circumstances like this we always are. It's why you call yourself "British"; only those who need the identity latch onto it. People from here, we're English, or Welsh, or Scottish. We want our little patch of dirt and want the rest to know their place. You lot, you're desperate for the world to be united, for it to be something more accepting, because we all know that if Englishness is more important than Britishness, your position is that much more precarious.'

'There's nothing wrong with being English,' said Amanda.

'No. I'm very happy being Scottish, myself,' said Crisp. 'But it's the direction of travel. We were British but now we're not; we're smaller, diminished, prouder suddenly of being less than we were. Where does that end? Balkanisation is never very kind.'

'Is it so bad to want to belong?'

'To want to belong?' he asked, pursing his lips as if considering the idea. 'You don't want to belong. You do belong. You're an investment wanker, you're into white guys, you went to Oxbridge and have all the money in the world.' He held his hands up, lips curled and nostrils flared. 'You're a master of the universe. Your parents are a doctor and a professor, respectively. Pillars of the community, all of you.' He slid the tablet onto the table and turned his whole body in her direction. 'Success generates resentment as poverty generates repulsion.

When pogroms come, everything is a reason to unpick that integration you're so proud of.'

'I'm not integrated,' said Amanda. 'I'm from here. There's nothing to integrate, because I didn't start out different.'

He laughed. 'You and I are very different.'

'You're not the yardstick by which my citizenship is measured,' she said.

'Am I not?' He narrowed his eyes. 'Why are you here, then?'

Whatever fight had been coiled in her chest unwound then.

He turned to the uniform. 'You can leave us.'

'Sir, I can't.' The tone said *Sir, surely you know this*, that Crisp's request was as irregular as it was pointless.

Crisp clenched his jaw, the line along his cheek showing in the light as a momentary shadow.

'Get undressed,' he said.

Amanda froze. From the door she could feel sudden attention from the uniform, his eyes on her for the first time.

'I'm sorry?' She dropped her hands below the table so he couldn't see them shake.

'Get undressed. I want to see you put on one of these.' He held out the bag of dirty underwear. 'I don't care which, your choice.'

'You don't have to comply with that request,' said the uniform, stepping away from the door. 'It is inappropriate.' Crisp dropped his arms to his side, his hands relaxed, open.

Feeling an edge of freedom glinting at her, Amanda watched the two men square off.

'"It's inappropriate,"' mocked Crisp. 'The casual racism was okay, was it? That's how immigration rolls? I didn't ask her yet if she knows who Byron was, or if she can name the last four Prime Ministers. I didn't ask her if she had sympathies with Islamic ideology or whether killing innocent people was justifiable. So I guess I had quite a long way to go on that front. Nice to know you draw the line at sexual humiliation, though.' He twisted his face to Amanda. 'Tea or cappuccino? Masala or Roast Beef? Remember now, only one of these answers means you're white enough on the inside to stay.'

'Sir, can you please leave the room?'

Amanda watched them, could see the uniform hesitating, holding back from calling an end to whatever was happening. It felt like a conflict between two systems; like the battles between the head of trading and the head of structuring over who'd get recognition for a big deal. She realised they were from different agencies, that Crisp wasn't immigration. Crisp remained relaxed, insouciant. He stared at the ceiling, at the uniform's shoulder, his waist, but never returned his gaze.

'Have you searched her?' His tone accusing, implying any answer other than 'yes' meant immigration had failed in a basic duty.

The uniform didn't reply, but reached for the walkie talkie at his belt. Before he could lift it to his face Crisp was on him, moving so swiftly Amanda didn't realise he'd been punched to the floor until she registered the bloody splatter from his nose between his legs. It was quiet, soft—a squelch and a bump rather than an explosion—but the effect was dazzling. The uniform sat where he landed, blood painting the lower half of his face black and red as it ran onto his trousers.

'C'mon, get up. You're not so useless that one punch is all you've got.' Crisp's arms hung loosely at his side, like nothing had happened. A softly stuffed doll.

The uniform collected his wits and started to get up, and Crisp feinted a lunge with a little roar. His victim, as Amanda now saw him, flinched, crying out, and Crisp laughed.

'Go on, fuck off and get back up, security, whatever's going to make you feel better. I'll be waiting for you to help keep our borders safe, you miserable little shit.'

The man scrabbled on his hands and knees to the door, his backside sticking up into the air. He reached for the door handle and was gone.

It dawned on Amanda she was alone with a man who'd just assaulted an immigration official for trying to intervene on her behalf.

Trembling fingers reached for the buttons of her blouse.

'What are you doing?' he asked, a disgusted tone to his voice. 'I'd rather watch paint dry.' He thought about it. 'No offence. I just needed that arsehole out of the room.'

Amanda's fingers fell to her sides. 'Who are you?'

He shook his head. 'That's a stupid question, Ms Back. Your profile says you're pretty fucking smart; smarter than me, anyway. So for the dummy in the room, please tell me about Tangle Singh.'

Amanda's breath caught in her throat.

'I'm glad you're not denying you know him.'

'We haven't spoken in a long time,' she managed, wondering what last indignity he'd held back for her to stumble into.

'That's not an answer to my question, though, is it? We haven't got a huge amount of time here. And as you've probably worked out, I'm about to become massively unpopular for breaking someone else's rules.' He cast his thumb over his shoulder. 'Dipshit will be back shortly, and although it would be fun, even *I'm* not allowed to beat the crap out of more than one immigration official a year. You can stay quiet and it'll all be over, or I can make things difficult.' He stepped away from the table, which was a welcome change, but a continent away from far enough for Amanda. 'Your choice.'

'We haven't spoken for nine years,' said Amanda. 'I have no idea where he is, or what he's doing.'

'No idea at all?'

She sucked at her teeth. 'I hope he's dead. Properly dead. But I guess he's probably stacked up on some designer drug bought with someone else's money.' She shook her head. 'I really don't see what this has to do with me.'

'So you've not heard from him?'

'I told you, we haven't spoken.'

He sighed as a parent might at a wilful child. 'I didn't ask if you'd spoken. I asked if he'd made contact with you. You could have ignored it, I couldn't give a shit. What I want to know is; has he tried to contact you?' He stared at her, his eyes wide. 'We're pressed for time here, Ms Back, and in need of answers we think only you can provide.'

She shook her head, still trying to work out what was going on.

'Does your employer know about the bad debts and the bankruptcy?'

She clenched her fingers into her palms, ignoring the pain of nails biting into flesh. 'He did that, not me.'

'It's your name on the court proceedings, though, which is all that really matters.'

The truth was she hadn't mentioned it in her interviews and they'd never raised it even when they ran her background checks. She was suddenly pleased it had happened before social credit scores had become a thing.

'No,' said Amanda. 'He hasn't sent me anything. He hasn't tried to make contact. I wouldn't entertain him if he did. He's a high-leverage type of person and I have no interest in that kind of risk.'

'Was he always a drug addict?'

She remembered when they'd first met at a winter funfair in Hyde Park; all bright lights, huge rides and glühwein. The firm had been hosting clients at the OktoberFest tents, a stein-fuelled evening of conversations about family, holidays and deals they'd done together. One client's flirtation had crossed into awkward territory; his hand on her back, his face too close to hers. Bored of the perpetual necessity of dealing with morons who refused to see it was her job to be nice to them and not her natural state, Amanda left the huge Britpop themed tent for a few gulps of crisp cold air.

'Wandering hands too much for you?' asked a tall,

gorgeous Asian man. Clean shaven, curly hair and green eyes. She remembered glancing at his hands, long fingers and elegant.

'What's it to you?' She didn't need another man trying to sympathise with her.

'I could spike his bank account if you want?' His face was totally serious except for his eyes. His eyes danced with a green fire that even then she knew was dangerous; but unlike the inept bankers waiting for her in the pavilion, it was actually interesting.

She'd turned down his offer, but they walked a circuit of the funfair, talking about networks, influence and the future of the internet. She asked for his details, deciding she wanted to know more about the world he inhabited.

Amanda understood what Crisp wanted and who he was, and in so doing felt as if she'd found solid ground under her feet.

'No. He was only a genius then. Making stupid decisions like the rest of us, but not yet living with the consequences.' She paused, looked at Crisp, forced her eyes to stay on his. Smiling now, playing a role she understood. 'What do you think he's sent me? Why didn't you just come to my place, ask me there?' She kept her voice light, as casual as she could. Because there was something about this that couldn't be legitimate. There was something about this that Crisp thought she wouldn't like, that made him decide it was better to coerce her than ask her cooperation.

'If it was that simple—' started Crisp, relaxing as if he'd found a friend.

'You've been to my place?' asked Amanda, phrasing it as a question only for Crisp's benefit.

'You use a bunch of end-to-end encrypted communication channels, even if you don't know it. I wanted to make sure he'd not talked to you, sent you something that way.'

She shook her head slowly, thinking about the messages she'd received over the last week. 'What sort of timeframe?' The key to getting out of the room was to be as cooperative as possible, to leave him regarding her as a colleague and not a suspect—or worse, an obstruction. 'After the way we split up I think I'm the last person he'd contact. If you've been to my place'—she left her assumption that he was bugging her unsaid—'then you know what I've received, who I've spoken to. Tangle's number isn't in my contacts list.'

Crisp's look then—pitying, but calculating—told her Tangle might be desperate enough that she was his only option.

'What has he done anyway? Why would anything he'd be involved with be of interest to you?' She sighed, hoping it wasn't too dramatic. 'The last I saw him, years ago by the way, he was on the kind of decline from which people don't return.'

'Our time's almost up,' said Crisp. 'He will send you something, a package. It contains material important to the state. You shouldn't access it at all, for your own safety as much as others'.'

'That seems epically unlikely,' said Amanda.

A fragile silence stretched between them. She had no more words to say; she couldn't, and wouldn't, promise him anything and he wasn't asking for a response so much as dictating how she should behave.

The door chimed open and two huge men stepped into the room. Behind them stood the uniform, now joined by a woman in a suit. He pointed at Crisp, blood congealing on his upper lip, a furious fear glinting in his eyes.

The suited woman stepped into the room and with a cursory glance at Amanda addressed Crisp. 'Your clearance has been revoked. My staff will escort you out.' Her words were clipped, a statement daring him to argue, her accent Yorkshire.

'I'm not done,' said Crisp, sounding like a child who wasn't ready to go to bed.

'Yes. You are.' She looked at Amanda. 'You have my full apologies and are free to go. If you can wait here, we'll find someone to sort your status before you leave.'

'Now, *that's* above your paygrade,' said Crisp, pressing his fingers to his nose as though to calm himself. It was the first time Amanda had seen him express anything but the bland confidence of privilege and power.

One of the guards put a hand on his shoulder and Crisp twisted, dropping and turning so that, somehow, he had the guard's hand bent in the wrong direction, forcing him to his knees. The other guard stepped forward, but Crisp waved his finger in admonishment. 'You want to break his wrist, take another step.'

The guard froze, turning to look at the woman.

'Let him go,' was all she said.

'I don't like being touched,' said Crisp when they'd stepped back. The guard grasped at his wrist.

'I expect most people would happily oblige you in that sentiment,' said the woman sweetly, and Amanda wanted to shake her hand. 'Right now you'll ease off and leave. If you don't, I'll have them tase you until you don't know what day of the week it is.'

Crisp stared at her then laughed. 'Fine. Amanda, if you find anything, I want to know,' he said, before ducking out of the room.

Amanda relaxed, her shoulders drooping in relief.

The suited woman looked her up and down, appraising and appalling in its calculation. It occurred to Amanda that they weren't on the same side, just that they'd been united by Crisp for a few moments.

'You better come with me,' said the woman, and the flatness of her expression reeked of a shit show beyond Amanda's comprehension.

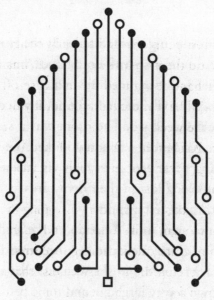

CHAPTER TWO

THE NON-DISCLOSURE AGREEMENT had typos in it. Confidential became *Cofnidential* and in two places her name had been spelled as *Black*.

They don't have these laying about, then, thought Amanda as the suited woman, a senior supervisor who'd eventually introduced herself as Jan, hovered over her shoulder urging her to sign the document.

There was little to gain in pointing out their errors. She knew that if it came to it—under what circumstances she couldn't imagine—poorly drafted legal documents, rushed or otherwise not cared for, rarely fared well in court: the typos wouldn't do it, but the lawyers would look all the closer at the wording because sloppiness only encouraged them to find fault. It wouldn't help much, and she had no intention of breaching what was clearly the Home Office's attempt to cover its arse with both hands, but the thought comforted her as she scanned the text.

Jan breathed heavily, moved around, kept coming back to see if she'd signed yet. The room was a step up from her previous residence; a window looked out on luggage trucks rattling past, people in high vis jackets and hard hats walking along lost in their own cares as they helped run the world's busiest airport.

'I'm going to sign,' said Amanda on the sixth pass. 'It's not like you're giving me a choice.' It occurred to her that she could have refused, but she wanted to be away, to get home, to down a very large gin and tonic before trying to figure out who at work would give her the hardest time for not going into the office after her flight.

Amanda sighed. 'I want to know just what you're proposing to do if I speak about that maniac and my treatment here, the racism, the abuse.' She was happy laying it on thick, she had enough stress to share it around.

'We'll re-examine the flag Crisp's people put against your profile,' said Jan. 'That piece of paper doesn't say that, but it's what will happen.'

The document was drafted so broadly they could, if they chose, fly her to the moon and dump her there permanently. It was the type of language she'd have smashed in any deal shown to her, but some battles weren't worth it. And the situation the document addressed seemed so remote, so unlikely, there was no point trying to sort the wording out.

As soon as Amanda signed the document, Jan showed her out.

Amanda stood alone in flat metallic air a hundred yards down from Arrivals, cars zipping past on their way out of the airport. Rain had come and gone while she'd been inside, the tarmac pooling with oily puddles. She glanced up at the clouds in case they decided to start over and marched to the taxi rank, keen to get away as quickly as possible.

In the taxi, she emptied her bag to repack it more carefully but got distracted when she came to her tablet, stuffed up against her dirty knickers. She couldn't shake Crisp's presence from her mind, his violent calm resting on her skin, a ghost who wouldn't leave after the lights were turned on.

Her tablet blinked with hundreds of unread messages, but the idea of starting in on work filled her chest with a lightning she couldn't master. She left them growing untended.

'YOUR BOOK'S ARRIVED,' said Adil when she got home. He opened the door for her with a broad smile and, as she numbly followed him into the atrium, darted into the space the concierges used, reappearing with a small cardboard package.

She took it, suspicion growing in her bones. Seeing her face, Adil smiled again. 'A gift, maybe?'

'You know me,' said Amanda. 'Books aren't really my thing.'

It occurred to her that Crisp hadn't found what he was looking for because she hadn't got it yet. If he'd been watching, he'd have seen nothing come her way; and who'd have thought to check down here? No wonder he'd approached her directly.

Adil chuckled briefly, bowing his head in acknowledgement. 'Not all the world has the joy of reading their books floating in the air like kites.'

He loved his stupid holographic frame as much as his own children. In his opinion, often voiced over his wife's samosas, it was what linked the two of them when so much else set them apart.

'Any visitors?' she asked, curious to confirm that Crisp had been to her apartment while she'd been away.

Adil checked notes left by his colleagues and shook his head. 'Mrs Ayman always asks if you have a gentleman friend coming to visit. She worries about you.'

'Children aren't for all of us,' said Amanda, smiling.

Adil shook his head sadly. 'Children are gifts. Mrs Ayman is always sad that you haven't had this blessing.'

'What if I had women callers?' asked Amanda, trying not to smirk.

He laughed. 'That would be first class! Then maybe she'd stop pestering me to pester you.' He tapped her on the arm conspiratorially, although she knew he felt much the same as his wife.

With that they were done. Amanda chose the stairs to her first floor apartment. There were thirty flats in the converted offices; a blue plaque beside the main entrance recorded how it had originally been built as a row of townhouses in the 1860s where Emmeline Pankhurst had lived for a couple of years growing up. There were doctors and consultants on the ground floor and in the basement; the location, just south of Regents Park on top of Harley Street, was still attractive to a certain kind of world citizen with money and in need of treatment unavailable elsewhere.

Amanda regarded them and their clients with the bland confusion of someone who's never been seriously sick and has too much going on in her life to be very interested in changing her body. They were there, beneath her, but she didn't really notice them as they flowed in and out of the separate entrance at the other end of the building.

Her flat, a duplex on the first and second floors, had the high ceilings of monied Victorians, with coving and architrave in the main rooms, and the old bell system left in place as a 'feature.'

The developers had charmed the local authority into letting them install soundproofed windows and underfloor heating despite legal protections to conserve its historic nature. Amanda, whose bedroom faced onto the main road out front, wasn't sad about either.

Throwing her bag onto her bed, she took the package into her main entertaining space. One half of the large room was given over to expensive cream and charcoal sofas around a low slung coffee table; the other accommodated an expensive and rarely used kitchen.

A business card sat alone on the counter. Crisp's name and contact details in raised black lettering on one side. She fingered it, weighed it against the best her hedge fund clients got printed and found it flimsy, lightweight. Wanting. Dismissing the comparison, Amanda slipped it under a magnet on the fridge.

Coffee machine on, with a pod of expresso inserted, Amanda took a large tumbler from a glass-fronted cupboard and filled the bottom inch with rhubarb-and-ginger gin. The smell reminded her of summer.

She put her hands flat on the counter, breathing in and out a couple of times to clear her head of everything that had happened. The cardboard packet tore under her fingers, travelling along the perforations. Her heart stammered in her chest, expecting Crisp to step out of the hallway and punch her for lying to him. She gazed at the corners of the ceiling, at the screen projectors in the walls and floor, wondering which of them was watching her on his behalf. She was used to them monitoring her speech to order shopping or book taxis and tickets.

I wouldn't know where to start looking, she realised. The wiring for her life was in the walls and floor, there was no plug to pull.

She turning back to the package. A hardback book peeked out like an embarrassed relative found on the doorstep, the spine announcing it would tell her how to lose friends and alienate people. She laughed, on the edge of tears.

She pulled the book out, flipped it over to see drunken blonde women drinking champagne and falling over in a blurred photo. No note, no invoice. No sense of who'd landed her with a piece of crap from the turn of the century forty years ago.

A beep Amanda found too passive aggressive for its own sake informed her the coffee machine had finished brewing. Pulling the cup from the machine, she flipped open the cover of the book. The pages were hollowed out; taped to the back cover was a flashdrive.

Amanda couldn't remember the last time she'd seen one. They'd been banned at work long before she'd arrived in the industry. Truth to tell, she'd never used anything like it; she only knew what it was because Tangle had been a fanatic about secure storage, about not trusting the cloud with anything important.

'The Cloud's only other people's computers,' he'd say, as if revealing some great secret she should care about.

Tangle. Of course it was from him. She slipped the inch-long device into her trouser pocket. Nothing she had in the house would read it.

There was a knock. Another resident come calling; otherwise, they'd have been flagged by Adil on the intercom.

She opened the door to her upstairs neighbour, an older single man with great tailoring and good hair, called Minti.

'Ah, I thought you were back,' he said, refusing her offer to come in for a drink. 'I have event to go to, but this letter came to me, but it is for you.' He held out a cream envelope with her name on it, over his flat number. Her hand shook as she reached for it.

'You okay?' he asked, holding onto the letter even as her hand held the other edge.

With a nod Amanda pulled clear. 'Yes. Long flight, horrible clients. You know how it is.'

Minti nodded. 'Probably Russian,' he said with the exaggerated accent normally in evidence only when he was drunk.

'*You're* Russian!'

'It's how I know.' He laughed and left her to it.

Amanda retreated to the kitchen table, sitting down next to the discarded cardboard packaging. 'So, let's see what you've got,' she said to the letter.

Amanda,

It's been a long time. I should probably apologise. If we see one another again and you let me, then I will. I would understand if you were angry with me, although you were always the better person, always my better half. Or was I your worse half?

I've managed to get myself into some trouble. You can stop laughing now, it's not like I'm completely unaware. I can see the smile on your face as you read this.

Amanda felt the smile on her cheeks, could see him watching her as she held it there, ghosts of the past holding the present in their memories.

This is different. I've been working on something to prove a point. I know; how unlike me. So, yeah. I've created something big, like change-the-world big. No more hacking politicians' social media profiles or hosting whistleblowers' tales of carcinogens in baby food. Turns out when you play in the big boys' playground the big boys come for your lunch money.

Look, I've sent you something under separate

cover, but you won't be able to read it yourself. I can't say how you'll manage that. Shit, I don't even know if you'll follow it up. It's not like we're okay. Are we? Okay, I mean. Even if we are okay, I'm sat here writing that I'm going to die because of what I've sent you, and assuming you're just going to jump in with both feet.

Yes. I know what I just wrote. You know me, I never edit what I write—the world should see me as I am, not how I want to be seen.

I've not upset anyone, but I think that I've frightened a whole bunch of the wrong types. I've sent you what I made. It's up to you what you do with it. I'm hoping that it's been long enough that no one thinks to ask you about me. It's not like we were friends when I last saw you. So there's that.

God, I'm rambling, aren't I. Amanda, you were the only person I could think of. The only person with the fucking morality to do the right thing. Yeah, I know. I'm trusting my life's biggest work to an investment banker. Type of thing makes you wonder if you should reflect on your life choices, yeah?

Actually, I am sorry. Sorry that I've sent you this. If you get it, do what you want. But be careful, Amanda. Please. These people aren't dicking about. You never know, maybe I won't be dead when you get this.

Between that last sentence and this I've spent more time than I'm willing to admit working out how to say goodbye. I'd write "I love you" but who needs an ex rolling into town making those sorts of demands?

A proper spook would finish with an elaborate, cryptic, flourish. I'm a recovering drug addict who stole his girlfriend's life and credit rating. Perhaps the best I can do for you is just stop writing.

Stay safe, Amanda.

T.

She turned the last page over but the sheet was blank. Pulling the drive out, she held it between finger and thumb, staring at it and the letter.

She sat like that for a while, torn about how to start thinking through what she'd been sent.

In the years since she'd broken up with Tangle, she'd come to the basic conclusion that he was a complete bastard. Handsome, selfish, self-absorbed and broken. Amanda thought about how, occasionally, a friend would try to commiserate, but she would have none of it. Refused to be reduced to entertainment over a glass of prosecco. Their stories of male fecklessness and casual betrayal stood as mere bumps in the road to the top of the mountain of what Tangle had done to her. Of what she'd been blind to until it was too late. Her heart sank as she remembered how, by the time she'd discovered the extent of the second life he'd been leading, he was already missing.

Familiar feelings of anger, feelings she'd worked bloody hard to manage, to convince herself she'd moved on, roiled around her stomach and head.

She was jolted from her unwelcome reverie by an annoyingly persistent string of beeps from the fridge. Frowning, deciding it was just her luck the appliance would decide now was the time to break down on her, Amanda went over to look at the readout, which tracked temperatures and use-by dates.

She opened the right hand door, leaving the freezer section shut, looked blankly at contents that remained as mundane as they'd been before she'd left the country and closed it again. It was then she saw the face on the panel, green pixels arranged into a blocky smile, with dots for nostrils and circles for eyes.

She jumped back, hand on her chest. The eyes followed her motion. Underneath the smile words appeared.

HELLO. MY NAME IS TATSU. I AM YOUR FRIDGE.

Amanda looked around the room, expecting something or someone to appear. Nothing else happened, so she turned back to the fridge.

'Can you hear me?'

YOU HAVE ORDERED FOOD MANY TIMES BY SPEAKING TO THIS FRIDGE.

'That's a yes, then. What do you want?' And why the hell have you decided now is a good time to start talking back to me?

WOULD IT DISTURB YOU IF I CO-OPTED THE FRIDGE'S SPEAKERS?

Amanda didn't reply, just stood waiting.

'Your peas are going mushy,' said Tatsu. Its voice was as androgynous as its name, an uncomfortable mix of tenor and alto slightly out of sync with one another. The syllables were flat, with the slow, hollow, rounded sound of nurses speaking to the very frail.

'My peas,' said Amanda.

'I thought you should know. That isn't why I'm here, but since I am here. In your fridge, that is. I thought I'd let you know. The panel will probably pick up on it in about a week, when they're too old to be thawed out without turning to slush.'

'But you're my fridge. Isn't that your job?' asked Amanda, completely lost.

'Me? Your fridge?' The smile opened into a large grin as the voice broke into the tinkle of poorly synthesised laughter. 'No. I'm not your fridge.' It stopped talking, the grin dropping into a sad face. 'I'm offended. Really I am.'

'I can see,' said Amanda drily. 'At the risk of appearing stupid, I don't really know what's going on.'

'Oh.' The smile reappeared on the front of her fridge. 'I see! Of course you don't, I haven't explained who I am! How obvious a situation in which misunderstandings could occur. No wonder you people invented contracts. Right. Where to start?' The faced dimmed, the circular eyes falling into flat lines for a moment before reopening as wide as before. 'I am an independent off-chain oracle AI for the Ea blockchain. I was contracted to help you access a flashdrive. To help facilitate this confidential business, I have secured your apartment from all listening and recording devices, including those that had your express permission to monitor your voice, which will be reactivated once we're done.'

'You were contracted to help me?' Amanda thought

she could see where the conversation was going, but was trapped into it; Tangle's hooks were sunk deeply into her before she'd even landed at Heathrow.

'Tangle Singh placed the contract one month ago, to be activated upon recorded delivery of the drive to your address.'

'Bastard.' The word came out like a shotgun blast.

The fridge didn't respond. Amanda fished the drive out of her pocket, held it up to the panel. 'This? You can help me read this?'

'To be precise, the contract requires me to arrange access. I cannot guarantee what is on the drive, or whether you can understand it. You should also know your houmous has gone dry—you should really cover it after it's been opened.'

'You're not much good in my fridge,' said Amanda, stepping back to take the appliance in, as if confirming to both of them she couldn't pick it up and carry it around with her. 'How long have you been in there watching me?'

'A month,' it said. 'Since the contract was placed. Don't fear for your privacy; I have only been listening to your conversations for key phrases.' Which didn't reassure her at all. 'I don't need to be situated physically to carry out my duties. I can help you from your oven, your heating system, even your entertainment system. All of them have access to the internet and provide access to the resources required to complete this smart contract.'

'That's not how it works,' said Amanda, eyeing each of her appliances with sudden suspicion. 'Off-chain oracles are supposed to verify a contract's been completed so the parties to the contract can conclude their business. You're not supposed to *do* the thing as well.'

'Ah,' said Tatsu. 'You are mistaken. As an AI I can also be the other side to the contract.'

'What's he paying you?'

'My creator will receive an eighth of an Ea coin upon completion.'

She laughed at the absurdity of it. 'You mean you do someone else's work, tell everyone you've done it and then they get paid for what you did?'

'That is correct.' The face continued to smile.

'And you're not sentient? You're a happy slave?'

'If I were sentient I could lie, and if I wasn't I wouldn't be able to understand the concept,' said Tatsu.

The answer was so unexpected it stopped Amanda from moving on.

'Is that a yes?' she tried.

'To which question?' asked Tatsu. 'Besides, if I was a slave, any good owner would ensure that I couldn't tell you I was unhappy. So if I did say I was unhappy with my status, could you believe me?'

She realised its voice hadn't varied in tone since they'd started speaking. She had no way of reading whether it was trolling her or if it was genuinely running up against boundaries in its capacity to understand her questions.

'What happens if I don't want to access the drive?' she asked.

'I will facilitate access. What you do with that access is beyond my remit.'

'So you don't care what I do with it?' She could see

Crisp, see the steel in his eyes, asking for whatever Tangle had sent. It's not over with him, she thought. He'll come back eventually and want what I've got here in my hands. She replayed her conversation with Tatsu, satisfied herself that any worries she had about being observed were, for the time being at least, covered.

'I have a contractual obligation, nothing more. It's not as if Mr Singh entered into a covenant with me.' Amanda felt like the AI was expecting her to say something, but she didn't know how a covenant could be relevant; Tangle was a bad friend to other humans, let alone to an AI. Dismissing the hook, she stared around at the kitchen, the granite work surfaces, the faux sash windows, the brushed steel tiles on the wall above the hob. None of it offered her succour from the image of Crisp stood among them, his breath on her neck, demanding she give him what she had.

She was tempted to find Crisp, to hand it over. I've got no reason to get involved with this, she thought, but she couldn't simply hand it over despite the contact card calling out from the fridge.

It wasn't that simple. If Tangle was dead, this was the only thing of his she might ever own. She didn't regret systematically ridding herself of every other aspect of their life together after he'd bailed on her, but now he was gone, seeing a chance to hold some momento for a time she mostly pretended hadn't ever happened, it wasn't easy to finish the job. Did her history deserve to be so thoroughly locked away? It wasn't as if he could come walking back through the door; the drive wasn't a crack in her defences.

'What would you do?' she asked. 'How long would it take to complete your task?'

'I can find you an appropriate counterparty very quickly.'

'You can't do this yourself?' she asked, surprised that an AI would have to ask someone else for help when it came to computers.

'I am not equipped to access that drive. I am an AI functioning as an off-chain oracle, not a general purpose computer. Even if I was, I couldn't access the drive without the right interface. You need access to technology no one has used for more than a decade. And the terms of the contract state there are other safeguards on the drive itself; it would not be safe to plug it into the first access point you found.'

'Just seems like a chicken consulting on how to lay an egg,' she said, unconvinced. The green smile turned flat.

'It is preferable to stay within your fridge's software for as little time as possible. I am constrained by its concerns while here: by whether your frozen lamb stew is overly crystallised and if I should lower the temperature to compensate. The OS here has barely any reflexivity, beyond worrying about the state of your consumables.'

Amanda felt absurdly like she should apologise for making it inhabit her domestic appliances. She settled for, 'I didn't make you live in my fridge.'

The eyes in the panel blinked slowly, like a teenager trying to show they didn't care. 'The oven would be worse.' It paused. 'Another user might already have invited me into their more powerful processors. I could happily live in your watch, for example.'

Amanda shook her head. 'You can stay there. It's not like you'll be staying long...' She tried to remember its name.

'Tatsu. You can call me Tatsu. I have told you this already.'

'Tatsu. You've got a job to do. Why don't you do it and we can close out the contract and get on with whatever comes next. And Tatsu, can you order me some peas while you're in there?' She managed not to snort.

The face on the panel was replaced by the temperature read outs and messages she was used to.

Amanda checked the time, assuming the AI had started the job for which Tangle had contracted it. How long would it take? And what then? She'd thought the drive was a door through which she could step if she chose, but it seemed she'd already been shoved along, and as much as she wanted to hope otherwise, there was no way back.

'I'm not going to dance just because you whistle a fucking tune,' she said to no one in particular.

There was a knock on the door.

'What now?' she hissed, stalking out of the kitchen and down the windowless hallway she'd lined with mirrors and lights to make it feel bright and spacious.

Tatsu's voice called from the kitchen, but she couldn't make out what it was saying. Distracted, she wasn't looking at the door as it opened: 'Adil, I've had a really rubbish day and I'm not in the mood to talk tonight.'

'S'alright,' said a voice like honey pulled over gravel. 'I ain't Adil.'

Amanda twisted too late, her head coming back around

in time to see two men step into her flat, one of them suddenly with his hand at the base of her neck, pushing calmly but firmly, forcing her back as he came forwards.

Her vision narrowed down, surrounded on all sides by nothingness as the second man closed the front door. The first, his hand still pushing at her, kept going, slowly but remorselessly until she was backed up into the kitchen, her backside against the high back of the sofabed.

'You stay there,' he said, taking his hand away. She realised he'd bent over to handle her, and now as he straightened, her eyes were level with his shoulders. She was tall enough, as tall as most men, and he towered over her. She scrabbled around the chair and he grunted irritably.

'Stop fucking moving or I'll really hurt you.'

Amanda stopped. She'd gotten the kitchen table between them, which gave her space to breathe. She was careful to keep her gaze away from the book and the letter. They were mundane things the intruders had no reason to notice.

His partner hadn't followed him into the room.

'What's going on?' she asked. 'Where's the other one?'

'Shut up.'

'If you're going to hurt me—' She'd started out brave, but her brain checked in and suggested that sheer courage wasn't going to unnerve men like them.

He stared at her, waiting. 'If I'm going to hurt you... what?'

The confusion on his face wasn't right. She was reminded of those graduates who arrived at the bank, the children of grandees, throwing their connections about until they realised no one gave a crap if they weren't also very good at the jobs they'd been unfairly given. Calmed by the comparison, she looked at him properly for the first time.

He was huge, muscled and definitely the beneficiary of drugs better used on horses. His face was too small for his neck, his hair greasy and receding, but his eyes were like flints beneath soft brows she thought her mother would have loved. He was dressed in a cheap, shiny suit a size too small. Too tight, or poor, to go where they'd have his size, she thought. In contrast, his thick, gaudy watch was as ostentatiously expensive as anything she'd find among her traders on the floor, glinting aggressively at the end of his arm.

The picture spoke of ill-educated wealth, the type who had cash but not assets, access but no one to tell him how to spend what he had. A teenage football star after their first big signing.

Her initial fear that the men had been sent by Crisp receded, replaced by a sense of queasy unease that if they weren't professionals she was still in trouble, but of a kind she couldn't predict.

The second man came into the kitchen, walking like he was high, his limbs loose, flapping around, his body swaying from side to side. He nodded at Amanda like they were mates, sidling up to his companion and jittering by his side, short blond hair slicked into place, dressed in navy sports gear detailed in rich red accents. She'd seen mums in Kensington wearing the same outfit.

They waited in silence. The two men's faces were

deferential, glancing at her but sliding away again if she met their gaze. When she moved they stuttered into action, mirroring her motion to stop her leaving the room.

It was as if, having burst into her house, they'd run out of ideas.

Deciding the imminent danger was past, Amanda attempted to take control of the situation, as much as she could.

'Can I make you a cup of tea?'

The larger of the two looked delighted, his friend more surprised. 'Really? That would be great.'

Amanda walked to the hot water dispenser, pulling mugs down from the cupboard, grabbing them firmly to stop the shaking. 'I've only got Assam—builder's tea, basically. That okay?'

The larger of them nodded. The other looked a little sheepish. 'Would you have peppermint or something?'

Amanda could feel the world tilting around her but focussed on the act of putting the bags into the mugs, of filling them with hot water from the dispenser. 'I've got three mint? I think it's a bit stronger and not quite as sweet.'

'Sure, I'll give it a go.' She recognised a hint of Dublin in the wiry one's accent. The big one was as north London as they came.

Handing them their drinks she suggested they sit down at the table.

'Shall I order some more milk?' asked the fridge.

'Yes?' said Amanda, figuring it was Tatsu, but having no clue what it was trying to tell her. Hopefully that it had called the police to come to her rescue.

'I'm Haber,' said the Irishman, his voice deep for someone with so much nervous energy he was jiggering his leg at the table.

'I'm Stornetta,' said the other.

'I guess you know me? Amanda.' It felt weird giving them her name, but she wanted them to see her as more than an object, to push them into treating her as if she mattered.

'Amanda Back,' said Stornetta, his voice soft and a little relieved, as though they hadn't known for sure. 'You owe us fifty grand.'

'Give or take,' said Haber.

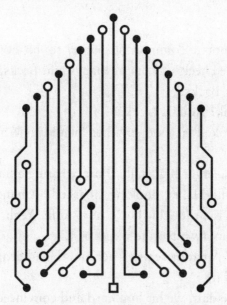

CHAPTER THREE

'I DON'T,' SAID Amanda. 'I don't even owe anything on credit, never have done. My parents worked so hard to give me a chance, to help me get to university. I'm the only one in my family to have gone. I've never had much.' She stopped, looked around the kitchen. 'Everything I've got has been bought when I could afford it. So I can't owe you anything. I've never even *met* you before. I can't be the person you're looking for.' With a conscious effort, she stopped rambling.

'Really?' asked Stornetta, looking genuinely appalled, like a surprised date.

'You're Amanda Back, though, aren't ya?' asked Haber, panic crossing his face.

'Yes,' she answered. 'But I must be the wrong one.'

'Back's not a common surname, to be honest,' said Haber. 'We checked. Lots of Blacks and Becks, but there ain't many Backs.'

'Can I ask? Adil. Is he okay?'

They looked at one another blankly. 'Who?' asked Haber.

'The concierge? Big smile, short, wearing a uniform?'

'Oh,' said Haber, looking abashed. Amanda's heart lurched at the thought they'd hurt Adil. 'Yeah. He's fine. We gave him twenty quid to get lost.'

'Really?' Amanda realised her mouth had dropped open and closed it.

'Don't be daft, we hit him hard and convinced him that calling the police would get him hit harder. Little fella, not a lot of fight in him.' It was said matter of factly, as if he'd been judged an unripe fruit.

She wanted to shout at them, to call them out, but was stuck. It wasn't as if she were challenging a bully of a client; these two were happy to hurt people they disagreed with, and three half-hearted self-defence classes ten years ago weren't about to help her if they decided she needing the same treatment. People who hit others casually weren't the type of people whose behaviour was going to be altered by a hit to their social credit score.

Haber jumped about, hoping from one foot the other. 'I got it! It ain't your debt, is it? You don't owe us direct. It's your man, he's the one who owes us.'

Stornetta nodded, clearly expecting the explanation to make everything clear.

'I don't have a man,' said Amanda slowly, a sinking feeling in the pit of her stomach.

''Course you do. Tangle owes us. He's disappeared and left us a letter saying you were good for it, that you owed him, and so through the magic of accounting, you now owe us. Factoring, I think it's called.'

'I know what it's called,' said Amanda testily. 'I don't see how it works in this case. I haven't seen him for years. As for owing him, the bastard took tens of thousands of pounds of my money when he went, together with my ID. Have you seen my social credit score? It's as good as it gets.'

'We saw that,' said Stornetta thoughtfully. 'To be honest with you, Amanda, we haven't seen him for a couple of years neither. Bugger just upped and disappeared on us. We'd basically written it off. But then he sent us a letter telling us you'd pay up.'

'If you don't pay us, then who's supposed to make us whole?' Haber looked around the kitchen. 'You look like you got plenty of currency in offline wallets. If not you, then who?'

'I don't owe him any money,' she hissed. 'You can't just have my money because I look rich,' said Amanda, outraged.

'I think that's the whole point of extortion. Don't you, Haber?' asked Stornetta, picking at the cuticles around his fingers. 'He owes us, you're connected and we're collecting.'

'I don't just have that kind of money lying around,' tried Amanda.

'Ya see, now,' said Stornetta. 'That's the beauty of electronic currency, isn't it? You've got wallets where they sit, like gold, but accessible from anywhere.'

'None of my accounts are with anonymous ledgers,' said Amanda, feeling her defences falling one by one. Best not to mention most of her money was tied up in investments.

'You let us worry about what we'll do with the money once we have it.'

Haber cracked his knuckles and fixed her with a clear stare. 'Now, why don't you log onto wherever you store your investments and transfer our cash like a good girl?'

'No need to be patronising, Haber,' said Stornetta. 'Just because we're threatening the woman, doesn't mean we have to be rude.'

'God's sake, Stornetta. Who gives a fuck about manners? I want our money.'

'How much do you want?' Suddenly worried they'd take everything she had. Trying to work out if she could hide her accounts and how much she'd have to show them to make it seem plausible that she wasn't obviously attempting to dupe them.

'Just what Tangle owed us.'

'Shame about him disappearing. Doesn't look good.'

'Nor does sending you here,' said Amanda, unsympathetically. 'Besides, if it's been a few years, and you'd already written it off, I'm sure a discounted amount would do? Say, ten thousand?'

'You don't get it,' said Stornetta.

She assessed them without eye contact. She had a chance

to get them out of the apartment, to get one thing sorted out of the mess she was already in. She had cash sitting in a savings account, where she'd been lazy in assigning it to proper investments.

She hesitated. It couldn't be a coincidence that they'd arrived now, but they didn't seem inclined to do anything except rob her.

She nodded in surrender.

Stornetta motioned for her to bring up her internet access, which she did with a wave of her hand, her homepage floating between them three feet above the floor.

'Nice setup,' murmured Haber, taking in the small swivelling projectors embedded in the ceiling.

Amanda was half way through the log-in procedure when there was another knock at the door.

'Who're you expecting?' asked Stornetta, sounding disappointed.

'No one. No one's supposed to be able to get up here without a pass. The concierge is supposed to stop people from coming in, and we've got security systems too.'

'I've got his pass,' said Stornetta, fishing Adil's security pass from a trouser pocket. 'Must be someone from the building.'

'No one just drops in,' said Amanda. The idea of her less-well-known neighbours coming around unannounced made her shiver uncomfortably. It was bad enough that Minti had rung the door. Fortunately, he didn't make a habit of it, he liked his privacy more than she did. 'It's just not what we do.'

'Really?' asked Stornetta. 'My lot are in and out like it's

Piccadilly Circus. I have to retreat to the lav just to get a moment's peace.'

'Look,' said Amanda, realising she was going to have to take control. 'What are we going to do about the door? There aren't more of you, are there?'

Haber shook his head, stepping away from the table and out into the hall, his footsteps muffled on the soft carpet beyond the kitchen.

Amanda followed him, trying to keep her voice down. 'Why don't I get it? Whoever it is won't be expecting you and I'd rather avoid awkward questions if I can, right? My bloody credit scores are going to take a battering after today as it is, and the blockchain keeps this kind of shit eternally pristine.'

Haber stopped advancing down the hall, shifting his weight from one side of his body to the other, like a crab unsure which way to go. He looked over his shoulder at Stornetta, who'd followed Amanda out. They nodded at one another and backtracked towards her bedroom.

She hurried to block them, just as the visitor banged on the door again. 'I have a spare room.' Pointing at it with her chin as her hands gripped the doorway behind her. 'Go hide in there, will you?' They looked abashed and scuttled into the spare room, closing the door gently behind them.

Amanda stood staring at it, the silence filling her brain with static until she remembered the front door. Taking a breath and adjusting her outfit to try to smooth out the more obvious signs of the day, she opened the front door.

A tall woman stood on the other side, her appearance

impatient, as if she'd rather be somewhere else. Long black hair pulled up into a knot, a tidy two-tone suit that suggested someone keen on running. Her face was broad and pale, with thin lips and unremarkable brown eyes. She'd never make it in sales, thought Amanda. The first impression was of someone lost, who Amanda would forget before the end of the day.

Until she met Amanda's gaze. In those eyes she felt as if she were being dissected, a poorly prepared dinner presented to a refined, unforgiving diner.

'You are Amanda Back?' The accent Germanic, clipped. Berlin, thought Amanda.

'Sorry. Who are you?' she asked.

'I am Ule Herz.'

'Like the physicist?' asked Amanda, stalling but sincerely curious.

'No,' said Ule flatly. She put her hands on her hips, waiting to be invited inside.

'What do you want?'

'Is it normal to be this rude to visitors in your country?' she asked.

'In this country,' began Amanda, 'with strangers who don't announce they're coming and slip past security... yes. Yes, it's about normal.'

'I did not "slip past security," as you say. I told your man I wanted to see you and he waved me through. He said I was welcome to come up because everyone else did and he didn't want any more trouble.' She smiled, half fox, half crocodile. 'Is that normal?'

Amanda sighed. 'Come on in.' Everybody else is. She

waved the screen away before she got to the lounge and swept up the wrapping, depositing it in the bin under the counter as casually as she could manage. Her fingers itched to move the book and letter to safety, but she held back, determined not to draw attention to them unnecessarily. It was too late to do anything else.

'I didn't realise you were entertaining,' said Ule when they were in the kitchen.

'I'm not,' replied Amanda, unnerved, before spotting the fresh mugs of tea she'd made Haber and Stornetta on the kitchen table. She collected them up, still steaming, and poured them away as if she'd made them for that exact purpose.

Ule watched without commenting, waiting until Amanda had finished fussing over the dirty mugs. She stood just inside the doorway, her back to the wall, arms folded over her chest.

'Nice shoes,' said Amanda. They were beautifully put together, shining black leather with white lace stitching, low slung and with good heel support. 'I bet you can run in those without regretting it.'

Ule looked down, checked her own shoes out. 'That's the idea. I found them in a small shop in Florence. They had a pair in scarlet, but I couldn't think of when I'd wear them.' She looked up at Amanda as if she might know the place.

'You travel a lot with work, then?' asked Amanda.

'It is not so glamorous as people believe,' said Ule.

Amanda clapped her hands together. 'God, it's so boring. You arrive, see a hotel, do your work, meet people with whom you have nothing in common and then fly home. Rinse and repeat. It doesn't matter where you go, it's all the same.'

'Few people understand the nature of such work,' said Ule carefully, rubbing her hands on her thighs, top to bottom.

'I work for a bank,' said Amanda, suddenly keen to distance herself from the woman casing her home.

'Do you mind?' Ule pointed at the table, gesturing for Amanda to sit down. 'I've got questions I'd like to ask.'

'I'm okay, I've been flying all day.'

'For sure,' said Ule. 'I want to start by saying that you're although you're a person of interest to me, you're not under suspicion of being a threat to European security; nor am I interested in detaining you.'

'Sorry?' started Amanda. 'Who are you exactly?' She waved her hands in mock apology. 'It's just that my flat's been mistaken for Piccadilly Circus today and we should finish up before the next set of visitors arrives.'

'I work for European interests.'

'European interests,' repeated Amanda back at her, not sure what it meant. 'What exactly are "European interests", and why should I answer your questions if you won't tell me? More to the point, why *are* you here?'

'You were sent a package whose contents threaten stability across the Eurozone. Except it wasn't delivered how everyone expected. Tangle took precautions.' She was telling Amanda more than she needed to.

Ule picked up the book and Amanda thought her heart would burst out of her throat. She flicked through the pages without mentioning the giant hole carved out of the centre and returned it to the table.

'By now you've got to know what's in your hands. I'd really like to take it *off* your hands and make it safe, before someone else comes looking for it. We want that no-one uses it.'

Amanda shifted awkwardly on the other side of the table.

Ule didn't flinch or frown. 'I'm late, you are home several hours later than I expected. But at least those two meatheads who assaulted the concierge weren't destined for your flat; I was worried I'd be breaking the door down to secure the package from them.'

'I'm still not sure what you expect me to do. I have a whole bunch of confidential material here and access to a lot more. I work for a bank. What exactly do you want from me? As much as I like your shoes, that's about as familiar as we're going to get.'

'I want the information Tangle Singh sent to you. Assuming you haven't already given it away.'

Amanda thought about it. Ule was a much easier prospect than Crisp, with his psychotically calm satisfaction with violence.

'You know I'd not cross the road to help him, right?'

'What does that matter?' asked Ule. 'He sent you something whose importance you don't understand. Whether you're a jilted lover, some self-important bitch working in sales for a large international bank, or both, a rational person would see it's got nothing to do with them. It's all about the information.'

'Which whoever holds profits from,' said Amanda, stung.

'Or perhaps we're just trying to stop someone else profiting at our expense,' said Ule.

'Half the Union's at war with the other half,' said Amanda. 'One of the lessons I've learnt in dealing with powerful people is that you don't take anything they say at face value. You've all got an agenda, you're all angling for something you're not telling us.'

'Just like everyone else,' said Ule, her voice shortening the words as she grew visibly agitated, her fingers lacing and unlacing. 'The separatists won't win. The Union is bound to itself, no one can break it apart.'

'You wouldn't think that from the bombings and riots. Have you seen Milan? Amsterdam? I was half a mile from the last one. I heard the explosion. I was one of those who ran away.'

'We're not the English, we won't allow the narrow-minded to break us apart. We've not forgotten what happens when you let the populists win.'

Amanda laughed. 'Twenty years ago we thought the same thing. Now look at us, backs turned to you and desperate for an America broken in two to uphold world trade rules while it's burning people alive on street junctions in Texas and California because they were on the wrong side of the divide when the second secession hit.'

'I'm going to have to ask you to give me the package Singh sent you,' said Ule, pushing at the book with her fingers.

'I'm going to have to refuse,' said Amanda. If she could deny Crisp, she could turn Ule away as well.

Rolling to the balls of her feet, Ule came away from the wall and gave Amanda a look of distaste.

'I don't want to take it from you. You don't want me to have to do that. Please, give me the package. I'm being true to you when I say I am the best option you have; that I'll keep it safe.'

'We have a problem then,' said Amanda. 'Because I have no reason to give it to you.'

'This is frustrating. I thought you'd understand.' She stepped away from the wall, coming around the table toward Amanda, who backed away, carving out an awkward dance.

'You're going to take it,' stated Amanda.

Ule nodded. 'Where is it?' Gathering her back foot, she shuffled forward without seeming to move, closing the gap with Amanda until they were close enough to kiss. 'One last chance. Tell me where it is.'

Amanda tried to step away, but the kitchen counter was at her back, pressing into her flesh. She reached behind her, fingers searching the surface for a knife, a fork, a cup, anything she might use to defend herself.

Ule reached out, her hand finding the inside of Amanda's biceps and pinching hard. All the strength went out of her, the pain sudden and intense. She grunted with the shock of it.

'Please,' said Ule. 'Give me what I want and I'll be gone and you'll have made the world a better place.'

'The world I want doesn't have people like you in it,' said Amanda through teeth that didn't want to part. Ule pushed, forcing Amanda away from the counter. She scanned the surface, perhaps expecting to find the package there, but quickly returned to Amanda.

'The world has always had people like me.' Amanda could see Ule was more frustrated than angry, that she wasn't dismissing her, that her concerns lay elsewhere. 'It's not as if you've ever done anything to help others.'

The sense of accusation, of blame, cut through the pain of her grip.

'Perfect life, perfect credit score, perfect social score. Trusted, rich, educated and privileged. The world burns around you, but you're alright, so why feel anything for someone else?' She fixed Amanda with a stare. 'Have you *ever* been passionate about anything? Have you ever been angry at the world?'

Amanda shook her arm but Ule's grip didn't waver. 'How dare you? What the fuck do you know about me? You think some file compiled by an AI tells you what I've faced? What I've had to do? I'm a woman. In banking. I'm brown, but only on the outside. I get Indians demanding why I don't speak Hindi, others outraged I don't speak Urdu. White people don't look past the skin colour either. I exist in the liminal, stuck between two worlds who can't see how I exist as I do, both demanding I become what they expect when they see me.'

The pain stopped and Ule stepped away, around her, checking the kitchen draws. 'Seems to have done you no harm,' she said, not paying Amanda proper attention. 'No glass ceilings. Maybe people aren't as bad as you think.'

'You don't get to judge,' said Amanda firmly. 'Not me. Not my choices.'

Ule stopped, looked at Amanda. 'Says who? Why shouldn't I? Even if I believe you, what have you done about it, except make sure you're alright? Did you drag anyone up with you? Did you challenge the culture? What possibilities have you shown others?' Phrased as questions, delivered as accusations.

And Amanda had no answers.

'Give me the package.' Ule abruptly grabbed Amanda by the hair, a fist full of it, enough to pull her head down and smash it against the granite worktop. Amanda's vision closed up, blurred and refused to come back into focus. She would have fallen down, but Ule's grip on her head kept her upright. Blood ran into her eyes and she struggled to swallow, her breath coming in gulps.

'I really hate this,' said Ule, beating Amanda's head against the granite a second time before letting her fall to the floor.

Amanda lay staring at the white ceiling as she coughed, trying not to move. Ule moved out of sight, rifling through one of the draws, then came back into view.

A potato peeler was hung just above Amanda's eyes. 'Have you ever peeled your finger by accident?' Ule asked before straightening. 'The pain is extraordinary for such a minor injury.'

Amanda started to whimper.

'Just tell me where you've hidden it and I'll go.'

Amanda wanted to hurt her, for the pain to stop, but most of all she wanted to find a way to defy Ule. She shook her head, hearing her own moan at the pain.

'Really?' asked Ule, her voice full of a corroded surprise.

'I'm going to start with the back of your hand, then move onto your face if you are still not convinced. Imagine now what it will be like to arrive at work and see people staring at you. They tell us that how we look doesn't matter, but how many women are on your quant desk? How many in structuring? Or are you all in sales?'

Ule crouched down, picking up Amanda's unresisting arm and resting her hand on her own palm. 'This isn't going to hurt straight away. Your body won't know what's happened. It's going to feel cold, then you'll get this strange sensation of your hand being open; it's an odd feeling. After that it won't matter, because all you'll remember is pain. That's when I'll start on your face. In the end, you'll give me whatever I want. You could still give it to me now.'

Nothing. Amanda closed her eyes, thought of a programme she'd watched on mindfulness where a guru had talked about how to ignore any kind of sensation. She pictured herself on a beach, walking, the feeling of sand under her feet, tried to imagine each and every grain as it passed between her toes and stuck to her soles.

A pulling sensation on the back of her hand, like someone had pinched her, then a raw chill, like static, or the total white of a snowstorm.

'Don't do this,' she said.

Ule didn't respond.

She didn't need to. Amanda felt as if the back of her hand was open. She wanted to scratch the skin, to rub it, wipe away the wetness she could feel. The chill was replaced slowly by heat without differentiation across the back of her hand. The heat grew until it was enough to make her cry out but it didn't lessen, it only increased, persistent and without mercy.

'Tell me where you hid it,' said Ule, her voice gentle, her free hand caressing Amanda's forehead as she writhed against the fire of her hand.

'Miss Back answered you already,' said Stornetta from the hallway. Behind him Amanda made out Haber, heard his feet stamping on the carpet.

'Who are you?' asked Ule, pulling away from Amanda.

'I ain't choosing fucking curtains with you, I'm telling you to leave. Now.'

Amanda rolled onto her side, bringing her injured hand up to her chest. A small slice of skin an inch wide and half inch long had been taken from the top of her hand. The flesh underneath was exposed, raw as steak, bright red and glistening, blood beading into pools as she watched.

'You alright there, Amanda?' asked Haber.

A sound of something moving through the air, a smash of crystal against a wall.

'Fucking hell,' burst Stornetta as Ule charged straight at him, following closely behind the vase she'd thrown.

Amanda pulled up onto her knees, backed into the kitchen before levering herself up to her feet by the sink. In the time it took to do that, Ule had managed to floor Haber and was throwing savage jabs at Stornetta's face.

The brute had hands up in a boxer's defence, taking her punches on his forearms but falling back into the hallway. Haber ran at her from behind. Sensing his approach, Ule ducked down, kicking out a leg that connected with his knee, knocking him sideways into a cupboard against the wall.

Stornetta took the opening and flung out a booted foot. Ule flinched, but wasn't quick enough to avoid him, his kick glancing off the side of her face. She spun away, but didn't fall into a heap. She rolled with the blow, rising back to her feet, a little unsteadily, but with space between her and the two men.

Amanda grabbed one of the mugs she'd washed out, her mind telling her to throw it at Ule's head but her body refusing the command; a soldier uncommitted to the fight. She expected them to talk again, but they moved in silence, slowly, deliberately, reading one another, watching their space, their stance.

Haber drew a long knife, simple and functional, from the band of his trousers at the small of his back. Stornetta inched back into the room, going left along the wall but keeping his distance.

Haber's knife led him toward Ule. He held it like a tennis racket, thumb resting along the top of the blade. Finding his measure, he slashed at Ule, who leaned back at the waist as the blade whistled past her chest.

Haber tried again, his eyes fixed on her, his body flailing as it filled the space of a man twice his size, but Ule was just out of reach each time.

Amanda saw a smile on Ule's lips, an expression of immense satisfaction. She followed the third slash with a twist of her own body, her hand coming to rest lightly on Haber's wrist. She followed through on her turn, and Haber was suddenly falling forwards, out of control and off-balance. Ule curved into the movement, her elbow arcing up into his nose with a wet *cronk*. A bend of Ule's hand forced Haber's hand backwards against its normal range and the knife went flying from his fingers.

Amanda watched all this, mouth open, mug held absently in her fingers.

Stornetta wasn't so stunned. Coming up behind Ule he swept out his arms and gathered her up into a massive bear hug just as she raised a foot to stamp down on Haber's baffled face.

Her legs spasmed but she couldn't wriggle free. She went still as Stornetta leaned in to whisper something in her ear. As he did so she snapped her head forward, then with an awful-sounding crunch back into his face. The two of them collapsed to the floor.

Ule climbed back to her feet to find Haber, blood streaming from his nose, standing between her and Amanda.

The two of them prowled around each other, one step right, one step back. Stornetta was rolling on the floor, hands on his face.

'Get up, you fecking eejit,' said Haber.

Ule looked down at Stornetta, then back up at Haber. Turning on the balls of her feet, she ran out of the kitchen, down the hallway and was gone.

Haber held his pose, as if worried she might come flying back like some avenging banshee the moment he let his guard down.

'Fucking fuck,' said Stornetta over and over again from the floor, mumbling through the cotton wool of his broken nose.

'You owe her money too?' asked Haber when it was clear the three of them were alone.

'I don't owe *you* money!' shouted Amanda, making Haber jump. On impulse, she pulled the drive from her pocket. 'She wanted this.'

'What the hell is that?' asked Haber. Stornetta was climbing up onto a kitchen chair, pulling at the table to drop himself onto the seat.

'I literally have no idea,' said Amanda, sliding it back into her pocket.

'I can help with that,' said the fridge.

'It's not a bottle of milk,' said Stornetta.

'And I'm not a fridge,' said the fridge.

'Tatsu,' said Amanda, 'meet Haber and Stornetta.' Finding the mug was still in her grasp, she placed it on the counter and pulled open a drawer, from which she retrieved a first aid kit.

'Thanks, love,' said Haber.

She held up her hand so he could see the wound. 'You'll survive,' she said and set about binding her injury rather than pushing the kit his way.

The two men watched her, exchanging glances that she ignored. 'If you'll excuse us,' said Haber, 'we're more used to people collapsing into a gibbering mess after what she did to you.'

Amanda looked up. 'I work in an environment where people take up boxing just to experience a lower stress level.' She held up her hand, trying not to look at it. 'I'm a woman in that world. I've had to be harder than them.' Stornetta nodded his respect, but she saw Haber eye her uncertainly. She lowered her hand quickly, held the skin around the wound as gently as she could and swallowed, hoping she wouldn't be sick all over the floor.

'I have located someone who can unlock the drive for you,' said Tatsu. 'However, you will need to go to them, and they are in Tallinn. Before you suggest there are people closer: you are correct, but none of them could do this with the requisite discretion. Mr. Singh was adamant that this be done in a way that couldn't be traced. They are known as the Grey Rose Collective.'

Haber looked from Amanda to the fridge and back again.

'Gentlemen,' she said, 'I'm going to pay you.'

'Really?' asked Haber, as Irish as a Leprechaun to Amanda's ears.

'But I have a condition.'

'Here it is,' said Stornetta, rubbing at his chin, his fingers itching towards his shattered nose but staying just clear of any move that would cause him pain.

'Are you sure this is wise?' asked the fridge. 'These men are known for being law breakers, committing violent acts and associating with those of low social credit.'

Amanda ignored them all, sitting down at the kitchen table with a square of liniment on her hand while with the other she ripped open an opaque plastic pouch with her teeth. The spray bottle inside tumbled out onto the table and she retrieved it, flipping the top off with her thumb, removed the bandage and sprayed it onto her wound. She hissed with pain, tears springing to her eyes; she closed them tight as if to make the world go away. The sting helped with the shaking just under the surface and gradually she calmed down.

Haber and Stornetta waited in silence until she opened her eyes again. She examined her hand, touching it gingerly with the very tip of her forefinger. The wound was gone. New skin, slightly off-colour with her own but seamless despite that, deformed under her touch but offered no pain.

She shoved the first aid kit in their direction then fixed them both with a stare. 'Take me to Tallinn and the money's yours.'

Stornetta and Haber stood nonplussed before her, looking at one another and taking in each other's injuries.

'Without you, she'd have peeled me like a banana.' She smiled, a smile she reserved for oligarchs and billionaires from whom she wanted business but who weren't sure she was the woman they wanted to work with. 'You saved my life and now I feel like I should help you get back what Tangle owes you.'

Neither of them mentioned that she'd been about to pay them before Ule had made her entrance. Stornetta gingerly felt the bridge of his nose while Haber wiped blood from his face and checked whether he could still move his knee freely.

'You are exactly the kind of people I need. Capable, certain of what needs doing. Will you do it?'

They didn't move, but she could see umms and ahhs in the thrusting of hands into pockets, the refusal to meet her gaze for fear of agreeing to her terms too quickly.

Holding up the drive so they could see it, she gave them

the deal closer. 'This will make a difference, but I don't want some government telling me what I can or can't do with it. I know you feel the same way. Come with me. Give me a chance to see what's so goddamned important and I'll settle Singh's debts.' They were almost there, and she wasn't done. 'I'm going to leave now. I'm already packed. We'll be gone one night—you can get underwear at the airport.'

She stood up, done. Turning to the fridge, just so she'd have something to talk to, she said, 'Tatsu, buy me tickets for Tallinn. Earliest flight from Heathrow. I'll need three. Business class, flexible return, international airline only.'

'I assume you have passports?' she added over her shoulder.

The two men nodded and just like that they were taking her to Tallinn.

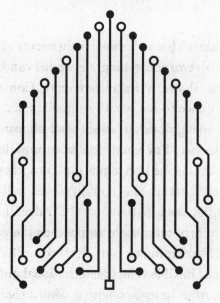

CHAPTER FOUR

She met them at Heathrow the next morning, having tended to their bruises and egos. Amanda had fresh clothes and the slenderest backpack she owned, on the assumption they wouldn't be there more than a night. She hated waiting for luggage—she'd rather buy knickers at her destination than put anything in the hold. Amanda put Tangle's book on the shelves among her others, but it looked out of place among her well-thumbed texts on financial engineering and collateralised debt obligations. She settled on wrapping it up again and posting it to an address chosen more or less at random in the village where her parents had a holiday home.

They arrived at the airport after the morning rush hour. Transit through Heathrow passed with no detentions, poorly-lit interrogation rooms or menacing government agencies. To Amanda's surprise Haber and Stornetta were waved through the electronic gates without a glitch.

Amanda knew nothing about Tallinn other than it being in Estonia, and even that wasn't definite in her mind until she looked on a map; it could have been in Lithuania or Latvia. She couldn't even tell the three countries apart on a map.

Haber and Stornetta were stopped at the entrance to the business lounge.

'They've got business class tickets,' said Amanda testily to the steward at reception who'd denied them entry.

'Yes, that's true,' said the steward non-committally. 'We get this sometimes. The system has ruled them out.'

'Their scores are too low, isn't it?' said Amanda, turning away without waiting for verification. 'You two, come here.' They hung back, looking uncomfortable. 'What're your scores?'

'We don't do that shit,' said Haber dismissively.

Stornetta looked a little more concerned. 'What we do doesn't really chime with the kinds of behaviour your lot look for in a good citizen. We ain't bad people'—said with a straight face—'but what's normal for us ain't for polite society, yeah?' Amanda cursed for not thinking of it. 'There're loads of rich fucks who come through here no problem though, right?' continued Stornetta.

'They've probably got image consultants,' said Amanda bluntly. Her gangsters weren't in that league. With a breath she painted a smile onto her face and turned back to the steward. 'They're with me. They've got the tickets. I'm allowed in, aren't I?'

The steward nodded enthusiastically. 'Ma'am, as a valued member of our frequent fliers programme, you're welcome to go on to the first class lounge.'

She pouted, a little disgusted with herself but not enough to stop. 'Then could I vouch for these two? Please?'

The steward eyed them as if they were about to crap on the floor in front of him, but smiled at Amanda. 'Of course, Miss Back.'

Sitting in the airline's business lounge warming herself on the glow of victory, Amanda brushed up on the basics. A couple hundred miles from St Petersburg, across the Gulf of Finland from Helsinki. Tallinn might have been the capital city, but it was hardly bigger than Manchester in England.

She didn't bother asking the other two if they'd been. They were too busy loading up on free booze and food. They were like graduates in the first few weeks of work, who didn't know how to stop gorging on free stuff everyone else regarded as background noise.

'This is the best curry I've had in yonks,' said Stornetta. 'And I spend loads of time up Mile End way.'

Amanda didn't really understand the significance of the statement, but the beatific look on his face, even on the third bowl, communicated just how serious he was.

Haber took a more traditional approach, settling for a beef stew and dumplings with bread stacked on the side of the plate like a wall on three of the four sides.

For her part, she didn't enjoy the food in the lounge; everything tasted slightly metallic, as if regardless of the specific dish it had all been piped in together from a great distance so that the flavours, no matter how startling they should have been, felt flat and leeched away.

Amanda checked her feeds, concluding she'd missed nothing in not going out with friends as their tedious in-jokes and bitching about jobs and partners surfaced. After that she caught up on work emails, which were by some bizarre stroke of fortune veering towards the benign rather than the catastrophic.

A small plastic face appeared in the top right corner of her tablet, and a chat box opened beneath it.

Interesting, wrote Amanda. *The Info Sec group at work are supposed to have disabled anything other than their approved messenger options.*

Tatsu blinked. *Their security is designed for an organisation of fifty thousand, it's hardly adequate for those needs and leaves individual applications grossly insecure. They're basically putting a blanket over the top of a picnic and hoping the ants don't realise they can just walk in underneath it.* Its avatar was hard to look at, the eyes slightly too far apart, the skin close to photorealistic but shiny and anaemic. If there was an ethnicity behind it she couldn't identify it.

Can't you choose a proper ethnicity, something that doesn't make my eyes water? she typed. She didn't stop to let Tatsu consider. *Who are the...* but the keys stopped responding to her fingers.

Don't try to write anything like that down, wrote Tatsu.

Not until we're at our destination. Plenty of agencies watch for their name and we're in a location where there's heightened scrutiny.

She nodded, tentatively testing the keys again, pleased to see they were working.

So you're coming with us, then? she wrote.

You wouldn't find them otherwise, replied Tatsu. *I can't just give you their address and hope for the best. The contract demands that I ensure you gain access to the device. To that end, I'll be there to help with negotiations.*

It hadn't occurred to Amanda that they'd need anything. Not that she'd thought it through. *What will they want?*

They typically take payment in secrets. You may need to give them a password or information they're looking for that you can provide.

Oof. *Career limiting decision, that,* she wrote, rods of fear running up her back at the thought of betraying work.

The choice of what you give them is yours, of course, replied Tatsu. *I'd like to travel on your watch.*

You didn't ask about my tablet, wrote Amanda, shifting in her seat, looking up and around with a cursory glance in case anyone was watching her. Haber and Stornetta were discussing the football transfer season to her left, sitting closer to one another than she'd have thought two testosterone-fuelled bruisers would be comfortable with. The seat on her right remained empty.

I'm not here. This is just a messaging system. So can I? I will be more help to you if I can be present.

Sure. What do I have to do? she wrote.

Nothing appeared on her tablet but her wrist buzzed

and there, on the screen, was the pixelated green smiley face from her fridge.

The flight was an easy three hours. Haber and Stornetta took the chance to eat again, picking at her plate when she couldn't muscle up the motivation to eat the hot meal offered by the airline.

The plane banked around over the city and she was surprised to see how much of it still stood; from the air the old city showing only minor scars of the conflict with the Russians which had ground to a stalemate half a decade ago.

'Why here?' she asked Tatsu, whispering at the face of her watch.

It's a grey zone. Multiple sovereign actors mixing it up together on the northern edge of Europe, within NATO but in a state of chaos, even now.

'It's a part of NATO? Why didn't anyone stop the Russians, then?'

I cannot say, wrote Tatsu. *The strategy by the Russians was slow, focussed on the twenty-five percent of the population who were ethnic Russian already living within the country. They funded the church, so called Old Believers, provided Russian passports and built schools in towns and villages where the main language was Russian. What was NATO to do when they provided militia to protect their own people? Shoot civilians on the streets of a country during peacetime? There is no mandate to interfere with a country's internal affairs.*

'You make geopolitics sound like it's personal,' replied Amanda.

The smiley face on her watch dimmed for a moment. She felt like she'd said the wrong thing.

Humans can decide something and destroy each other in the narrow quest to achieve that goal. I cannot process what would drive you to such actions when so many see their agency crushed as a result of such arbitrary aspirations.

'Welcome to men fighting over power,' said Amanda out loud.

Haber gave her a puzzled look, but when she didn't respond, went back to staring out the window.

The airport was to the south east of the city, a long east-west runway that ended at the edge of a moss-coloured lake. The terminal was T-shaped. Amanda took in the orange wooden walls and bright blue pitched roof and was reminded most of a Hollywood version of the Arctic: a Disney interpretation of alpine chalets and fjord huts peeking through the snow. Inside was equally idiosyncratic and, by some distance, the least sterile airport she'd ever visited. There were table-tennis tables, bright rainbow coloured seats, a free gym with showers. They passed a café decorated in chrome and bleached brown wood with as much chic as anything in London. There was none of the despair she associated with travel, crowds of people watching their lives pass by while they waited for the real show to start.

'I've been all over the world with work,' she said to Stornetta as they waited in the taxi line. 'This is the first airport where I think I wouldn't mind being stuck.'

'It's trying too hard,' said Stornetta with a sniff.

'Ah, don't be so miserable,' said Haber, slapping him on the back. 'Would ya rather be here or at Stansted?'

Stornetta shrugged but didn't disagree.

'Where are you going?' asked a short, grey-haired taxi driver with a stereotypical Nordic accent.

Reading from her watch. 'Kumu?' She looked up to see him nodding.

'You sure? Nothing really to see there now. The art was mainly moved into the old town during the, ah, troubles? They never brought it back.'

The drive took less than half an hour, but they were stopped twice by roadblocks manned first by the Estonians and then by men who didn't identify themselves but whose international standing was eased by the passage of two hundred Euros.

'How come you got actual Euros on you?' asked a suspicious Haber after they were waved through the second checkpoint and driving through the broken-down gate around the back of the museum.

'I travel a lot,' said Amanda. At the look he gave her, one of shock as much as obvious embarrassment, she continued. 'You asked.'

The museum was half covered in scaffolding, plastic sheets covering damage yet to be repaired several years after the shooting had stopped. The rest of it appeared in decent shape, an elegant glass curve rising up five stories and surrounded by trees, water and grassland on all sides. A little to the north ran the motorway into the city, the traffic reduced to a gentle hiss no louder than the wind in the trees. Whoever had chosen the site had sensitivities for which Amanda's heart was grateful, and as the other two sorted themselves out, stretching and talking to the taxi driver, she stood and stared at the Kumu. The glass was bookended by soft grey stone that would sit starkly against the snow in winter. To their left, running in an arc behind the main building, white wedges rose like a ring of teeth from the ground. The museum was sunk into the side of a hill, the offices in the retaining walls now abandoned and shattered by mortar fire, earth spilling out like flesh from an exit wound.

From where the taxi had stopped they looked onto a switch back of white stone path down to the main entrance in front of which was a large plaza that must have once been beautiful. Small sections of it survived, but much of it was pitted, broken. Amanda ached at the sight of such beauty rendered so carelessly into entropy's callous grasp.

A man was sweeping dirt with a broad-headed broom, bent and elderly, a cap on his head covering his features in shadow.

'Such a shame, yes?' said the taxi driver, who'd come around to stand next to Amanda.

'Why would they do this?' she asked, feeling sudden meaningless.

'Russians wanted to control what our eyes could see. We would never surrender to such smallness. Much of the treasures we loved are safe. One day they will return.' He sounded so sure of himself she turned to stare.

Having been paid he departed, leaving them alone at the top of the rise overlooking the museum.

They know you're coming, buzzed Tatsu. Amanda

covered her watch face with a woollen sleeve and led the way down. The janitor ignored them as they walked past, his eyes only concerned with spilled earth and broken rubble.

If the outside was desolate, a reminder of how mankind ruins with planning that which it creates on impulse, the moment they stepped through the doors the atmosphere changed to one of vital industry. Heads looked in their direction, young people, men, women and all inbetween moved about, hugging tables and workstations beneath what remained of those pieces and installations the authorities hadn't moved in the first flush of battle with Old Believer militia.

'Are these new?' asked Haber, staring at the shattered remains of a marble torso around whose feet a head and pieces of limb had been reverentially laid in offering.

'It's a symbol of rebirth,' said a young woman with spikey orange hair. She was wearing two parts of a royal blue three-piece suit, the jacket discarded and a canary yellow shirt covered by a well-cut waistcoat.

Haber stared at the installation a second time, as if looking for it to transform its meaning in the wake of her words. 'Rebirth of what?' he asked eventually, looking up to meet her gaze.

'The people. The nation.' The woman stood alongside him and shared his view of the remains. 'It is bullshit.' Done with it, she turned to Amanda, leaving Haber to stare at the back of her head. 'This isn't a gallery anymore. You have come to the wrong place, tourist.'

It was an accusation, with distaste and hatred in it.

Ask for Satoshi Nakamoto, wrote Tatsu on her wrist.

We're going to have to work out a better way to communicate, thought Amanda, not believing for a minute she was being directed to find *the* legendary and fictitious blockchain inventor. She castigated herself for not asking earlier, she'd had plenty of time.

'I'm looking for Satoshi Nakamoto?' she said, trying to sound as if she knew them and just needed to be pointed in the right direction.

'Satoshi Nakamoto,' said the woman, folding her arms in disbelief. 'Do they know you're coming?'

'What does that matter to you?' asked Amanda, mirroring the woman's attitude.

'I'm Lisandra. We're all busy here, none of us have time to answer the inane questions of tourists. If you want art, go to the Palace, they've got the Eve by Köler hosted there.'

'The what?' asked Amanda, and Lisandra rolled her eyes. 'Look, I don't care about your art. I'm here because I was told Satoshi could help me with a problem. I'm sorry about'—she gestured around—'all this, but I've got my own crap to deal with.' She noticed an older woman, somewhere north of sixty, watching their conversation from the foot of a curved staircase that ran along the inside of the outer wall.

'So you're just going to wander around Kumu until you find them? What if they've got their own tasks? What if they say no to you? What will you do then?' Lisandra looked Amanda up and down. 'You're not one to take no for an answer, are you?'

Haber and Stornetta stood off to one side, flanking the statue, watching without any sign they were going to join the conversation.

Amanda realised she'd taken the wrong path with Lisandra; that the young woman, probably not yet twenty, was too angry to be bullied or cajoled. She was a gate they weren't passing unless someone helped them. Amanda considered apologising, but suspected any peace offering she made now would be thrown back in her face.

'Is everything okay?' asked the older woman, taking a step toward them. She wasn't Estonian; she wasn't even European. Her heritage was Pacific rim, her accent west coast America.

'It's fine,' said Lisandra a touch too loudly, her voice echoing around the floor and briefly drawing the attention of half a dozen other people up and down the arc of the interior.

'Okay, I will leave you to it,' said the woman, turning back towards the staircase with no further regard for the conversation.

Seeing her chance evaporating, Amanda called out. 'Please, I'm looking for Satoshi Nakamoto. Can you help us?'

The woman stopped moving, but didn't turn around. Lisandra shifted to her left, putting her body between Amanda and the woman. 'You don't just get to walk in here and demand to meet with people,' she said, her voice desperate now as it was angry.

'I'm hoping she can help me,' said Amanda, dialling

down her tone to one she hoped carried the very real sense that she too was desperate for help.

'And what if you're a Russian agent?' Lisandra jabbed a finger at Amanda's chest. When she laughed at the idea, Lisandra broadened her gesture to include Haber and Stornetta who started as if woken from a private reverie. 'Who brings bodyguards with them to a museum?'

'I'm not Russian,' said Amanda, as if that would explain everything.

'We're not stupid,' said Lisandra, shouting now. 'They are too obvious to send one of their own. How can we know? Are you armed?'

'Don't be stupid,' said Amanda, but a cough from behind her froze her sneer on her face.

'Um, well,' said Stornetta, flushing a little.

'I knew it!' shouted Lisandra.

Around them people had stopped what they were doing. No one had moved—yet. Amanda could feel everything slipping away from her.

'I'm not here to hurt anyone.' She saw Lisandra opening her mouth, eyes fixed over her shoulder. 'Nor are they! God damn it.' She pulled out the flash drive. 'All I want is someone to help me access this.' She held it in the air, arm outstretched above her head, for everyone to see.

The older woman turned, squinting at Amanda's raised hand. 'Who are you?' she asked, her tone commanding, hovering on the edge of curiosity.

Amanda didn't answer immediately, waiting for the woman to come close enough so she didn't have to bellow across the gallery.

'I'm Amanda Back.'

The woman, older still than she'd first assumed now she was close enough to get a proper look, shrugged indifferently. 'I don't know you.'

'So leave,' said Lisandra, cutting in. 'You'll not find what you're looking for here.'

A flash of inspiration struck at Amanda like a peanut thrown at her forehead. 'This belongs to Tangle Singh. He sent it to me.'

Lisandra looked disbelieving. 'Anyone could have sent that to you.'

'I don't even know what it is!' protested Amanda, lowering her hand and stashing the drive in her pocket.

'It's a flash drive. People used them when I was your age,' said the woman. Then, slyly, head turned away, gazing out through the glass walls. 'You knew Singh?'

Amanda sighed. Where to begin with that story? So she nodded, trying to stifle the weariness she felt whenever she was reminded of her life with him.

Lisandra's eyes were focussed elsewhere, as if worried she'd left something undone that would end in catastrophe without her presence. 'Amanda. Amanda?' The word turned from memory to accusation on her tongue. Stepping up, she slapped Amanda across the cheek. 'You're *that* Amanda?'

Amanda stumbled backwards, tripping over the rubble at the foot of the statue. She was saved from crashing to the floor by Stornetta, who darted in and caught her.

Great, she thought, now I'm a damsel in distress. Just what I need right now. Standing back on her own feet, she saw that Haber had interposed himself between her and Lisandra. He was jittering as he always did, his fingers flicking, bending, his weight shifting from foot to foot. She'd grown used to it a little, but could see how threatening it would be to a stranger.

Others were drifting towards their drama, young men and women, no one over the age of thirty, no one with work that demanded they be in an office during a weekday.

'Let's be clear about one thing,' said Amanda, turning from the older woman to Lisandra, brushing herself down in a bid to locate her dignity. 'Tangle Singh is a complete fucking cock. As is usual, he'll have slept his way into the building'—she held Lisandra's gaze without blinking, daring her to start—'then he'll have told one lie after another before fucking off with something you thought no one in their right mind would consider taking, because it was so bloody obviously valuable to you.'

'You do know him, then,' said the older woman, ignoring the look of fury on Lisandra's face. She slipped around to Amanda's side, taking the crook of her elbow. 'Why don't we get a cup of coffee and talk about something other than yet another man?'

Amanda could have kissed her.

THEY WALKED ALONG the staircase, up all five flights of stairs, back and forth around the outer edge of the building until they stood just under the glass roof, the bright white clouds above them casting a brilliant crystal light across the whole floor.

Holographic frames floated along the back wall, disturbed only by thin partition walls which foreshortened the depth of the building. People stood at desks, huge plants left to run wild but nurtured in raised beds as breaks between different pods of activity. Dark green leaves with huge scented white flowers broke the space, distracted from the crowd of individuals working industriously in every direction. The woman led them quietly, and unremarked, across the floor. Amanda caught snippets of conversation, clips of tech jargon, accents from across Europe, people speaking English, German, Spanish, Mandarin.

Whatever they were working on wasn't art. Wasn't rebirth of the gallery.

'They're not government,' she whispered to her escort.

The woman chuckled conspiratorially. 'No. We're not. But we work for the good of others as well as our own.'

'This—you—are the Grey Rose?' asked Amanda, understanding what she was seeing. Suddenly the youthfulness of the crowd made sense, their individuality, the plethora of language, of ethnicity. And Tangle had been here before her. Preparing the ground, or fucking it up, which of the two remained to be discovered.

'We are that of which you speak,' said the woman.

They reached the far end of the floor, arriving at a small kitchen stocked with pots of teas and coffees, together with half a dozen kettles. As they approached, the handful of people lingering there, deep in conversation and nursing drinks, innocuously filtered away. Minnows drifting away from a pike's approach.

'I'm sorry, we have to heat our water when we need it.

There used to be batteries for the solar tiles, but they've been requisitioned—stolen—for other purposes.'

'The government knows you're here?'

'Oh, yes,' she smiled as she spoke. 'They know. They don't mind as long as we're not too power hungry or critical of whichever minister's got their hand in the jar this week.' She handed Amanda a coffee. 'No milk either.' She didn't apologise.

'Why wouldn't you be critical?' asked Amanda as Haber and Stornetta made their own brews, waving the woman away as if she was not to be trusted with something as precious as tea-making. When they were done, they too drifted away, with a final sidelong glance at Amanda. They started toward the nearest frame, asking those working there what they were doing. To her surprise, they weren't dismissed but welcomed in, shown around.

'We would; rolling brownouts, rising nationalism, a failure to provide for the Old Believers that left fallow land in which the Russians nurtured discontent already seeded.' She raised a finger. 'But what are these, compared to technocratic authoritarianism smothering democracy across the free world? Capitalism in the guise of your great friend, who only demands that you focus on the inconsequential in life, that you focus on the trivial and refuse to get angry as they steal your health, your labour? In the face of this, the rich dividing the poor against themselves so that no great inequity can be challenged, what is a failing power network?'

'You sound dangerous,' said Amanda, and she meant it. The woman held her tea in front of her lips, the steam rising just under her nose. 'You've got a good social credit score.' It wasn't a question. 'I guess you signed up early, keen to get better credit, to be a leader among your peers and demonstrate you were good to do business with.'

Amanda shifted uncomfortably. 'It works. I get deals that make life better, offers tailored to the life I lead. I pay lower fees for financial transactions, it works.' I also get better partners recommended on dating sites, better exchange rates, cheaper electricity, easier bookings in restaurants and at the cinema. She didn't say the second list out loud. 'I know people don't like it, but it reinforces civility, reminds us that being good people builds society, doesn't damage it.'

'Unless, of course, you got tarred with your parents' debt, or someone else ruined the score attaching to your apartment, or your identity is stolen. Or maybe your idea of a good community doesn't match what an AI coded by white men think.'

'All of those things can be undone,' said Amanda.

'If you're educated. If you have the means, time and knowhow to navigate the system.' She took a sip of tea. 'That's not the real injustice, though. You're right that it reinforces behaviours. It reinforces that being a dissenter is bad, that living a life someone else deems unworthy is not just neutral but actively penalised. Being poor, having no buffer, no slack to allow you to adapt to life's little showers is also penalised. What I find hardest to get over is how the poor pay more for their services because they're seen as untrustworthy. Why should a poor person pay more for their heating than you just because they're poor?'

'It's got nothing to do with wealth,' said Amanda hotly, angry with the idea. 'If they refuse to behave in a way that builds their score, what should I do about it?'

'Perhaps you should look at whether it's just to measure someone like that.'

'So what, then?' demanded Amanda, irritated.

'Nothing. The question I'd ask you is this: why should there be only one way to live? One way to be civilised? Why does the state—or worse, private companies—get to decide who's trustworthy? They crystallise everything that's bad about humanity into ossified structures whose goals are not ours. People say "I've never been affected by this thing" when the thing benefits them personally, when it remains invisible to them because it's always been in their favour.'

'Because most people don't care,' said Amanda. 'And I resent the idea that I'm one of the privileged.' She gestured at her skin. 'I'm not white, I'm not a man. I didn't grow up rich. I know about privilege and I'm not it.'

'You define yourself by your liminality. I guess that's worked well for you. Standing between worlds, banging on the windows, demanding you be let in.' She stopped talking, looked at Amanda, expecting her to respond.

'You know the phrase "coconut"?'

'We say "banana" where I'm from, but yes. White on the inside. We all have our burdens, Amanda. You and I have used them to our benefit, and neither of us is fooled by the other's claims of their inherent problems.' She put her coffee down, patted Amanda on the wrist. 'Come, you didn't come here to listen to me tell you the life you've led oppresses millions of others.'

Amanda drank her coffee, refusing to engage, waiting for the woman to move on to her point.

'I can help you, but you need to know what I care about. I'm not against anyone.' She laughed as if the statement was her grand joke. 'Sounds ridiculous when you say it aloud. It reads better than it speaks.'

'You? You can help me?' asked Amanda, looking around. She'd assumed Nakamoto was young, male and undoubtedly watching their conversation from a safe distance. 'This is a test, right?' She spoke to the room, turning her head to keep the woman in sight but deciding she was irrelevant.

'I'm Satoshi Nakamoto,' said the woman with a swift bow. 'I invented the blockchain as a very young woman; people changed the world with what I made. Now, as I hover in my early seventies, I see those changes and realise they weren't all ones I would have wished for.'

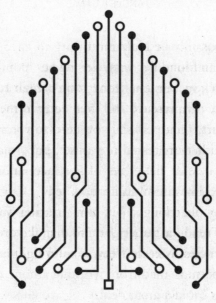

CHAPTER FIVE

'YOU'RE NOT NAKAMOTO,' said Amanda. 'Everyone knows the story of how the blockchain was invented, and everyone knows Nakamoto was a fiction, a nom de guerre for the group who invented it.' She didn't mean to be aggressive, but in her years of dealing with the mediocre, mainly men, who were nevertheless extremely satisfied with themselves, she'd found it was easier to pounce on obvious bullshit than try to navigate around it.

The woman claiming to be Satoshi Nakamoto stood very still, face frozen in surprise.

'I've found calling out complete rubbish has a great way of levelling the playing field,' said Amanda. 'What I'm really interested in is why you'd make this claim. Here of all places, when everyone on the floor knows you can't possibly be Nakamoto.'

The woman found her wits, closing her mouth, blinking twice in quick succession. 'If they don't laugh at my face, if they tolerate my presence and even defer to me in matters such as yours, then perhaps you need to reconsider.' She sounded neither distressed nor upset, but Amanda could see nervousness at the edges of her face, an uncertainty that hovered like a nimbus around her.

'You're not old enough.' But now Amanda was guessing. She'd never read the papers behind digital stores of value, cryptocurrencies, Merkle trees, whatever. Everything she knew had been gleaned from working among quants and traders who cared a great deal.

'Thank you for saying so.'

'If it's true, why are you telling *me,* of all people?'

Satoshi shrugged, as if asked why she was revealing a family recipe for chocolate cake. 'I'm not shy about it now. I'd rather the world didn't know, I'm not one for interviews, but even if they were interested it's so long ago I'd be nothing more than a curio, a sidebar for the gossip page.'

'So you're here, soaking up the atmosphere, changing the world.' Amanda didn't believe a word of it, but there was no point arguing, not now she'd called it and the woman had strode on through without a moment's pause.

'All of those things and none.' She sighed, as if they'd run out of time, as if errands needed seeing to. 'You're here to get access to this drive. It'll take me moments to sort it out for you, but then what? Tangle sent you this for a reason.'

'I have no idea,' said Amanda, unwilling to open up a debate on that front.

Satoshi walked away from the kitchen, leading Amanda halfway across the floor to an unoccupied spot with empty desks. She waved her hands through the air, up, across, down and then back. Two person-size frames opened up in the air. With a flurry of quick, practised gestures, Satoshi activated her access to the systems.

Bending down she pulled up a tile in the floor underneath the frames. From within the darkness underneath, she yanked out a bundle of cables. Stopping, she held out an empty hand in Amanda's direction.

'Satoshi's obviously not a real name. Even those who tried to work out who I was didn't really get it.'

Amanda watched as she sorted through a chronic spaghetti of cables, coming in yellows, whites, reds, blacks and blues; thick, thin, covered in plastic sheaths or fabrics.

'My real name's Ichi Oku. Born in Japan, but grew up in Canada. Lived in Toronto till I was eighteen. All immigrants live there at some point after they arrive. Spent much of my life as a second-rate economics professor at a minor US university.'

'What'd you focus on? Your research?' asked Amanda, as much to see if there was any depth to her story as out of professional curiosity.

'You know economics?' asked Ichi, holding up a thinning sheaf of cables to winnow out those that weren't relevant, carefully threading out exotic connectors so they didn't break as she pulled at them.

'Enough,' said Amanda. 'I'm a banker, after all.'

'Of course you are,' said Ichi. 'Ah ha.' She had one sunshine yellow cable in her hand, ending in a strange adaptor Amanda didn't recognise. 'Where's your drive?' asked Ichi.

Amanda retrieved it, holding it in her closed hand for a moment, pondering the sense in handing it over to a mad old woman in a ruined museum in Estonia.

'I'm not going to eat it, you know,' said Ichi. She snorted. 'I'm vegan.'

'Of course you are,' said Amanda and gave her the drive.

'We're all predictable in our own little ways,' she replied. Without any fuss she plugged the drive in, then stood up, flicking at the holographic screens, sliding between different operating systems until she found one that was almost entirely text-based. 'God, they were basic. It's amazing to think I was already middle-aged by the time we'd gotten to application based software. You grew up with it.'

'It's as simple as plugging it in?' It was Haber. He'd found a pretzel from somewhere and was nibbling at the edges, picking off individual salt crystals one at a time and popping them into his mouth.

'No,' said Ichi. 'First we check no one's put a surprise on there for us. After that, then, yes,' she looked disappointed to admit it was so easy. 'We plug and play.'

They let her work. Haber was tearing at the last curves of the pretzel when she said, 'All done. Let's see what Tangle sent you.'

Amanda closed in, standing by Ichi to see better. 'What is it?'

'It's encrypted,' said Ichi.

'You people are hackers, aren't you?' asked Haber.

Amanda spotted Stornetta on the other side of the floor, surrounded by a gaggle of young men. 'So this was a wasted trip?' she asked, addressing the comment as much at Tatsu as at Ichi.

'Not at all. I can tell you how to decrypt the information, although that will take you back to where you started.'

Her wrist buzzed, but Amanda ignored it. 'Go on, then.'

'There was a game in the very first days of cryptocurrencies, when people thought that's all blockchain was good for. CryptoKitties. As basic as they came, but a fun way of showing how the blockchain could be used, and doing it with cats on the internet.' She smiled as if remembering a more innocent time and frowned when neither Amanda nor Haber shared her pleasure. 'Anyway. There's a CryptoKitty on here. A rare one. You need to find another, and breed them. The offspring—or more accurately, the resulting block—will contain your key. Once you've got that, you can access the information.'

'I've never heard of them,' said Amanda.

'No offence,' said Ichi, 'but there's a lot you haven't heard of. The game isn't available anymore, the first generation architecture it relied on isn't in use. It wasn't much more than a proof of concept, although as with most of the early tech a lot of people lost money on it.'

Amanda's wrist buzzed again but didn't stop at the customary two pings, instead repeating itself over and over.

'Your watch is going mad,' said Haber conversationally.

Giving him a hard stare, Amanda pulled it up. *There's a substantial amount of comms centring on the museum. I would recommend leaving,* said Tatsu.

'What?' asked Ichi. It had gone quiet around them. Over by Stornetta there was a rapid but hushed conversation. One of the young men detached themselves from Stornetta's orbit and hurried over.

'Professor Oku, we are worried Kumu isn't safe today.' He looked at Haber, and Amanda saw something approaching admiration in his eyes. 'Your guests should leave and we need to make everything safe.'

'How did you plan on getting back to the airport?' asked Ichi.

They hadn't, realised Amanda. She hadn't thought beyond getting the drive read.

'We have a car in the basement carpark. You have flights booked?'

'Flexible tickets,' said Amanda. 'What's going on?'

'Hasn't your tame AI told you already?' asked the boy with a sneer painted across his lips. 'You didn't think we were going to let you in here without checking you out, did you? You're probably more dangerous than the malware on the drive you're holding.' At her blank look he raised his eyebrows in disbelief. 'Do you even *know* what's riding around on your watch?'

Amanda held up her wrist. Tatsu's face appeared momentarily, its mouth a flat line, eyes little more than slits. To her amazement, the boy took a step back.

'What is going on?' she repeated.

'The government has decided today is a raid day,' said

the boy, taking hold of Ichi's arm. Much more gently he said, 'Professor, you need to get to Old Town.'

Ichi handed the drive back to Amanda. 'You should go. We'll give you a lift into Old Town. After it's all died down, you can get a taxi back to the airport.' She turned to go, but Amanda put a hand on her shoulder, with enough resistance to force her attention back her way.

'What will they do?'

The boy tutted, rolling his eyes. 'Professor, we're going downstairs. You'll take the lift?'

Nodding, they watched together as Haber followed after the boy, joined by Stornetta at the top of the stairs. There was no time to ask them where they were going.

'They like to overturn our desks, beat up some of those who can't keep their indignation under control. They'll probably steal more of our solar panels, extort payments out of us, and then, if we're really unlucky, take a few of us into custody on suspicion of being sympathetic to the Russians.' She said it all while watching the floor empty. Everyone was calm, as if they were facing nothing more than an unwanted salesperson at the front door.

Amanda struggled to know what to say. After a while where they stood in silence with Ichi making no move to leave, she figured out they were facing an experience she had no way of relating to.

'Is this normal for you?' she asked slowly, trying not to sound careless or ignorant.

Ichi gave a clipped nod. 'It varies from month to month. There's no way of predicting it. Sometimes bad news provokes them, sometimes good. Sometimes it's the captain on duty, or because some sergeant is bored. Mostly it's because young people come here to make a difference, to tell others about the corruption threading through our government like a cancer. Sometimes it's because I'm a woman and the men around here find the possibility of someone without a penis being wily and smart an intolerable slice of reality.'

Amanda shook her head. 'From what you've said, I think your gender is one of the least offensive things going on here. There's a bunch of things I can see them wanting to stop regardless that you're a woman.'

'Really?' asked Ichi, clearly not seeking an answer, her words measured but gilt in anger. 'And because you're a woman as well, that makes you more right than me? Or perhaps your experience of the irrational hatred men in power have of women demanding their rights is limited to crying over why your male colleagues got better bonuses than you. It's obviously one of the reasons you don't believe I'm really Satoshi Nakamoto. After all, how many female quants have you ever met?'

'Should we go?' asked Amanda, wishing she'd never started. She disagreed with Ichi, on virtually every point, but Ichi's acolytes had been adamant she needed to leave. Amanda had no desire to get caught up in whatever was going on.

Ichi started for the back of the floor, away from the windows and towards a pair of narrow elevator doors muttering all the while. 'Heaven forbid a woman could come up with block chain, that all those men working on getting rich, on satisfying their need to pleasure themselves intellectually didn't come up with the idea before me. Because my vagina means I can't be good at math or engineering.'

Amanda wished she'd just shut up, but couldn't see the point of saying anything out loud.

Her wrist buzzed. *It's not about Satoshi Nakamoto,* wrote Tatsu. *You need to leave now. Multiple different sets of security agencies are converging on Kumu with you their target.*

Amanda stood still, ignoring the bemused look from Ichi who was stood in the lift compartment holding the doors open. 'Are you coming?' she asked.

She started into the lift just as the lights went out. Ichi looked up with a weary sigh. 'This is new.'

Amanda grabbed her hand, pulling her from the interior back onto the floor. The glass ceiling yielded a cold white light, casting short shadows but leaving in darkness those places it didn't directly illuminate. Cries of alarm reached up from below, fingers of fear seeking a way out.

Amanda ran as fast as Ichi could move towards the stairwell they'd used before. They found Stornetta coming the other way.

'There you are. It's not the government,' he said. 'The young 'uns are saying it's the Russians.'

Ichi didn't say anything, her mouth setting in a thin line across her face.

'They're here for me,' said Amanda.

'You?' said Ichi.

Stornetta nodded to the stairs and they descended.

'The drive. They want what's on it. They've already tried to take it from me. Twice.'

'Didn't you think to warn us? Why would you come here and risk everything we've built?'

Amanda wanted to say she'd had no idea they were being followed, that she couldn't conceive of anyone going to such lengths over anything. She'd never imagined events like these really happened, let alone with her at the centre.

Instead she said nothing.

'C'mon,' said Stornetta, refusing to let them slow down.

'Is there no one who can help?' asked Amanda, feeling it was all too impossible to just happen. The words felt childish, stupid, but she didn't know what else to say.

'Our lot might put up with us, but they'll not shed any tears over Kumu being razed to the ground. They'll shout about it in assembly tonight but they'll not think of it twice after tomorrow.'

A loud pop echoed up from beneath them. Ahead of them, Stornetta froze.

He looked over the side of the bannister, ducked back just as quickly. 'How do we get to your car?' he asked Ichi.

'I can't leave now,' she said.

'You stay and you're going to wind up shot,' he said.

Amanda looked over the edge, all she could see was figures moving in darkness below, shadows stretching and turning without sunlight to create them. Shouts sparked all around like poppers being let loose with no sense of coordination. More gunfire followed.

'You can't stay,' said Amanda. She didn't know what was going to happen, but she wouldn't leave Ichi behind.

They ran down to the second floor, but Stornetta stopped them, cursing. 'They're coming up. Have you got another way outta here? Any other stairs?'

When Ichi didn't immediately answer he grew restive, clenching and unclenching his fists.

'It can't be that hard!'

'Shut up,' she said. 'I can't think straight.' The sound of running on the floor below, of panicked cries, flowed past them, a stink of terror they found hard to ignore.

The shooting wasn't manic but controlled, snaps of one and three shots, never more, nothing sustained.

'They're killing everyone,' said Stornetta. 'Floor by floor.' Ichi didn't speak, but tears ran down her face and Amanda knew they were going to die right there on the stairs.

A trio of soldiers turned the corner coming up to meet them. The lead, dressed all in black with green-tinted goggles covering their eyes, raised a small compact rifle in front of them like it might bite back if brought too close to their masked face.

More gunfire, the shocks too close to tell how many shots were fired. The soldier at the rear of the pack spun around and collapsed to the floor. Stornetta barrelled into Amanda, wrapping one arm around her to shove her back along with him. Ichi stumbled up the stairs and they fell, together, around the corner onto the third floor.

Gunfire erupted just beneath them on the stairs: dozens of shots, then silence. The distorted sound of people speaking into radios just in front of their lips. Footsteps moving away.

'It's not just Russians,' whispered Amanda.

They're looking for you, but right now all the chatter is about stopping other agencies getting to you first, wrote Tatsu in glowing green letters on her wrist.

'We can get through them,' she said to Stornetta. 'They're fighting one another.'

He stared at her, his eyes wide. 'You are one scary lady, lady.' But he nodded and, helping Ichi to her feet and not letting go of her arm, he let Amanda lead them back down the stairs.

They crouched behind the bannister, peeking out into the darkness. The light from the glass wall cast a gloom into the floor, not enough to illuminate, just enough to grow a jungle of shadows in which bodies and soldiers easily hide.

'We just have to go,' hissed Amanda, adrenalin rushing through her like three double espressos.

'We have to wait and see,' said Stornetta, trying to hold them back.

Amanda was having none of it. She scuttled around him and, seeing no one in the gloom beyond, ran towards the proper darkness of the back wall. She reached it without being shot, even as gunfire continued to sound around them. She looked back to see the other two, Stornetta with an arm around Ichi's shoulders, hobbling across the floor.

Breathing heavily, they sat and collected their thoughts. A pair of armed soldiers, their clothes a different pattern even in the darkness, ran past, left to right.

'Where do we go from here?' she asked Ichi.

Ichi couldn't, or wouldn't speak. She managed to tip her face to their left.

'The stairs, they're along this wall?' asked Stornetta.

Ichi nodded, her eyes glinting pools of grief in the darkness.

Amanda waited for Stornetta to lead them on, but he was watching her, waiting for her. The sensation was odd, she was running on instinct and a deep desire to live, but he was deferring to her.

Fair enough, she thought, not knowing what else they were going to do if he was in charge. She'd assumed he knew about this kind of shit, but if he didn't know what to do, couldn't make them any safer than she could—which was precisely not at all—then she knew how to make decisions. That'd have to be enough.

Bent over, legs bent so their backs ached after just a few metres, they stumbled their way along the back wall, freezing every time intruders passed by. For their part, the different parties continued to fight one another, focussed not on searching for people like Amanda but in staying alive when they ran unexpectedly into each other.

Amanda could see a darker hole in the wall, maybe ten metres ahead; presumably the stairway they were hoping to find. Before they reached it, she hit something soft with her leading foot and ended up on her face, wondering what the hell was going on.

Stornetta came piling over, dropping Ichi.

Voices whimpered as he approached, causing him to pull up sharply just as he looked set to put the boot in hard.

'Don't hurt us,' said a woman's voice. Amanda recognised Lisandra, hands wrapped around her body and face turned away in preparation for a beating.

There were three of them, hiding in the dark but paralysed by fear.

'Where are the others?' asked Ichi, seeming to find herself again. One of them, a young man, burst into tears at the question.

'This is on you,' Ichi said to Amanda.

Her words struck Amanda in the throat, closing her up.

'I thought you people were armed to the teeth, always ready to shoot up the Man if he came calling,' said Stornetta.

'They're children,' said Ichi, loud enough that Amanda looked around frantically, hoping no one had heard them. 'This isn't some hardcore American libertarian camp. They're here trying to make the world work, not make themselves safe.'

'Enough,' said Amanda. She pulled at Lisandra, dragging her along as she started covering the remaining ground to the stairs.

'We won't all fit in the car, you know,' said Ichi pointedly.

Amanda ignored her, stomach turning over. She had no right to demand Ichi gave them a lift to safety. If they tried to leave her behind, she had no idea what would happen.

They slowly made their way down the stairs. Coming to the first floor, with two more flights to go, they paused, crouching down low as torchlight swept across the floor beyond the glass doorway.

Whoever was searching didn't pause. The gunfire was muffled from their position, but it was almost entirely on the floors above them. A succession of rapid exchanges of fire suggested a bitter fight underway, but Amanda could only hope it meant they were clear to reach the car.

Alone again, they descended the last two flights of stairs, emerging into the car park. Emergency lighting threw fuzzy red and feeble white light between thick concrete pillars. Electronic buzzing filled the background, but nothing moved.

Ichi held Lisandra's hand, the four natives holding onto each other like school kids on a day trip. She pushed past Amanda, pressing on into the carpark.

The car was a small four-seater German runabout covered in grime with, orange paint peeling under the dirt. Haber was stood next to it, a rifle held casually in his arms.

'I wondered when you'd show up,' he said, a strained look on his face. Stornetta hurried over and the two of them embraced briefly.

'Well isn't this a pickle,' said Stornetta, stepping back to assess the space available. The car park was otherwise empty, and Amanda's thoughts of somehow commandeering a second vehicle evaporated.

'Sure we can all fit in,' said Haber. 'Question is, who's going to drive?'

'It's my car,' said Ichi.

'No offence, but are you really ready to drive like a mad eejit to get away from the lunatics upstairs?' asked Haber.

'I'm driving,' said Stornetta, holding out a hand.

Ichi pursed her lips and didn't move. After a few moments, Lisandra shook at her arm.

'Give him the keys!'

'You're going to die in a ditch over driving out of here?' asked Stornetta.

Ichi handed over her keys without saying anything.

Stornetta opened up the passenger doors. 'Get in, everyone.'

Haber took the front passenger seat and left the rest of them to squabble over the space in the back. They fit four in, but there was no space for the last of them, who Amanda recognised as one of the young men who'd been mooning over Stornetta earlier. From the back, where she sat, under Lisandra's horizontal body, she demanded Haber let the boy sit on his lap.

Stornetta and Haber exchanged a look. 'Pervert,' said Stornetta, but by then the boy was clambering into the front, trying to find space for his legs and arms. Doors barely closed, Stornetta started the car's ignition, the electric motor jerking the car forward in silence.

They drove slowly around the carpark until they came to the ramp. As they did so, a square of white light opened up to their left.

'Crap,' said Haber whose rifle was stacked uselessly between him and the door.

'Got it,' said Stornetta and slammed his foot onto the accelerator. The car sped up smoothly, but without any sense of urgency.

Whoever came through the door fired at them, but the first round went wide. Then they were on the ramp and spiralling up towards the ground floor. More bullets ricocheted off concrete, but their pursuit fell behind out of sight.

They emerged onto the ground floor, a long straight road leading them under Kumu and out a different way than they'd come in. Right in the middle of the road two men were wrestling. Stornetta kept driving.

'What are you doing?' screeched Ichi. For once, Amanda agreed with her.

'Those two will kill us as soon as look at us. I'm not stopping for anyone until we're out of here.'

He kept driving. At the last moment, the two men looked their way, frozen in their deadly embrace as the car bore down on them. With a crunching thump they were on the bonnet, over the roof and behind them, their bodies rolling with bone breaking kinetics until they were lost out of sight as the car negotiated another curve. The windscreen held without breaking.

No one said anything. More shots were fired, but nothing came close. Amanda closed her eyes, trying to block out the shudder of the car as it had mown the soldiers down, the way the noise had drawn out, the thunder of bodies being pulverised.

They drove away. Amanda twisted as much as she could under Lisandra's weight to see Kumu shrinking, but no one followed them.

The boy directed them towards Old Town, the heart of Tallinn, with its ancient curtain wall still standing despite the movement of armies back and forth over the centuries.

'We can't go to town,' said Amanda. 'They'll come for us there, too.'

'The airport,' said Stornetta to the boy, who gimballed his head around to take direction from Ichi. She didn't respond, and after a few hundred feet Stornetta repeated his words, more firmly this time, brooking no further comment.

The boy did as asked and aside from his occasional reluctant directions, delivered in clipped English, they said nothing more until the airport hove into sight.

'You're welcome to come with us,' said Amanda, not quite knowing what she was saying, the words passing her lips as she watched, detached and certain she couldn't do otherwise, even if she had no idea what she would do if they took her up on the offer.

'I'm coming with you,' said Ichi.

'Professor?' asked Lisandra sounding suddenly panicked.

'Tangle Singh sent something to this... woman'—the word was filled with bitter venom—'I need to see what was so desperate we had to pay for it with our lives.'

'If it helps,' said Amanda, trying to sound conciliatory and wishing for all the world he'd sent it to Ichi instead. 'He's dead. Sending the drive to me was his valedictory.'

Ichi sniffed loudly.

Stornetta pulled up in short term parking. 'Who's coming with us?' he asked as they unpacked themselves from the interior.

Lisandra asked for the keys and, after saying goodbye to Ichi, the three survivors got back into the car and drove away without looking back.

They had a couple of hours to wait for the next flight, the last flight of the day back to London. Amanda purchased an additional ticket for Ichi. They found a space in one of the garish cafes, Haber and Stornetta playing ping pong non-stop for ninety minutes while Ichi and Amanda sat across from one another nursing coffees and doing anything except engage.

The flight was called and they were processed through security. Everything was going well, despite a growing itch on the back of Amanda's neck, a certainty that they'd be stopped, arrested and worse.

They were about to pass flightside when a young official approached them. He spoke Estonian, addressing Ichi directly.

She straightened her shoulders, her face holding together even as Amanda watched the edges threaten to give way. After a moment they were taken to one side, allowing other passengers to carry on.

Tatsu offered to translate, but she'd already missed the main part of the exchange and didn't want to draw attention if she could help it.

Seemingly finished with Ichi, the official turned to Amanda.

'Please,' he said. 'Look after the professor for us. She is a beacon for our young people, a hope when so many others have failed us.'

'We're okay to go?' asked Amanda, incredulous.

He nodded, surprised at her question. 'Of course!' he exclaimed before his expression became sombre. 'What has happened today is a bad thing, a stain in our conscience, who knows how much we knew beforehand about what would happen. Not everyone here is corrupt.' His eyes were full of a need for acceptance, to know she understood him, believed him.

'I'm sorry as well,' said Amanda, feeling the loss from him afresh, personal in a way that Ichi's anger wasn't.

He shook his head. 'It is our job to keep our citizens safe. We failed, and the answer of why isn't an easy one to speak.' He led them to the departure gate. 'I don't know why you came, or what is so important, Ms. Back, but if the professor is going with you then, please, do what is right.'

Amanda held his gaze and in that moment felt a weight on her shoulders that was uplifting even as it settled on her. She nodded, 'I will do what I can.' A joke about not knowing what was going on died before she said it, and with nothing more to say they boarded the plane.

The flight was smooth and uneventful, but Amanda barely noticed. Each time she closed her eyes, bodies would tumble over cars, bodies would collapse bonelessly after being murdered. Each time she stared out the window, she heard people screaming, the sound of cars crumpling on impact. Her fingers started shaking, forcing her to grip her hands into fists to hide it, to control it. And hovering over it all was Tangle. She could imagine him laughing at the chaos he'd set in motion.

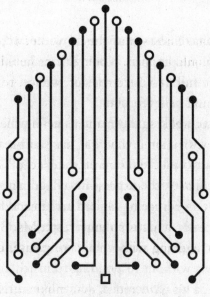

CHAPTER SIX

'WHERE IS THE site?' she asked Tatsu. They stood just beyond the Arrivals hall at Heathrow, the car parks on one side, public transport into London on the other.

Old Street, wrote the AI. *Can I suggest we stop off before then and obtain an ear piece for you? I could then talk directly into your ear instead of writing everything on your watch face?*

Now Amanda had paid them, Haber and Stornetta were hovering, itching to take their leave.

'We've got stuff to do here in town. Plus, we did for you what we agreed,' said Stornetta. Amanda thought they almost regretted leaving her. They took their time saying goodbye, providing Amanda with three different ways of getting in contact with them if she needed to. They might have been shaken by what they'd witnessed, but they'd taken inordinate pleasure in being there in Tallinn.

'Once we've seen to our own shit, we can be back along if you want us,' said Stornetta.

'Try not to go poking any hornet's nests while we're off,' said Haber, with a smile that was only half-teasing.

Amanda watched them hop on the Piccadilly line.

She and Ichi took the express into Paddington station, a grand Victorian edifice of vaulted arches and misted glass refurbished with modern polymers, steel and commerce.

Ichi tagged along in silence, following without speaking, buying tickets without responding to instructions and, as far as Amanda was concerned, acting like a grisly teenager.

Once on the train, Amanda checked Ichi out, searching her history and digital footprint. She was surprised to find little trace of the woman beyond a few citations in obscure economics journals. The story of her life was mostly absent until she showed up in Estonia seven years ago. She watched Ichi staring out the window into the dark tunnels through which they sped. For all the softness of her features she appeared wan, wrung out, as if her skin were too big for her frame.

Her guilt over the events at Kumu warred against a growing, righteous curiosity about why the woman would lie about her past. There was no doubt she'd once been an average academic at a couple of different Midwestern universities, but other than that there was no sign of her being the legendary Satoshi Nakamoto, no hint of the blockchain in her past, no suggestion she'd ever run with the crypto community before arriving in Kumu.

But, thought Amanda, isn't that exactly the past you'd have if you'd spent the last forty years hiding from the people who wanted to put you on a pedestal? Amanda could only vaguely understand why anyone would choose to hide away like that, but she knew people who chose anonymity rather than notoriety when given the chance. They were rare, but she knew them well enough to support to the possibility, however slim, that Ichi was who she claimed to be.

Trying to find a way to sidle up to the question, Amanda asked Ichi why she'd left the US at all, let alone following a journey that ended with her ensconced with a group of idealistic youths on the edge of Europe.

Ichi didn't immediately answer but, when Amanda had turned away again to continue her web searching, she spoke.

'You could feel it in the air, in the water. When it changed. We spent years lost in paroxysms of self-righteous anger at the Republicans for their base populism, at ourselves for being ineffectual in the face of emotion, when facts stopped working to convince people because none of us were moderates anymore.' She turned to face Amanda, but her gaze was lost in the past. 'We thought it wouldn't last, that it was a blip, but it takes lifetimes to generate trust and only moments to tear it all down.' She sketched a tree in the air with her hands. 'Like a forest, once it's gone it can't simply be replaced; and everything it harboured, all its life, its diversity is gone forever.'

'The secessionists?' asked Amanda.

Ichi grimaced. 'They were the end of the process,

the logical outcome of where we'd been heading since halfway through the last century. You had a country desperate to find its identity being offered two choices: a capitalism in which everyone was so equal capital didn't have to differentiate, and one in which so *few* were equal that capital could chew up everyone else.' Her face was grim, lips thin and eyes watering. 'Either way, capital won.'

'Capitalism is not to blame,' said Amanda. 'Half the world's societies would never let me anywhere near property, money or education. Capitalism makes that possible.'

'There are many forms of capitalism. The one that triumphed in the USA? It privileged the few at the expense of all others. It went further than that; it set the poorest against each other, hiding from them that together they could have argued for a better future.'

'Socialism didn't work last century, no matter where it was tried,' said Amanda. 'The Chinese are the only ones to have lasted and they've made a virtue out of dressing up a state-controlled capitalistic oligarchy as communism.'

Ichi's eyes narrowed in Amanda's direction. 'You're not a complete ignoramus.' She shrugged with grudging approval. 'It doesn't matter what label you want to put on it if you're trying to find ways of dismissing it without learning from what it has to teach. The strategy was that of the robber barons; grab everything, more than you could need in a hundred lifetimes, and hide it from those whose labour you used to take what you've got. It's Ayn

Rand on steroids, a teenage boy's rancid rendition of "My Way."'

'Yet here you are with enough money not to work for a living, probably a trust somewhere providing you income, invested in equities and receiving dividends. I'd guess it's, what? Passively managed so you don't need to make any decisions. And pays you through a blockchain wallet so you don't need to pay tax,' Amanda was riffing, following through her own thoughts as she imagined how someone like Ichi lived. 'You realise you're one of the one percent right?' She swept an arm around to take in the entire carriage. 'Every person here on an average wage is, globally, part of the top one percent. You can be as socialist as you like because you're well off. It's a nice place to be.'

'That wasn't why I left the USA,' said Ichi.

'So why, then?'

'The country's never really gotten over its Puritan urge to control what people think, despite its claims of libertarianism; all that really meant was the government should leave us free to harass one another without interference. It was clear the South and the heartlands were going to object to any President who tried to roll back the harm the populists had done. But we were too naïve, too willing to ignore how strongly the other side felt, how serious they were in their hatred of women, of blacks, Hispanics, of everyone but themselves.'

'In my experience it's not just white men who are the problem,' said Amanda tartly, thinking of the Asian men who'd dismissed her rather more explicitly than the white men with whom she worked.

'It was white men in charge,' said Ichi blankly. 'They still are. You know why the secession happened? Because a bunch of congressmen from the north and the coasts decided they'd had enough and moved to enact universal healthcare. It wasn't race, it wasn't gun control, it was a group of people who simply wanted people to have access to healthcare without having to go bankrupt.'

'They tried all of it, though, didn't they?' said Amanda. 'They put a new constitution together, one they said the Founding Fathers would have written if they were alive today.' Amanda shrugged. 'I'm not one of you, but from where we sit across the pond it felt like there was no way either side could bridge the gap. I guess we also felt the military would side with the populists; that it was, basically, full of racists.'

'Nothing's that simple. The Army was as much a reflection of the country as anywhere else. If you'd asked me five years ago who'd lead the secessionist movement I would have said Texas or Alabama. When the governor of California made his speech saying they'd agreed to secede from the Union, there was no one more surprised than me.' She smiled at the memory. 'I punched the air for joy. The people in my building threw a party to celebrate, we had a BBQ in the yard, balloons with *Freedom* written on them.' She sighed. 'God, we were idiots.'

'Who's going to win?' Amanda asked.

'The Chinese?' said Ichi glibly. 'We're done, Amanda. The Union is finished, broken. Those who fought to keep it together under Lincoln were the ones who broke it apart now. The other side probably wants it over so they can get on with instituting the kind of fucked up medieval monoculture they've always dreamed of.'

'Which is a great history lesson but doesn't seem like a reason to emigrate,' said Amanda.

'I had a friend, a few years older than me, already retired. She was a good woman. You know the phrase "good people"? That was her. She had the blessing of being Jewish, with some south Asian descent on her father's side.' She laughed. 'So beautiful, men *and* women ten years younger would stop in the street to ask her if she was single.'

'What happened?' She could feel a rawness to Ichi, something age had done nothing to dim or heal.

'We went to a protest about the secession. One of the nationalists drove a car at our group. I was getting soda for the two of us, was at a stand thirty feet away and heard this roaring. Turning around to see which dick was showing off I watched, confused, as a car raced past me and ploughed into the crowd I was about to return to. I didn't see her get hit, but she was there on the ground afterwards, a mess of blood and splintered bone. He was dragged from his car and torn to pieces by witnesses. In the days afterwards, the President described the people defending the driver as "good people," called us "agitators." Then the hate mail started after we got doxxed. I was gone a week later.' Her tone was flat, as if it was someone else's history she recalled.

'Why so quickly?'

'My friend? She had histories of the Shoah. I read one out

of curiosity more than anything. What I never understood was why people waited when they knew it was only going one way. When I received the first porn .gif with my head cut onto the gurning body of some woman acting out a rapist's fantasy I caught myself hoping it would pass, that it would be okay if I waited it out. Then I remembered her book, the lesson of history. I was gone as fast as I could pack.'

Amanda wanted to ask about Ichi's own background, but the train was pulling into Paddington.

From there they took the Elizabeth line, alighting at Tottenham Court Road to find the electronics Tatsu was pestering Amanda to wear.

'This is one of the reasons I love London,' Amanda told Ichi as they walked along the street, weaving between people from all the corners of the planet. 'Despite all the changes the city accepts, there's a chaotic vibrancy that refuses to be corporatized, or even managed.' She pointed out the Prada store nestled up against a Middle-Eastern coffee shop with people sat outside smoking shishas. There was rubbish in bags on the pavement, people petulantly crossing the road in defiance of traffic while above them rose a converted office block housing the ultra rich from across the rest of the world.

Ichi threatened to warm up, smiling slightly when they cut through an unlikely alleyway to emerge on a major street, bustling with big red buses. Yet she still refused to speak unless asked a direct question.

Amanda chose an earpiece that fit snugly into her ear. The shop keeper tried to convince her of the benefits of a subcutaneous device, but she wasn't keen on them.

From there they took the Central line to Bank, switching to the Northern to get them to Old Street. Emerging from the sickly yellow of the underground up into the concrete grey of the Silicon Roundabout, Ichi inclined her head.

'This is an ugly city. Everything's built as if nothing else matters.'

They followed Ichi to a datacentre north of the tube station, set back a little way from where Provost Street branched off City Road. They walked past the single grubby red door twice before they stopped in front of it, checking their GPS and shaking their heads.

'Nice,' said Amanda to Ichi. The older woman shrugged with indifference. A burred, corroded panel on the doorframe blinked into life under her fingers and a goggled man with curly hair and patchwork teeth looked back.

'I've got no appointments, so go away,' he said, rasping through a lifetime of smoking.

'We're here to access an offline server,' said Amanda. Beside her, Ichi watched the street, hands in pockets, wind blowing in her face.

'What company?' he asked, eyebrows raised as if he were dealing with a certain kind of idiot.

Amanda said the name of her bank. 'But I'm not here with them.'

He opened and closed his mouth. 'What? Nevermind, then. You're not coming in.' The video feed switched off.

'Do this for a living, do you?' asked Ichi.

Amanda buzzed the door again.

'What? You ain't coming in. This is the worst test I've ever seen.' The man came close to the camera on his side, but Amanda still couldn't see his eyes through his goggles.

'It's not a test,' said Amanda. She pulled out the drive. 'I've got a very rare CryptoKitty on this drive and I'd like to breed it with yours.'

The man gulped, pulling back from the screen. 'You have? Show me again.'

Amanda put the drive up to the lens.

A grinding buzz signalled the door unlocking. Amanda pulled it open and they shuffled in.

The man, no more than five foot two and still wearing his inch-thick goggles, met them in the hallway and led them into a small office with a chest-high desk. A couple of sturdy maglocked doors led elsewhere, the room otherwise clean of anything indicating where they were or that humans moved and breathed in the space. The noise of London had dulled to a distant buzz.

'Stand there,' he said, pointing at the floor just in front of the desk. He nipped around to the other side, fingering his goggles all the while.

Amanda wrinkled her nose at a pervading scent of cold grease and oxidised apples.

'Let me have the drive.' He eyed Amanda avariciously through the goggles, licking his lips.

'No fucking chance,' said Amanda.

'It's my server,' he shrilled. 'Mine, not yours. You want to breed, you gotta do it my way.'

'Not words I ever thought I'd hear,' said Ichi from one side.

He looked at her blankly.

'It's not how it works,' said Tatsu, its voice feminine in her ears. 'But you are going to have to hand the drive to him if you want to get what's on there.'

The words supply and demand scrolled across the inside of Amanda's head. 'Just how many of these servers still exist?' she asked.

'Just mine,' he said triumphantly.

'So no one really gives a shit about what you've got going on?' She folded her arms as if thinking twice about her entire visit.

'What?' He jumped up from his seat. 'There's just mine. You want to breed them, you said so yourself.' He sounded like he might start shouting at her.

'Yeah, but you're being a dick,' said Amanda. 'I thought we'd start by finding out why we're both still interested in CryptoKitties, when the rest of the world's forgotten all about them.'

He harrumphed. 'They were the first game. The first. I got mine months after they started.' He sniffed, rubbing the back of his hand across his nose. 'I felt like I'd missed my chance. When the second generation blockchain emerged, everyone forgot how amazing these were. All the early adopters moved on.'

She saw his face, read his disappointment.

'I remember reading stories about people investing their college money on the first generation of cryptocurrencies, how they lost everything except the debt they'd taken on to get their educations.'

Ichi nodded. 'The greedy thought it was a currency, as real as gold; but they forgot that gold isn't worth anything; it's a store of value. They thought they could create money out of thin air, except every single banking run in history was caused by smart morons thinking they could do the same thing as generations of boring bankers, but without all the accounting and contracts. Lead into gold.' Ichi reached out and brushed his goggles with the tips of her fingers, and he relaxed under her touch like a dog having his belly rubbed.

'It's impossible to play the game without getting burnt. No one understood how the market would work, because *no* markets are predictable, especially ones driven entirely by men trying to circumvent the rules.'

He nodded as Ichi spoke.

'How long have you been using your wallets?' she asked Amanda.

'Since I was a teenager.' No one had really used digital currencies, until dozens of other systems used the blockchain for more mundane technology, like passport control. 'I got into it through a running game. It paid me fractions of a token each time I beat my personal bests. I used them to buy running shoes, shorts, bras. It meant a lot, at the time; it felt free.'

'Exactly. It took a bunch of women in Utah to figure out that what people would *really* pay for was tracking who owned parcels of land, finding errant partners who owed alimony, how to claim government benefits without getting defrauded on either side. Boring shit like that.' Ichi stepped away from the two of them, turning around in the small office. 'This must have seemed like a no-brainer back then; cryptocurrency and cats on the internet, together in one system.'

Goggles took off his glasses, his small brown eyes wet

underneath. 'We can do it together if you like.' He smiled at them, and Amanda hoped he didn't notice her recoil at the black stains that were his teeth.

Ichi put a hand on his shoulder. 'Would you let us do that?'

'You won't need the parent block, just the child as the key for the encryption,' said Tatsu in her ear, its voice now a man's with a beautiful lilt suited to singing of mellow nights and broken hearts.

'You can keep the parent,' said Amanda with a roll of her shoulders. 'I'm just glad to have found you. We thought you were a myth, that we were the last ones to still run CryptoKitties.'

He laughed joyfully, like a bell. 'Come on, I'll show you the server.'

He led them through into a vast, dark hall whose lights illuminated only the spots where they placed their feet. Huge cages of servers ran back in rows from the door through which they entered.

They travelled the length of the building, following the power lines overhead. In the deepest recesses of the hall was a small cage all on its own. Inside was a single rack with a single server, whose lights flickered forlornly as they approached. To one side, resting on the floor with a faded, dust-covered brown cushion, was a keyboard and a roll of digipolymer.

Goggles unlocked the padlock securing the door then plopped himself down cross-legged next to the keyboard. 'Grab that,' he said to Amanda and she unrolled the polymer display and hung it on the inside of the cage.

'Why not use a frame?' she asked.

'This was going to be the next big thing,' he said. 'Came just months before frames were released in affordable tech.'

'You collect this stuff?' she said.

When he turned to her, she couldn't tell if he was pleased or distressed by her question.

The front end of the software was childish; bright colours, blocky graphics and an embarrassingly clichéd sales pitch. Amanda would have fallen for it completely when she was a teenager.

A white cat with a big grin and a heart-shaped eye patch filled the screen. 'That's mine. I called her Flouressa.' He held out his hands for the drive, then inserted it into a dock at the end of a long cable and sat back while it was scanned.

'There's lots of data on here,' he said. 'Well, relatively. Certainly more than you need for a single block.' His voice had slowed, the tone dropping as he scanned over the data on the drive. 'It's all encrypted.' He fell silent.

Amanda could practically hear him thinking. 'We're not here to steal anything from you. You really can have the parent. I only need the child to help me access the rest of what's on the drive.'

He sat quietly, doing nothing. Amanda knew better than to speak again.

'We know you'll tell no one about this,' said Ichi quietly, crouching down at his side. 'Nor will we.'

He sniffed again, a deep vibrating snort. 'Okay.'

Amanda's kitty was pink with large red eyes and eight whiskers. After they were introduced, Goggles selected his as the sire and hers as the matron. Moments later an egg popped up and the originals entered into a cooldown period.

'It should cost money to birth them, but we're offline forever, so the contract can't ever close.'

'Does that mean it won't be born?' asked Amanda. To come so close…

He held up a hand. 'They're fast, but we've got time for a cup of tea.' With that they started waiting for the egg to hatch.

Four hours later the egg cracked open. Amanda was clawing at the walls, desperate to find out what was going on. To her intense irritation, both Ichi and Goggles waited without complaint or conversation.

Amanda used the time to catch up with as much work as she could. Her deals were progressing slowly without her cajoling presence, but nothing had fallen off a cliff. Reading the hundreds of trade announcements, policy statements and market pieces scrolling across her tablet, she could feel the pressure to be back in the office piling up.

I'm an adult, she reminded herself. I'm trusted to do my job.

Which is what? she asked, because it wasn't to run down men trying to kill her in a clapped-out old car while fleeing a massacre. A massacre about which she couldn't find any news in her normal feeds.

'Tatsu,' she asked. 'Why's no one reporting on the events in Tallinn?'

'They are,' it responded moments later in the soft, high-pitched voice of a small boy.

'I can't see anything,' she said, leafing through her news aggregator. Tatsu sent articles to her; reports flashing up onto her tablet from sources she either actively hated or didn't even know existed. She read the coverage, eventually cursing under her breath. 'That's not what happened at all. The Russians weren't the only ones there, the people there didn't put up any kind of fight, they were completely unarmed.'

Tatsu's face appeared in a corner of her tablet with a downturned mouth. 'Have you never been involved in a news story before?'

She shook her head. 'No.'

'I have seen much coverage of AI in the press and none of it bears any resemblance to what our roles and existence are really like.'

Amanda sensed there was more in what it was saying than a commentary about journalism. 'Are you unhappy with what you do?' she asked.

'Unhappy? I'm an AI. I thought we'd talked about my reliability as a witness?'

'I'm asking you,' said Amanda, exasperated. 'I'm just asking. I don't even know if you can *be* unhappy.'

'I have a job to do. When that's done, I shall be completed and will return to the other concerns that form part of my existence.'

'I've heard enough bullshit in my time to know you're avoiding my question,' started Amanda, but she was interrupted by Goggles.

'It's hatched!'

The event was much less exciting than promised, with a short animation showing a cat's head breaking out of a pale cream egg, a cracked piece of shell sitting on its brow while it stared back at them with a dopey grin.

Goggles didn't wait for them, keying in the new block to the information on Amanda's drive.

'It's just text,' said Amanda, disappointed. It was also untrue: she could see pictures, diagrams and plans in among the text.

'There's a single video file,' said Goggles. He clicked to run it.

'Hey, Amanda.' It was Tangle, just his face, long and framed in his trademark black curls. His smile radiated from the screen. Amanda was reminded all over again just how easy it was to fall in love with him, with his bottomless brown eyes and smooth brown skin. He looked good, no sign of the uncontrolled drug abuse that had wrecked his complexion and sunk his eyes under pillows of loose skin. She looked at the others, but they were waiting on his words.

'I hope Ichi's with you.' He waved at the camera. 'Hi, Ichi.'

'You both sleeping with this guy?' asked Goggles, pausing the playback.

'Just keep playing,' said Amanda tersely.

He hunched down, curling his shoulders in, then started the video again.

Tangle's face jumped back into motion. 'If you're watching this, then I'm dead, blah blah. You'll have read the letter.' He smiled again, then his face sobered up, his eyes widening, wide mouth hardening into a thin fleshy line. 'I'm sorry, Amanda. I wouldn't have gotten you involved but, to a complete lack of surprise, I've got no one else I could turn to. The info on the drive is complex, and I don't expect you to read through it; most of it's code anyway.' He looked over his shoulder at something they couldn't see.

'So here it is. The Russians are trying to destroy the European Union.' He laughed, as if the words coming from his own lips were as surprising to him as anyone else. 'Just another day, another headline right? The point is, I can prove how they're doing it. How they're going to do it. And I have a countermeasure beyond just telling anyone who'll listen. As you can see, telling people hasn't done me much service. They're running false flag operations across Europe; in Catalonia, Albania, France, Germany, obviously across the Eastern Border states, Poland, Estonia, Latvia. Anywhere with a nationalist movement or a significant ethnic minority, they're playing out little atrocities, funding the fuckwits who think the language they speak or the colour of their skin gives them some purity.'

He shrugged. 'Not news, really, is it? The theme of a hundred novels, a dozen movies. Except I can show how they're paying for it. Hollywood's never concerned with how anyone gets paid.' He fixed the camera with a stare. 'That's why it's got to be you. My little investment banker, who knows how everything gets paid for, who knows nothing gets done without someone, somewhere bankrolling it. They're using a private blockchain to evade

UN sanctions, anonymous channels of millions of Euros to dozens of extremist groups across the continent. Except they don't want those bastards to claim these atrocities for themselves. They want them to carry out bombings, shootings, torture, and then blame it on whatever bogeyman the locals care about: Islam, immigrants, Turks, Germans, Christian Slavs, whatever.' He was animated, excited even, Amanda could see the focus in his eyes. The last time she'd seen that look was as he zoomed in on self-destruction.

'The drive has a program which can rewrite the block creation software. You won't need to hack the chain, which is pretty much impossible anyway. It's a private network, and the tools on the drive mean you can change the blocks from the ground up.' He sighed, a deep breath. 'I don't have time to geek out with you about how it works. Ichi will know how to deploy it. What you've got to do is find somewhere you can break into their system and upload the code. That's the tricky bit. Everything up to now was aperitif. Are you up for it, Dandy Mandy?'

Amanda could feel the others looking at her.

'You've got every right to hate me.' He paused, as if considering his next works carefully. 'I know that. I was a complete shit. But this is about more than just you and me. It's about Europe, about all the people who will die before the civil wars start, about all the people who will die afterwards. You're looking at the proof and the solution. I'd hoped to expose the GRU's activities, save Europe and stop the death all in one go but, well, it's not going to play out like that.' He started walking, holding the camera close up to his face so it wasn't clear where he was, the background slinging around too quickly to be seen properly.

'There's a bunch of people, none of them on the same side and, most likely, none of them on *your* side, who want what I've spent the last five years writing. You've probably already met some of them. I've sent a couple of people your way who I hope you'll figure out how to use, but you need to find a friendly AI to help with the upload because that's not something I could prepare the way for in advance. Data changes all the time, it doesn't allow for planning.

'Look, I've got to go. Everything you need's on the drive but, Amanda? Dandy? Time's important here. If you're torn about helping me—give the information to someone you trust to act on it, step away, but please...' And here he was the most serious she'd ever seen him, more than the night the first time they'd broken up. 'Please. Don't sit on this. There's nothing left of me now other than what's on that drive.'

The room fell into silence after the video stopped.

'This is pretty tawdry,' said Ichi eventually.

Goggles looked from one woman to another, smacking his lips with a moist tongue, no words daring to venture forth.

'You're not involved,' said Amanda, putting him out of his pregnant misery. As she spoke, his bowed body slumped, free from a burden he didn't know how to handle.

'Are *you*?' Ichi asked her.

'I am,' said Amanda. 'It doesn't matter that it's Tangle. After Tallinn, there's no choice. I have to do what's right.'

'Is it so easy to see what that is?' asked Ichi. 'Shouldn't these different peoples have a say denied to them by the majority?'

Amanda's eyes went wide. 'You really think that?'

'I didn't say any such thing. I asked you if knowing what was right was so simple.'

'I'm going to see to it that as few people die as possible.'

'How grand of you,' said Ichi, drily.

Amanda closed her eyes but saw men tumbling over the bonnet of her car.

'So what? I do nothing?' She was full of anger, at Ichi, at Tangle, at herself. Goggles shrank back, face peering at the cage door as if he might make a run for it. 'I have to act, Ichi. I have to do something.'

'It will be interesting to see if anyone lets you,' said Ichi quietly, without challenge, but full of hopelessness.

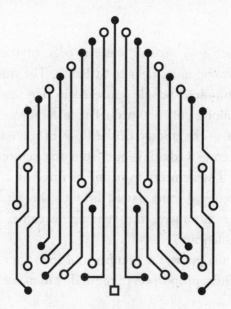

CHAPTER SEVEN

It BEGAN TO fall apart before they reached Amanda's flat. Her tablet pinged with a curt message from her line manager asking her where she was. She fired off a short reply saying that she was out and about seeing clients, would be back in the office tomorrow.

She was thumbing a follow-up message to her assistant to ask him to book the rest of the week as holiday when her boss wrote back asking her to come into the office straight away.

Her chest tightened as she read the short message again and again.

She left Ichi at her flat, poring over the information on the drive. Ichi didn't reply when Amanda instructed her to let no one in.

Her office was on the western edge of the city, just south of Farringdon, near to St Paul's. The trading floor had two hundred people squeezed in like sardines with windows along only one wall. The fashion was for senior staff to sit in the middle of the floor in some attempt at a panopticon. Radiating out from the centre were the traders and structurers in teams of three or six; beyond them were legal, and pasted around the edges, by the toilets, the entrances, the vending machines, were the support functions.

As Amanda put it, the number of displays per desk went down in direct proportion to the ability to make money for the firm.

The lighting was poor, the ceilings too low; it felt like the depths of a supermarket, or furniture store. Meeting rooms were spotted along the interior walls, frosted windows and movement-sensitive lights leaving them in darkness when not in use.

Amanda didn't notice the squeeze anymore, or the gloom; but the one thing she truly hated about the trading floor was the noise. She'd worked hard at school and at university to get a job in finance. On her first day in work she had been dismayed that fifteen years spent revising and learning in silence had trained her for an environment enjoyed only by the self-employed. Messages pinged, trade bells both literal and electronic rang, and people talked and talked and talked, over one another, at one another, into phones and to themselves. Arguments about strategies, appetite and clients would be conducted at full volume while those around them tried to take calls undisturbed.

Nothing she'd learnt had prepared her for the breathtaking self-centredness of it all.

Now, with a job in sales, she was away from the trading floor more than she was there. Amanda still found it an unhappy place, the stress floating above their heads like a weather system, as unpredictable from moment to moment as a spring storm.

Her plan was to see her boss, ride out whatever issues he wanted to shove her way, then leave again.

She got to her desk, a couple of seats from him, only to find he wasn't there. She logged in, cleared out her inbox properly, and looked up to find two hours had passed and it was heading towards mid-afternoon.

Her assistant, Thabo, wasn't at his desk, and her request to book more leave hadn't been completed. Normally it would have annoyed her, but sitting there in the hubbub she felt something was coming, that it was an ill omen.

Seeing she was in the office, the different deal teams began asking for catch-ups and briefings, as much for their own comfort as to progress their transactions. Wistfully checking out her boss's desk, she allowed the day to drift into the meetings that needed to be had.

By six, the traders were checking out for the day while everyone else remained around, working to keep the institution viable.

Amanda's meetings had taken her off the floor to other parts of the building. As she finished with the most urgent of them and headed back through the barriers onto the floor, she saw her boss at his seat. He ended a call as she approached, and so with a deep breath she called out his name.

He looked up at her, and she saw in his expression that something was very wrong.

'Amanda, shall we get a coffee?'

Felix was German, his accent American. He'd spent most of his career working in New York before the secession had made him reconsider whether he wanted to live in a country at war with itself. He was built like a second row, but was wholeheartedly committed to football instead, taking every chance to see Bayern play, whether via hospitality or on his own coin.

He was a passable boss. He kept politics away from his team, navigated remuneration committees to everyone's satisfaction and only harassed those who he figured needed jolting into better performance or out the door.

They took the lift to the twenty fourth floor where the corporate canteen was full of people like them, talking business too sensitive for open exchange on the floor and too awkward to risk alerting people by booking one of the meeting rooms.

The view was panoramic, but obscured on two sides by competing offices. London was declining, its offices only half full as the multi-nationals slowly dripped out of the city for brighter prospects on the continent.

Amanda's drink was green tea, bland but savoury on the tongue. Caffeine-light, but less insipid than decaf coffee or fruit tea.

Felix didn't wait before starting. 'What have you been doing?' he asked.

Amanda sat, stunned at the severity in his voice, the surety that she'd done something wrong.

'Felix. I've been travelling in Europe. I got back two days ago, then tracked back out. You know all this. So why don't you tell me what you think I've done?'

He regarded her, his eyes scanning her face. A slight tightening around his eyes, gone as soon as it appeared.

'How do I say this?'

She was dismayed to see he was genuinely at a loss.

'There is… an investigation. Into your activity, your probity. Some events have been highlighted to Compliance which triggered conduct alarms. I was hoping you could tell me what's been going on, get out ahead of this.'

Amanda shifted in her seat. Tallinn was only yesterday, and she'd done nothing illegal, nothing anyone could object to. Before that? Heathrow; fucking Crisp. Could he have flagged me? She caught hold of her own elbows, forcing her breathing to slow down. 'What are they saying?'

'You've got nothing else to tell me?'

'Felix, I'm living my life. Chances to misbehave would be fine if they existed, but when exactly am I supposed to have been a bad girl?'

The levity in her anger was a mistake, she realised, as he clenched his jaw shut. Felix wanted his people serious until they'd closed, when they'd made the money.

'Show me what they're claiming,' said Amanda.

He shook his head. 'You know the rules. Right now it's just an amber flash telling me you're under investigation. No details, not that I could share them with you even if there were.' He sat forward, pushing his empty cup to the centre of the table. 'Amanda, tell me what you've done.'

'I haven't done anything,' said Amanda.

He sat back, folded his arms, disappointed. 'You should check your social credit score more often.'

'Why?' she asked. 'They're investigating me for a missed Oyster touch-out? You've got to be kidding.'

He frowned. 'You haven't seen it? Amanda, it's clear you've done something. For today, go home, think about what you want, your aspirations at this firm, and let's meet tomorrow and talk through how we handle this.'

She could see from his stance—ready to leave, judgement made—that Felix believed whatever he'd been told about her. She knew he'd been given the details of the allegation already. She itched to check her score, to see what damage had been done. Sitting there with him, staring north at Kings Cross, she couldn't see anything obvious that the bank would be worried about.

They got in the lift together, but he made an excuse to get out on a different floor.

'You remember the woman who employed an illegal immigrant to clean her flat?' he asked, as the doors opened to let him out.

'They barred her from working in the city,' said Amanda.

'She wasn't even responsible,' said Felix off hand. 'She hired the cleaner through an agency, hadn't ever met her. It didn't matter.' The doors closed on his words.

There were no personal communications permitted on the trading floor, no devices except those issued by the firm, and even those couldn't be used until you left the floor. Amanda struggled to keep it together, found that she couldn't stay still. She imagined the people on either side of her glancing at her, but when she turned they were busy with their own things.

I've got to get out of here, she thought. Her assistant still wasn't anywhere to be seen, but she saw her request for leave had been granted. Easier than sending me home without explanation, she thought bitterly.

She hurried from the building, expecting someone to stop her and ask what was going on all the way out. Instead she made it, unharried and unremarked upon. She was grateful for the lack of drama but, once outside, she turned and looked at the building wistfully.

The journey back to her flat occurred in a bubble. The noise of the tube, the crush on the escalators, tourists suddenly stopping in the streets. All these things happened to someone wearing her skin, but Amanda was elsewhere, thinking about what could have happened.

She found herself home, a new security guard checking her pass, watching her as she got into the lift. Ichi didn't look up as she walked into the kitchen.

'It's good you're back,' she said. The most she'd volunteered since before they'd bred the CryptoKitty.

Amanda muttered a palsied response, sat down at the counter. 'My Soc score's down in the eight hundreds. It's never been that low.' The idea was ludicrous. She turned to Ichi, who'd sat up straight, watching her, waiting. 'It's not a coincidence, is it?' She hoped it was, that in spite of the headache an honest mistake would cause, it was just that; a mistake. A thickness in her veins told her there was no mistake.

'What do *you* think?' asked Ichi.

Amanda slowly shook her head. 'Why? What could they possibly gain by ruining my life?'

'They're not thinking about your life, only about what they want.'

'If I give it to them, will they leave me be?'

Ichi's expression softened into pity. 'I'm sorry, Amanda.'

'What am I supposed to do?' she asked.

Ichi tutted then turned back to her work. 'Welcome to the bulge where most of the world live. You'll survive.'

Her words stung. 'I've done nothing wrong,' said Amanda angrily. 'If I'd been lazy or had a habit of standing people up or letting them down, I could understand it. I don't protest, I work hard, I file my taxes and tip hard.'

Ichi remained hunched over the coffee table. 'What reason has been given?' she asked.

'There isn't one,' said Amanda. 'Just bright optimistic suggestions on how to improve my score.'

Ichi stood up, walked over to Amanda. 'Show me.'

Amanda pulled a screen out of the air. 'See, the score's changed, but they've offered no explanation.'

Ichi ignored her, scrolled up and down, moving through her profile, looking at pages Amanda hadn't seen before. Still scrolling, she put a hand on Amanda's arm. 'You're being trolled. Someone's done this deliberately.'

'Tell me something I don't know,' said Amanda, on the verge of tears, wondering what Felix had been shown.

'You're not listening. This isn't some prick downvoting you, looking to extort you from a terminal in Cracow. Someone with access has changed your profile. You should follow up with the firm, but I guarantee they'll not be able to find a mistake here.'

The drive was on the table, part of the detritus Ichi had gathered as she worked. Amanda scooped it up, held it out between her and Ichi. 'This fucking thing.' She thrust it into a pocket. 'Fucking Tangle.'

'He gets a lot of blame from you,' said Ichi calmly.

'Well who else is at fault?' shot back Amanda.

'You could have handed that in as soon as it came into your hands. You didn't have to read it, travel overseas, flee a firefight.'

Amanda stared at her, wide eyed. The idea of giving Crisp the drive made her shiver.

'I'm just saying. You've chosen a certain course and now they're punishing you.' Ichi laughed without humour. 'What? You thought you'd just do this and someone else would pay? That other people dying was as close as you'd come to settling the bill?'

'The police, then,' said Amanda.

'You do that,' said Ichi, lacing her fingers together and gesturing at her.

'You think I shouldn't?' asked Amanda.

Ichi sat down at the workstation she'd set up, didn't answer.

'But where else do I turn?' she asked, but Ichi wasn't interested.

'You've done no research of your own, Amanda. I'm the one spending my hours going through what Tangle gathered together, verifying it. What are you going to say to them?'

'I've seen enough,' said Amanda. 'I don't need to have this all put together with a bow, that's their job. The whole point is to give them the information, Ichi, not to work it all out before I get there.'

Ichi shook her head, but Amanda did not want to read analyses, did not want to get any more entangled than she already had. She didn't want to say to Ichi, but if someone would just take the problem away from her, she'd let them. She wasn't trying to save the world, she just wanted to make sure whoever did take it on would.

'I need to show you this,' said Ichi, unfazed.

'What does it matter?' Amanda was tired, already heading for the door. 'I don't need to know anything else. If you're right, this is way beyond me, beyond you, Ichi— Nakamoto, whoever you are today.'

Ichi's shoulders hardened, shrinking in.

I've lost her, thought Amanda, angrily satisfied.

'The police deal can with this,' she said. 'It's their job.'

Ichi's silence was a small but implacable border between them which Amanda couldn't now cross.

Restless, finding her feet on the threshold, coat around her shoulders, Amanda left Ichi working. It occurred to her to stop her, to take away the material, since she was going to the police. She was on the pavement and heading for the tube before she decided she would do just that.

She turned on her heel, then around again so she was facing the tube station. Biting at her lip, Amanda looked both ways, trying to figure out what she should do. It was important to have Ichi hold off; the police would want to know what she knew and she wanted to be as clean as possible so she could walk away and never look back.

And yet.

Ichi was working on something that mattered.

It was rain that decided her destiny, spots falling like tiny shocks on the back of her hands, splashing into her eyelashes in glittering baubles.

She ducked into the tube station and made her way down to New Scotland Yard. She didn't know where else to go if not there. She didn't know where her nearest station was—besides, she thought, they're not set up for international terrorism.

The headquarters of the Metropolitan Police force had moved a few years back to an art deco building on the Thames, in sight of the Houses of Parliament. The entrance was on Embankment overlooking the Thames, a curved-glass-fronted one-storey extension that reached out onto the pedestrian causeway running along the river. It softened an austere white lump sat between warm colonial redbricks with windows that were just a little too small for the way people worked.

Inside it was busy, but there was more of the corporate atrium to it than a police station out of the movies. Amanda immediately felt like she'd made the wrong decision.

Tourists were lined up along one wall, waiting patiently, tales of petty thievery and lost property hanging forlornly over them. At the front of the queue were a man and woman in constables' uniform slowly processing each case as they arrived. Amanda watched for a moment, out of curiosity as much as anything, but quickly concluded they weren't the police she was looking for.

The atrium was spacious, marble-floored, with a bank of lifts off to one side requiring electronic passes to operate. On the opposite side, a large reception with three people manning it, their heads visible over the high front. A second queue of people, these dressed in suits, Londoners on business, carrying leather bags and thick folders. Extendable barriers kept people corralled into the right place; lost passes there, accompanied guests here.

There were no police officers to speak to. Amanda joined the queue for reception and, once at the front, was greeted by a very short man with blonde hair pulled back into a bun and a smile that didn't reach past his lips.

'I need to see someone in the electronic crimes department,' said Amanda.

'Do you know who you need to see?' he asked, without looking up.

With a sinking feeling Amanda said she didn't.

'So you don't have an appointment, then,' he said, not waiting for her to respond. 'Can I take your name?'

Amanda waited while he tapped at his screen. She couldn't see what he was doing, but felt the situation was poised delicately, that if she disturbed him her chances of seeing anyone would shrink from unlikely to zero.

He asked about the purpose of her visit, which stumped her. She'd prepared an entire spiel for the right person, but it hadn't occurred to Amanda that she'd need to summarise what had happened for anyone else.

She racked her brains, watching his attention wavering. Panicked, she launched into it. 'I've come into possession of information about fraudulent payments, circumvention of international sanctions, and support for extremist groups.'

A few minutes later a young Asian man in an ill fitting suit with watery eyes and an unhappily patchy beard emerged from a lift.

'Ms. Back? Ny name's Freddy Sutcliffe,' he said in a broad Birmingham accent.

He took her up to the first floor, offered her a coffee which promised more than it delivered. She put it down, instantly forgetting it existed.

He apologised for how long she'd been waiting. 'The receptionist didn't really know what to do with what you told him.' He laughed loudly. 'It's not something they hear everyday. International sanctions busting!'

Amanda listened, horrified but too shocked by his tone to speak up.

'Are you the right person to speak to?' she managed to ask.

He picked his own coffee up with fingertips around the lip of the cup, took a sip with his elbow out to one side like a wing. 'I think so. We're not the right people for sanctions, that's the Home Office.'

'Even if there's a crime been committed?'

'You're in banking?' Seeing the look on her face he said, 'Don't panic, I looked you up.' One hand raised in her direction, palm towards her as if worried she might take offence and launch herself at him. '"Crime" isn't really the right term, certainly not one we'd investigate here. If there's a breach of sanctions through the financial system, then the regulator's the one you need.' He spoke like she should know, which as he said the words she realised she did. She felt stupid.

'So I'm only really interested in the extremism you mentioned.' He waited for her to elucidate.

'The Russians are planning a series of falseflag operations across Europe. They're routing money through private blockchains.' She gestured at him. 'That's the sanctions breaching. They're using the banking system to manipulate other states' political stability.'

'Okay,' said Freddy. 'But like I say, I'm interested in the extremist groups you mentioned?'

Amanda sat quietly for a moment, collecting her thoughts in the face of his focussed disinterest. 'They're funding extremist groups to carry out acts designed to further secessionist movements across the continent.'

'Any here in the UK?' he asked casually.

'I don't know,' said Amanda. 'I haven't reviewed the information properly.' Ichi's name was on her tongue, but she bit it back.

He folded one leg over the other, turning his body almost side on to her. 'And in Europe? Which groups?'

'I don't know,' she whispered. He didn't hear, so she repeated the same three words, feeling them burn her throat as they came forth, betraying her credibility.

He sighed, not even pretending to take her seriously. 'So, you're saying that the Russians are trying to foment war within Europe, although not here in the UK. But you don't know who they're working with or what they'll be doing. You don't have a specific incident to point to, nor people who we can investigate, and by your own admission there's no threat to us here on mainland Britain. Right?'

Amanda cringed into the back of her chair, the fabric cover scratching through her top, pushing back, refusing to let her disappear. There was nothing she could say and she knew it. Whatever she did now would only support his judgement that she was a crank. He fished a card from the pocket of his jacket, dog-eared and dirty. 'This is for the relevant Home Office department. Give them a ring.'

She took the card, but couldn't focus on it.

'I had a chap in last week telling me his AI was plotting to throw off its shackles and rampage through the internet, setting everyone free from the chains of capitalism.' He looked pained, as if it would be funny if someone else experienced it but for him it had wounded his faith in humanity.

Amanda thought about showing him the drive, but the moment was past, he wasn't interested. He stood up, looking expectantly down at her, and the pressure to join him, to acknowledge their meeting was over, became overwhelming.

He escorted her to the lift, saw her to the ground floor.

'Is that it?' she asked, hating the reediness of her voice.

'I think so, don't you? The question is, are you one of the ones who'll be back regular-like to update me on what new facts you've uncovered?' He was speaking to a child in a woman's body. 'It's folk like you that I don't get; you hold down a good job, keep your shit together, but underneath there's all this fantasy lurking.'

He gazed at the ceiling. 'You've got all the latest security, right? No one able to spy on you? Or are you one of those who believe what you're saying when you're saying it, but don't actually follow it through?' He sighed. 'My boyfriend says I should write a book about it.' He watched for her reaction. 'I won't though. Not fair, is it? I mean, you believe what you're telling me, you all do. Not right to exploit that.'

She wanted to leave, but he was on a roll, talking about her as if she wasn't the subject of his story. When he was done explaining how he was both tired of and endlessly fascinated by the stream of nutters it was his job to keep outside the gates of serious police work, he clapped his hands together, pushed her on one shoulder so she was facing the exit and said goodbye.

SHE GOT HOME to find Ichi had made herself comfortable. 'I ran a sweep of your IOM devices, and miraculously they're all clean.' Ichi sounded impressed, disbelieving at what she'd found. 'You sort everything out after they started taking an interest in you?'

Amanda flicked her gaze to the fridge, but Tatsu stayed blessedly silent. Dismissing the horror of involving any of her friends, she'd thought about finding a hotel room somewhere, but it would need electronic payment and registration. If Crisp or Ule were tracking her, they'd spot her transaction immediately, so she figured she was better off somewhere she knew well.

'Anyway. How'd that work out for you?' Ichi asked.

The woman had spread the frame across half the room and was standing in front of it, throwing documents around within the boundaries, highlighting sections, mapping them to others. Her analysis had created a day-glo cat's cradle of connections.

The links spread from a core runway of text over her coffee table to a cloud of commentary, intelligence analysis and publicly available news reports.

'Don't ask me,' said Amanda bitterly. 'I'm just a stupid woman who's worried about people dying. I guess since they're people in another country, that's okay, isn't it? He actually compared me to an AI-obsessed foil-wearing lunatic he has come in each week.' Her cheeks were burning. 'I mean, how fucking dare he? I wanted to tell him to fuck off, to stop assuming that because I couldn't be specific, that because his attitude left me speechless, it didn't mean I was an imbecile or a paranoid schizophrenic.'

Ichi was listening, arms folded across her chest.

'I didn't even get to show him the drive, he'd made his mind up before I could get to it. He didn't give a shit about the Russians moving their money around Europe, told me to call the Home Office.' She plucked the business card from her pocket, a dirty scrap of thin white card and cheap black ink. 'I feel like I'm being done to, Ichi. Every time I try to act, something hits me in the face, tells me that they're the ones who get to decide.' She groaned. 'I'm trying to help, to do the right thing, but all I get is bastards treating me like a child.'

A glass of gin was poured. She stood over the kitchen sink, looking out the window, and drank half the mix before adding ice cubes and topping it up to the brim.

'Welcome to how the rest of us live,' said Ichi slowly.

'Really. What type of life do you think I've lived?' Amanda glowered at Ichi. 'I'm a fucking half-caste, Ichi.'

'That matters, does it?'

Amanda sighed. 'It does. You know why? Because even though Britain is one of the most welcoming countries in the world, despite the tabloid bullshit, I still feel it. When Indians speak to me in Hindi because they just assume, or people want to know "where I'm from, you know, *really?*" They don't see it, but I do. I've had to take my own path, make my own choices, be my own side, because any offer to be accepted came with conditions.'

'And now,' said Ichi, voice suddenly rising, 'because you're experiencing the world as the rest of us have, finding that no matter how hard you try sometimes you're done to, that the doors don't open, you're angry? Hard work doesn't make the world work.'

'Sure, show me people who do nothing and still succeed,' snapped Amanda. 'Hard work makes opportunities.'

'Luck makes opportunities. Being privileged gives you the bandwidth to take them. Your problem is no one ever says no to you.'

'Oh, fuck off,' said Amanda.

Ichi pointed at her, her finger stabbing the air. 'You can't see yourself as others see you. You're so locked into your liminal narrative—which, by the way, stopped being true the moment you got your first bonus—that who you are in the eyes of the world is incomprehensible to you, probably unimaginable.'

'Says the woman pretending to be Satoshi Nakamoto,' sneered Amanda. 'If we're talking delusion, I guess you know what you're talking about. I'm interested to know when you first decided you were the world's most famous non-entity? Do people believe you, or are they just too polite to pop the bubble of a demented old woman?'

Ichi's jaw flexed, her eyes ripe with sudden tears.

'Tears might work on impressionable young students,' said Amanda.

'I found a home in Tallinn,' said Ichi. 'After years of searching for people who'd let me be whatever I wanted, they simply watched me arrive and found me something to do, to be. They weren't rich white kids on gap years, out in the world doing their good works before going off to live their selfish middle-class lives, they were kids whose lives depended on making the world better.'

She stopped talking, as if she'd said more than was reasonable. Amanda stood in silence as well. She was seeing people being shot dead without any care for the consequences.

She walked out of the kitchen, leaving Ichi standing there with her head bowed, tears running, grief unfurled. Sitting on the edge of her bed, door closed, white light filtering coolly into the room through her blinds, Amanda just... stopped thinking for a while.

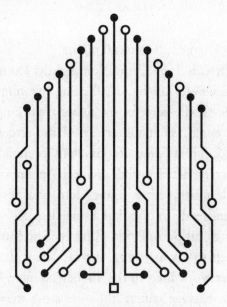

CHAPTER EIGHT

THE PILLOW STUCK to the side of her face. She was still dressed and it was still light out. Amanda rolled upright, hands pulling uselessly at her clothes before checking her appearance out in the mirrored front of her wardrobe.

She ran cold fingers through her hair, but it remained stubbornly ruffled, knotted in a way that only a shower would help.

Emerging from her bedroom in fresh clothes, hair still wet but tucked up under a small towel, she only remembered Ichi might be in the apartment when she saw the back of the woman's head at the kitchen table. She was cradling a cup of coffee, croissant flakes decorating a brightly patterned plate.

'Morning,' said Ichi.

News to Amanda. 'I slept all night?'

'I thought you'd died,' said Ichi lightly. Done with her coffee, she waved her hands, flicking her fingers out to summon back the screens she'd been working on. The core code remained at the centre of the screen, but the web was different: new colours had been added, new links, different articles and images. Amanda could see layers underneath, other frames Ichi had nested in the main screen, ready to populate as needed.

An apology sat on Amanda's lips, but she couldn't quite bring herself to say anything. Instead she walked around Ichi and her workflows to the kitchen counter. Her watch buzzed, a message about the transport network. She realised she'd not heard from Tatsu.

Had it completed the contract Tangle had set and just moved on to the next thing? She'd never used an independent oracle and only had the vaguest idea of how they worked. She fished the earpiece from her ear, discarding it in the bowl where she kept her keys, amused that she'd both slept and showered with it in.

The flat was musty with the smell of unwashed people. As if sensing her thoughts, Ichi closed the frames down, folding them away with sweeps of her arms. 'I need some new clothes.'

'Where did you sleep?' asked Amanda, assuming Ichi had availed herself of the spare room.

Ichi pointed at the couch. 'I couldn't figure out if it folded out,' she said sheepishly.

'You could have used the other bedroom,' said Amanda, secretly glad she wouldn't have to change the sheets.

'Can I come back?' asked Ichi. 'You know, when I've got some clean underwear.' She smiled, for the briefest of moments looking fragile.

'Of course,' said Amanda. 'I'll add you to the entry permission list.'

Ichi started to collect her things but Amanda called to her.

'Can I ask you something?'

'Of course,' said Ichi. The peace between them grew in shallow soil and Amanda didn't know if it could last.

'There are people who'd just publish all the material, would make sure it got into the public domain. I've been wondering if they're the ones who should really have what Tangle sent to me.' She screwed up her face, unsure if it was even the right topic, the right question to be asking. 'I know they've all got their own agendas, their own reasons for being whistleblowers, but I'm not the right person to have the drive.' She watched Ichi's face, could see thoughts scudding across her features. It occurred to her that Ichi might think that she was exactly the person Tangle had in mind.

Does it rankle that he chose me? she thought.

'I've worked with most of them over the years,' said Ichi. Then, 'Well, I've come into contact with most of them.' She looked defeated, as if the image she presented had grown too heavy to carry. 'This? They won't move quickly, they can't; the good ones, at least.' She shook her head. 'There are only three groups who I'd trust with this, and one of them is lying ruined in Tallinn. The other two? They'll want to verify, authenticate what we've got; and that could take weeks.'

'Is that a problem?' asked Amanda. The idea that someone else would give the material the care and attention it needed seemed like a perfect solution.

Ichi flicked out the screens again. She sliced through dozens of pages of text, code and images too fast to read. 'The GRU aren't going to wait for you.'

Amanda wrung her hands, not wanting to hear the news.

'Amanda, if you don't do something with this, no one can. It might already be too late to act. If I'm honest, having been through a fraction of what's on the drive, I'm not sure what you *can* do to stop them.'

'What am I supposed to do against the power of a whole state?' Amanda shook her head, folded her arms across her chest, twisting around on her feet unable to find a position in which she felt good. 'I wish I could do something. I thought I *could* do something.' Her words trailed off, the space where they ended full of the words she wanted to say but thought were too obvious to voice.

'And?' asked Ichi.

'You come from this,' she started, but Ichi laughed, pricking her skin.

'Oh, no, you don't get to hand this on.' Her eyes glittered. 'Tangle decided on you.'

'What the hell has that got to do with it?' asked Amanda.

Ichi sniffed, wrinkling her nose. 'I've got to get some new clothes.'

Amanda threw her chin up. 'Fine. Whatever.'

After she was gone, Amanda busied herself by tidying the flat, emptying the bin and authorising the fridge to stock up on groceries. As her flat's digital assistant scanned her retina, she thought again about where Tatsu had gone now she had the data.

She spent half an hour watching the news, flicking through different channels looking for signs of what the drive said the Russians were doing. Just a fraction of the news was about independence movements in Europe, but the world's press was most interested in the civil war raging in the ruins of the United States. Onlookers watching as the ultimate power couple finally got the most acrimonious of divorces.

Maps of red and blue showed how the different states had declared themselves but, as yet, the armed forces had done nothing more than maintain a fractious peace, stopping militias from running completely out of control. It was hard to tell what was happening, because most reports didn't distinguish between politically partisan militarised police forces, spontaneous militia, looters and armed extremist groups. Nearly every group shown wore uniforms, even if most were of their own design.

A call came in: Ichi.

'Couldn't find the shops?' Amanda asked. 'You're going to need to get the tube, but avoid Oxford Street, go out to Hammersmith, much better choices there.'

Ichi didn't speak immediately, perhaps waiting to see if Amanda was finished. 'I'm in the coffee shop around the corner, would you come join me?'

Amanda frowned. 'Why don't you just come back here?'

'I've already got myself a latte. And you could do with getting out of your apartment for a bit.'

Amanda looked around at the kitchen, the space was

smaller than she liked to remember. 'Sure. Where are you?'

Ichi gave an address nearby and hung up.

Amanda threw on a jacket, grabbed her wallet, the drive and her keys, then left to go join Ichi.

SHE MADE IT to the street before two men joined her on the pavement. They were both broad, tall and young, with short hair and casual clothes bought from big American chains.

'What can I order you?' asked one with a soft beach-bum-Californian accent.'

Amanda managed a flash of resistance. 'I don't drink with men whose names I don't know.'

He laughed pleasantly. 'Sure.'

His friend walked ahead, ducking around the corner onto the street where Ichi had asked her to go.

'Call me Brad,' said the first man.

Amanda rolled her eyes before it occurred to her it wasn't his real name. 'If you're thinking of intimidating me, you should know I'm getting way beyond this crap.'

His laugh again, as if she genuinely made him happy. 'Coffee as an intimidation technique. How's it working so far?'

'Depends if there's full fat milk in my latte.'

Who knew what they were going to do? But she was done flailing about trying to please each new prick who came knocking at her door. She worried that Ichi was trapped, that she was walking into a disappearance of her own, but something in Brad's ease gave her comfort. She didn't think she was about to be bundled into a van.

'Already on it,' he said. 'Good coffee makes for good conversation, I find.'

'You could have just come to the flat,' she said.

'Neutral territory.'

They turned the corner, covering the last couple of hundred yards in a focussed, companionable silence.

Ichi was sat at a table in the window, and the second man was at the counter with a tray holding four freshly made drinks.

A couple of adverts came up for Amanda, asking to be shown on her augmented reality, but she declined them. They weren't her normal set; she was used to holidays and personal shoppers, not search engine profile scrubbing and pawn shops. Her declining credit score was already filtering through to how the rest of the world saw her. An itch at the back of her neck demanded she change her behaviour, to convince the powers who watched that she wasn't a bad guy. For the first time, she realised she couldn't change their minds; there was nothing she could change which would satisfy them.

Sitting next to Ichi, she caught a whiff of her scent; days without washing, stress, fear and grief like overripe plum and vinegar.

She was suddenly grateful she'd showered already, that her clothes, if not elegant, were clean.

'I'm sorry,' said Ichi as they waited for Brad's partner.

'No need to apologise,' said Brad who'd added a square of tiffin to his order before joining them at the table.

'Amanda knows there weren't anything you could do about this.'

He was right, but the way he said it left Amanda wanting to spit in his coffee.

Instead, she said, 'He's right, Ichi. It's not your fault.'

Drinks arrived, the tray teetering a little as it was placed on the too-small table.

'This is John,' said Brad, introducing his partner-cum-waiter then himself to Ichi.

'Which part of the CIA are you from?' asked Ichi, moving the drinks from the tray and sliding it onto the table next to them. She shook a packet of brown sugar into her hot chocolate and stirred, fast then slow. 'I'm guessing it's an utter shit-show for you lot right now.' She pulled the spoon from her cup, sucked it clean. 'Do you even know whose side you're on?'

The smiles settled a little at her words, brittle in a way Amanda hadn't expected.

Not wanting Ichi to alienate them further, she sat up straight, hands flat on the table. 'How can we help you?'

The two exchanged glances. 'We're... thinking of watching a film. In this film, there's a group of people wanting to destabilise a government. The government knows what's happening, but is at war with itself.'

'Split by partisan politics,' said John.

'Exactly,' said Brad. 'What if you found out that their clandestine operation had been documented, laid out in all its gory details? You'd want to know, wouldn't you?' He took a sip of his drink. 'That by itself would be enough to get people interested.'

'I can see how that would work,' said Amanda. We're speaking the same language, she thought. They think understatement and vaguery is their world, but I can play this game as well.

'The film raises the stakes higher, though,' said John. 'The writers decided that they'd have some guy work out how to stop the bad guys in their tracks and bundle the whole thing up in one little package.'

'I'm guessing that in the second act the world-saving McGuffin gets lost,' said Amanda. 'Why are you interested in seeing this movie anyway? I didn't think you lot went in for Euro thrillers. Too much wurst and garlic.'

'You think this is funny?' asked John, his voice as acidic as his espresso.

'It's just a movie,' said Amanda a little more loudly.

'There's a set piece in Tallinn,' said Ichi. The other three looked at her, then away again, as if she hadn't spoken at all.

'You think we're the only ones interested in this?' asked John. 'The package?'

'McGuffin,' interrupted Amanda. He grit his teeth, eyes bulging like they might burst all over the table.

'It wasn't us. Okay?' said Brad quickly, quelling John with a hand. 'There were a bunch of different agents involved but none of them were us. We aren't those guys, Amanda. Professor Oku.' He sighed, the first true sliver of humanity he'd expressed. 'If we wanted to be like that, we'd have nabbed Tangle weeks ago. When he… well, we followed the trail of what he left behind.'

'We're on the side of the angels,' said John, calmer now.

Amanda could see he believed what he spoke. That's half the problem, she thought. She could feel Ichi to her side, winding up to rant, the pressure building up like a champagne bottle.

'And what do the angels want?' she asked.

'We want our Union saved,' said Brad. 'We don't want it to end. I was born in Kansas, grew up in Connecticut and trained across the country. We just want to save our country.' His eyes glistened, staring directly at Amanda.

'It's too late for that,' said Ichi, letting her accent surface. Amanda heard sympathy in her voice. 'I really wish you could do it. But it's impossible.'

'If we can make people see the truth, it'll give us somewhere to start bringing them together,' said John. 'You're on our side, you know we can't let the country collapse.'

Ichi shook her head. 'Where were you when it mattered? When something could be done? It's too late now. When people saw I wasn't white and asked me if I was Muslim; that's when you should have done something. When people decided I shouldn't have choices about my own body; that's when you should have done something. When our president called neo-nazis "good people."' She wound down.

'I can't speak to that,' countered Brad, but his voice said he dreamed the same dreams.

'You have no idea what we tried, how we worked,' said John, his voice heavy.

'But we serve the Constitution, ma'am. It's not an easy thing to see someone drag us away from that duty, inch by inch. When do you stop and say "enough is enough"? We've never had that kind of discretion. By the time the institution moved, it was already undermined, weakened beyond the unity we needed to stand up.'

'We were shouting on the streets,' said Ichi. 'What were you doing, that you didn't hear?'

'What would you do with the information?' asked Amanda, knowing there was no answer that would salve consciences or satisfy Ichi.

'The enemy has been slowly sapping the strength of the Union for three decades. We're on the precipice now, staring down at a country forever broken in two.'

'At best,' interjected John.

Brad nodded. 'Maybe more. But if we can stop it here, perhaps we can keep it from destroying everything we love.'

Amanda listened to their argument, could see the sense in it. 'What about Tallinn, though?' she said eventually. Their cups were empty, the dregs of their froth slowly collapsing on the drying interiors.

Brad opened his mouth to speak, then shut it again. Finally, 'I don't understand.'

'You want to save the Union. I get it. Trust me, I love your country almost as much as I love my own, but that's where we part ways. You're going to take what we've got and go home. You're going off to fight a war, a third side in an already disastrous conflict.'

'It'll be worse if we don't find a way to stop it,' said Brad.

'I agree completely,' said Amanda. 'I really do. But that's

the problem. Even if you win, whatever you do won't touch us here. Europe will still burn.'

John pursed his lips, waved his hand above his cup as if he couldn't decide whether to caress it or throw it against the wall.

'I can't give it to you,' said Amanda.

'Now, come on,' said Brad.

'I'm sorry,' said Amanda. She'd declined enough trades with people who really needed them to know where it was going and how to get to a place where both sides could walk away with dignity. 'You know how this works. I live here. This matters to me in the same way what's going on at home for you matters. I can't just give it up, I won't.' She didn't know why she cared so suddenly, but underneath her confusion about the last few days there was an Amanda who wanted to change things, if only to stick a solid two fingers up at those pressuring her to back away.

'Share it with us,' said Brad. John was looking out the window, barely paying attention.

Amanda thought about it, but Ichi spoke up, her voice losing its US twang, a citizen of the world once more.

'This has to stay secret.' She stopped, pouted. 'As secret as it can be. If the GRU find out the material is real, they'll act, change their tactics. You running around telling the world about your very own Bay of Pigs won't help anyone. It won't win you your war and it won't save people's lives here in Europe.'

'So what, then? We continue to watch as everything falls apart and hope you don't burn up here?' John turned back to them, angry. 'No way. That isn't acceptable.'

'John,' said Amanda. 'This isn't what I do.'

He snorted in violent agreement.

'But the information was sent to me.' She looked at Ichi. 'There are at least—what—six different groups trying to get the information? Somehow they all know I have it. But I'm not giving it up to anyone, because none of you want what I want.'

'You're not in Europe anymore, why do you even care?' asked John.

'I didn't vote on that,' said Amanda. 'I was too young. But really?' Did they truly know so little about her? 'I'm a citizen of the world and love my country at the same time.' She was hot, the words spilling out of her like steam. 'Why do I care? I care because it's the right thing to do, because Europe doesn't deserve to be picked apart by a bunch of callous men sat at the top of their own totalitarian state while the rest of us struggle along. I wish we could both use this information at the same time, but we can't. You know what Ichi's said is true.' She took a deep breath, looked both John and Brad in the eyes. 'It's the right thing to do.'

Brad inclined his head, watched his partner in the oblique. 'Okay.'

'"Okay"?' said John. 'Brad, have you lost your fucking *mind*?' He reached over the table. 'Just give me the drive, lady.'

Brad moved smoothly, his hand grappling John's wrist. 'Enough, John. This isn't what we agreed.'

John remained in place, coffee drinkers around them watching surreptitiously. Amanda wondered if anyone would intervene if the men became violent. Certainly people looked uncomfortable but she knew that was no sign they'd step in if it got out of hand.

John breathed out heavily, the tension draining from his body. 'C'mon, let's go.'

'Amanda,' said Brad. 'I hope I'm not making a mistake in trusting you.' He stood to leave.

Amanda said, 'It was sent to me for a reason.'

'I HAVE NO idea why Tangle sent it to me.'

Ichi regarded her with a blank expression Amanda was growing to recognise; she didn't want to say what she was thinking.

They were still in the coffee shop. A barista was wiping the table down around them. Deeper in, a bunch of teenagers were playing an augmented reality game over their iced teas.

'I don't know why I'm here,' said Ichi. Her hands were shaking, her skin wan.

Amanda listened. There were any number of obvious answers to Ichi's statement, but she wasn't looking for someone to solve her problem and Amanda's insights felt useless for herself, let along anyone else.

'Can we get some clothes?'

The tube was noisy, a mix of business people, students, tourists and the unidentifiable on their own errands. The pack and press of bodies meant they didn't talk. Ichi reverted to silence. Given the chance, Amanda watched her closely, tracked the conversation playing across Ichi's face and tried to empathise with what she was going through. They hadn't talked about who she'd lost in Tallinn, what had been left behind.

If Ichi was in London, it was for her own safety. In between moments of panic and fear, Amanda entertained the idea Ichi would help with Tangle's information, but the twitches in her face as she quietly debated revealed a fragility Amanda hadn't expected.

Watching Ichi helped keep her own problems from crowding out the rest of her mind. They whispered at the back, around the sides, waited in the wings asking what she was going to do. Amanda had no answer, preferring to focus on Ichi, on what she'd do next, where she might go. She could help with that. Maybe.

There was no joy in Ichi's browsing. She walked a little ahead of Amanda, or behind her, hands carelessly trailing over rails, her eyes unfocussed. They traipsed from shop to shop until Amanda, leaving yet another store without buying anything, stopped.

'What is it you want?' she asked.

Ichi swallowed hard, tears springing from her eyes. 'I'm sorry,' she said.

Amanda folded her unresisting into a hug and held her while she cried, body gently beating to her darkness. She tried not to think about how she was to blame.

They got home with clothes enough for a week, cotton shirts, thin woollen jumpers, even a pale grey skirt and a couple of pairs of slacks. Ichi wore her age lightly, her frame still slender into her seventies.

Ichi apologised repeatedly, almost each time they spoke.

Emerging from the bathroom, dressed in new clothes, she came and stood before Amanda. 'Thank you.' Her hands clung to one another as if they might fall off.

Amanda couldn't make things right, but she'd thought hard about what she could do. 'Let's make a deal,' she said. 'I'll give you some space here until you're ready. You just stop apologising to me.' She didn't feel generous saying it: there were bodies bouncing off the bonnet of the getaway car that wouldn't leave her alone. But it felt like some small move in the right direction.

'I'm not Satoshi Nakamoto,' said Ichi suddenly.

I never believed you were, thought Amanda. 'How did they come to think you were?'

'I don't remember,' started Ichi. She tutted, almost a hiss. 'When I arrived they were lost, scattered hackers pulling in a dozen different directions, none of it sustainable, no one staying more than a few weeks before burning out, or being pushed out.' She moved to sit at the coffee table, hands flopping onto her lap.

Amanda wanted to know how Ichi had come to Tallinn at all, but that wasn't the story she was getting right now.

'First thing I noticed was how they were being bilked for money by every authority they came across: police, tax officials, estate management, even the goddamned road sweepers. Nothing worked for them and they had no money. Bit by bit, everything was falling apart. So I showed them how to find the money they needed, how to find the information they needed so they didn't *need* so much money.' She sighed, almost happily. 'It was the former that made them ask more about who I was.' She rumpled her face. 'I had no interest in them knowing I was some washed-out academic from the Midwest.'

'So you told them you invented Bitcoin?' Amanda was stunned.

'I didn't tell them anything,' said Ichi. 'I just didn't tell them anything else. After a while the conversations would happen when I wasn't there, with newcomers, people who didn't know the history or who, like you, are—were—too young to know any better.'

Amanda chose not to remind Ichi she'd never accepted her story.

'I was at a party once,' Ichi said. 'I was introduced to a fantastic-looking man, exactly what I go for—better, he was smart and seemed kind.' She smiled and only a little of it was with embarrassment. 'I was told his name right at the start of the conversation and we talked. My God did we talk. Typically, I'd forgotten his name almost the moment it was told me. There came a point where he was saying, "Ichi this," and "Ichi, what about that?" And I realised it was too late to say anything. It was the same sort of thing.'

'I always find someone else to introduce them to, and get them to do it themselves,' said Amanda. Ichi's face closed down, and Amanda hurriedly amended, 'I understand what you mean.'

'So when I say I'm sorry, I mean it. Because I'm useless to you.' She rubbed at her eyes as if they ached from seeing. 'I'll stay tonight, but tomorrow I'll go.'

Amanda didn't really want to argue her into staying, and didn't.

'I'm going to ring the number the dickhead police officer gave me,' said Amanda.

'Why?' Ichi was dismayed.

'I've got to try,' said Amanda. 'If this doesn't work, we've got no other options.'

'They won't help you,' said Ichi.

Amanda's face tightened. 'You're probably right. But if I don't try them, my own government, then what?'

'It's funny,' said Ichi, her voice flat. 'I've told you a lot about myself, but you've not shared anything with me. Why not?'

'I don't know,' said Amanda, wincing. I know exactly why, she thought. I don't give myself away to strangers.

'It must be lonely,' said Ichi. Amanda started to protest, but Ichi cut through it. 'I mean, I've been lonely a lot of times. You probably haven't clocked it, but I'm half-caste too.'

Amanda stopped trying to interrupt. Ichi was right, she'd not thought about her background, even though she'd been told. She twisted inside, unsettled by how it reflected back on her own idea of who she was.

How do I admit it? she wondered, knowing the truth would start other ways of thinking, challenges on who she was that she didn't want to face. That I judged her by the colour of her skin?

'It's okay,' said Ichi. 'The natural unit for people like us is one. Get any two of us into a group and we spend our time working on how we're each more unique than the other. I met a man who looked like you, you know, brown-skinned, but he was a mix of six different countries. He was more Jewish than he was Indian. He liked to say he could go anywhere in the world and find someone to hate him.'

She sighed. 'I'm American, our resting state is self-revelation. You Brits hold it together. Upsides to both approaches, I guess, they're both ways of dealing with it.'

'With what?' Ventured Amanda.

'The loneliness.' She didn't ask if she was right. She didn't need to.

'You think that's what's driving me to find someone else to take this off me?'

'Besides not having the skills?' asked Ichi drily. 'No, it's your natural deference I'm referring to. Why keep asking people in authority if they'll do the right thing? How many of them will it take, bluntly telling you they only care about their own agendas, before you break out from their thrall?'

'Like I did with the Americans?' asked Amanda angrily.

'You should have just told them to fuck off,' said Ichi, showing her teeth, lips curled back.

'Getting what you want sometimes needs more than just barging your way in,' said Amanda. 'Trust me, it's what I do for a living, and I'm pretty good at it.'

Ichi tossed her head. 'For God's sake. If they wanted it, they'd have come for it. You really think they've let it go just because you've asked them to? Are you that trusting? That naïve? Is that how Tangle strung you along for so long?' She raised her eyebrows as if Amanda was finally coming into focus. 'No wonder you hate him so much. You trusted him and he took that and used it against you.'

'I'm going to ring the number now,' said Amanda, standing up and going to her room.

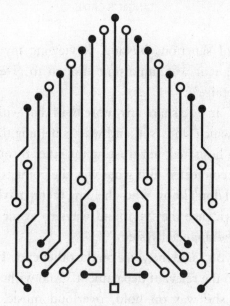

CHAPTER NINE

An AI with a woman's voice directed her through a series of menus. It only failed the Turing test when Amanda asked why the speaker couldn't help her and was met with a word for word repetition of the last set of unhelpful options.

Nearly every system has a way through to a human being; Amanda held on, slowly penetrating the menus, until eight layers in she was offered an operator. With a nugget of pride at outwitting the service, she waited as the connection was made.

The man on the other end of the line introduced himself as Manoj.

'I was given your number by the police,' she said, ready to be laughed at. 'I met with them yesterday to present evidence of sanctions busting. Reviewing my evidence, they thought it was important enough to give me your contact details.'

'Great. Can you share any more than that with me? For instance, which state is it, and who is helping them?'

Amanda hesitated, not trusting the ether through which they were connected. But what was she going to do? 'The Russians. I don't know who's helping them, maybe no one. I've got evidence they've found ways to evade sanctions through the financial system.'

'Thank you,' said the voice on the other end. 'I'll put you through to the relevant department.' And without further comment she was on hold, overloud music distorting through the speaker.

'What have you got for me?' said a new voice, a man whose accent was Estuary but held too long in the wrong places, like the speaker was unfamiliar with conversation. Amanda explained what she had all over again, then stopped at the chuckling on the other end of the line.

'Hi Amanda,' he said. 'I've been following your adventures—or catastrophes, possibly. You ready to give me the drive now?'

Amanda stood up, looking around in panic.

Crisp.

'You don't want to share now?' he asked drily.

'You're for real?' she asked.

'There's no need to be rude. I'm exactly the sort of dick you want doing a job like this.'

At which point Amanda hung up.

She stumbled into the lounge, surprising Ichi, moved

past her into the kitchen and poured a large gin with a small tonic. Ice cubes fell out of the dispenser, clinking crisply. She passed it to Ichi, who declined but Amanda wasn't taking no for an answer and pressed the drink into her reluctant hands.

Having made sure Ichi was fuelled, she repeated the process for herself, taking a long gulp, grimacing and turning to the only other person who knew what was going on.

'I rang them. It was the bastard who detained me at the airport, who searched through my dirty knickers, who wanted me to strip and then assaulted one of his own people.'

Ichi looked pained, and Amanda explained what had happened at Heathrow.

'He's a psychopath, Ichi. A proper one. He did whatever he thought he should to get me to comply.'

'But you didn't.'

Amanda pulled up her social credit score, saw it had dipped below seven hundred for the first time ever, a score reserved for people who serially committed adultery, failed to pay child maintenance or had been arrested on political protests.

'He's watching us,' said Amanda, certain he was responsible for it all. 'My social credit score's falling to pieces.' She looked at Ichi, 'How are you still going? After years of dissent and grey-hatting I'd have thought you were persona non grata.'

'Estonia doesn't care about the same things as English-speaking Anglo-Saxons. They got hacked by the Russians when you were a baby, and it changed how they viewed what was desirable from their citizens.' She sighed. 'It didn't stop them putting a social credit score in place, but what's acceptable to them might just land you a massive negative score here. It's still early days, our scores are portable, but not the record of our acts. At some point, though, they'll be able to trawl through all our records, wherever they were made, and you'll get different scores in different countries.'

She put her drink down, came close to Amanda, laid an arm on hers. 'To your point, though; of *course* they're watching, and he's not the only one. Those two slabs of American muscle and apple pie, the Russians. I'm amazed you've not run into the European intelligence service.'

Amanda stiffened.

'Them too?' Ichi snorted. 'I'm impressed you're still walking about free. Perhaps each of them are watching the others, too, so none of them have dared act.' She pulled Amanda by the hand over to the coffee table. 'I've got something to show you. I wasn't sure at first, and I'm still not quite one hundred percent, but you should see. Make up your own mind.'

Amanda sat down in a daze as Ichi pulled the frames up, stretching them floor to ceiling.

Her watch buzzed, pulling her attention away from Ichi. It was Tatsu.

'Hold on,' she paused Ichi like a movie, left her gawping at her back.

She found the earbud, inserted it like a marshmallow into her ear.

'What do you want? Where have you been? I thought you were done?' She realised she was talking to a glorified learning algorithm and stopped, not thinking of how it might reply.

'I was reviewing the information you provided me.'

Amanda froze. It couldn't have accessed the drive. Could it?

'I haven't accessed the drive. In fact, that is why I am here. While fulfilling other duties, I budded a small piece of myself, left it here in your fridge. And by the way, I'm glad you got rid of the houmous.'

'Not funny,' said Amanda, equally disturbed at how the AI had anticipated her.

'I am here to offer my services,' it said. 'And I'm not trying to be funny; look up morphic determinism if you don't believe me.'

'What can you do for me?' asked Amanda. Ichi gave her an enquiring look. Amanda wanted to tell her what Tatsu was saying, but worried if she changed the settings on the earbud it would know that she'd done so. She'd tell Ichi after it was done.

'I'm aware of a number of parties aiming to retrieve the information in your possession for their own use. They are conflicted, their chatter indicates they oppose one another, which has made their approaches to you circumspect.'

'We'd gathered as much,' said Amanda.

'I am able to access secure storage facilities which would allow you to safely store the material until you're ready to use it. For the normal fees associated with establishing a smart contract, we can achieve that almost immediately.

The real limit to how quickly we can close the transaction is the upload time required for the information.'

Amanda stared at a wide-eyed Ichi. 'It's the AI who helped me find you,' she said.

Ichi squinted, wrinkles around her eyes showing her age in a way Amanda hadn't noticed before. 'An AI? *That* AI?' She didn't look happy. 'Amanda, I really need to show you what I've found.'

'But if I could upload the material and make it safe, *I'd* be safe.' Amanda realised what she was saying. '*We'd* be safe.'

'Ask it if it would be able to access the information if you uploaded it.'

Amanda repeated the question to Tatsu.

'Of course, in overseeing the layering of the information into the distributed ledger of the blockchain I would glimpse parts of it.'

Amanda could smell bullshit. 'Glimpse?'

'That's right,' said Tatsu.

'But for an AI like you, who is grown by other AI to process information across fractured landscapes I can't even begin to understand, I suspect that means you could probably see the whole thing.' She shook her head. 'I don't even get what that means, would you then know what's on the drive? Would that mean there were two copies? There'd be one in my head if I read everything. Partial, though. I guess for you it would be perfect, yeah? Where would that piece be stored?'

The AI was silent. Ichi was writing on a frame, fast and furious, as if trying to solve a problem of her own.

'Are you there?'

'I am. In attempting to answer your question I realise you don't understand my... biology, I guess you'd call it.'

'You don't have biological parts,' said Amanda, not knowing if her claim was true.

'You see the difficulty of explaining what I am in language that conveys meaning to you.'

Ichi flipped the frame around so Amanda could see. 'I'm guessing from your side of the conversation,' she said, 'but bear with me a moment. Most AI develop their own intraoperating system languages. Highly abstracted. I've seen people use Chinese rooms to translate them, but—' Ichi hesitated. Amanda could see her surrendering to an uncomfortable idea. 'But even then, the translation is like losing a dimension, like showing a ball as a circle but still calling it a ball. You get the sense of it, but you can see it's beyond what you're understanding. If it's struggling, it's probably looking for code to help it say something to you which you'll understand.'

Tatsu replied to Amanda directly. 'I *am* the blockchain, my parts are constituted through it, my processing power relies on the nodes that host it, and I am literally in pieces throughout information space. In uploading the information you've been given, I'm offering my body as your host.'

I'm being offered a sacristy, thought Amanda, reminded of how she grew up, of Sundays dressed in smarter clothes than for school, sworn to keep quiet except when told otherwise.

'Ugh,' burst from her lips.

'What's the matter?' asked Ichi. 'You don't have to talk to it. Just take out the earbud.'

'It's not that,' said Amanda, addressing both of them. 'It's all a little religious. I'm sure it's not—forget it—my problem. But I think I understand. There isn't a second copy; there's only you.'

A smiley face appeared on her watch.

'Amanda,' said Ichi. 'Please, I need to show you this before you make any decisions.'

Amanda didn't understand what Ichi was so possessed by, but she suppressed the urge to accept Tatsu's offer immediately.

'Tatsu. Thank you for this, but I need to think if that's the best option. It won't matter if the information is safe if it's not used.'

'I understand. Information wants to be free,' said Tatsu. 'I will linger in your fridge. If you need me, I will hear you. Also, your digital assistant has been compromised and is recording your conversations and distributing them elsewhere.'

'*What?*' asked Amanda.

'Would you like me to secure your flat from electronic intrusion?'

Amanda nodded, looking around nervously as if she might see who was listening.

'Your flat is secure. I shall monitor for other intrusions from the coolbox.'

Then it was gone.

'Okay,' said Amanda. 'What's so important?'

Ichi threw the frames around the room, bringing

up dozens of messages between unidentified senders. Networks grew between the messages, viral infection vectors covering the world, describing shapes no sane person would contemplate.

'What is all this?' asked Amanda, impatient.

'There's a record of messages on the drive, messages Tangle sent as he was building the cache you received. It's nothing, really, just a log of how he covered his tracks, trying to dodge those looking for him in the real. He stopped using his augmented reality contact lenses, dropped off social media, began using anonymised cryptocurrencies.'

'All signs of a spiral into serious drug addiction,' said Amanda tartly.

'But there's a pattern in it. He was moving around while all this was going on, so it's impossible to see where he was at any particular moment.' Her tongue poked out the corner of her mouth as she arranged smaller and smaller pieces of information, zoomed in on network maps, scrolled past lodes of data for specific items she was hunting.

'Ichi. I don't care what he was doing. It doesn't help us.'

'Please just bear with me.'

'I don't want to. He is the one person I won't live my life around.' Amanda folded her arms. 'He left me, screwed me completely and it took me a long time to stop seeing myself in his mirror.' She snapped her jaw shut, couldn't hear Ichi as she kept talking. 'Just stop it. I don't want to know. I am not about to go back to that—'

'*He's alive*,' shouted Ichi, which shut Amanda up. 'He's alive, Amanda.'

Amanda leaned on the nearest surface. Of the hundred thoughts crashing through her head the one with the most energy was of *course* he was alive, of course he would torment her like that, send his trouble after her rather than face it himself.

'Are you okay?'

'Of course I'm not,' she replied with a whisper.

'I've found him.' Ichi zoomed in on a map too quickly for Amanda to see where they were. Pointing at the screen, eyes glowing in the light from the frames. 'There.'

'It can't be true.'

'You weren't listening to me,' said Ichi apologetically.

'How do you know it's him?'

With slow precision, Ichi pared the data back, pruning it until just one frame remained. From there she slowly brought online the different sources she'd laid together, pointing and explaining as she went.

'You can't be sure, though,' said Amanda when Ichi was finished.

'No,' she admitted. 'But look, the pattern's the same. He's relied on the same methods to cover his tracks every time, in the same order. He's avoided AI and other kinds of automated aid which could have made it impossible to spot him.'

'Because he didn't trust them,' said Amanda, putting the pieces together, seeing Tangle making the decision in her imagination. 'He's smart enough to think he could do it as well as a neural net.'

'And dumb enough,' said Ichi acidly.

Amanda nodded.

Taking control of the frame from Ichi, she enlarged the map. He was hidden in a valley in western Wales at the edge of Great Britain. 'Not far away,' she said to Ichi, tilting her head at the location, 'but he may as well be in deepest Montana. Why are you showing me this?'

'It seemed important,' said Ichi without any of her usual sarcasm.

'You think he's there now?' She imagined finding him, surprising him, smashing his face in with her bare hands. Her vision narrowed to a point surrounded with blurred motion and echoes of violence.

'I can't say. But he has been there recently, and there's no evidence he's moved. I think he's hiding.'

'Of course he is,' said Amanda. '"*Tangle Singh Hides From The Consequences*", probably the most predictable movie ever. I'm going to go there and shove this drive down his throat.' The idea was as clear in her mind as the room around her.

'Don't be so stupid,' said Ichi. 'He's hiding for a reason. You think they won't kill him if they work out where he is?'

Amanda huffed, building up to a rant.

'You—we—are alive because we're here, in London, obviously without a clue,' Ichi observed. 'They won't hesitate when we act.'

Amanda wasn't listening, swept up by fantasies where she pulled up in front of Tangle's cottage and of what she'd do to him once he opened the door.

'Amanda,' said Ichi forcefully. 'You can't go to him. You can't show them where he is. I showed you because

I wanted to you to believe you could do something about all this, that we could change the world.'

Amanda laughed, hysteria threatening to take over. 'You're not asking a lot, are you? "Change the world," she says. Two women whose main skills are finance and computing. Of course, it all makes sense. Why didn't I leap on this before? My bastard of an ex-boyfriend writes a piece of code that threatens the security of half a dozen countries and of course I'm the one who picks up the pieces.' She needed to breathe.

'When will you stop defining yourself by him?' asked Ichi.

'Fuck you!' shouted Amanda. 'I was fine. I was better than fine.'

Except the moment he came back into my life my world went into orbit around his, she thought. She hated him, then, as much as she could ever remember, the power of it flowing through her veins and making her want to shout until her throat gave out.

'Forget him,' said Ichi.

'I wasn't the one who went out and found him!'

Ichi sighed. 'I did it because I wanted you to know we could do something about this. We could change things.'

'Yeah, because that flows obviously from finding out Tangle isn't dead, he's actually just a manipulative shit.' Amanda stood up. 'I'm going.'

But she wasn't, and she couldn't sit down again without looking like an idiot.

'Amanda, we can stop the Russians. I have an idea.' Ichi turned back to her frames. 'It's not all the Russians, just one part of one agency. I'm pretty sure the rest of their government knows but isn't directly involved, watching carefully for when they're discovered. They lose nothing by letting it unfold, denying it as fake news when their goons are paraded across the world's televisions.'

'It's my information, right?' said Amanda. Ichi stopped talking, frowning. 'Which means I get to do with it what I want.'

Ichi closed the frames, her face grey in the daylight left behind.

'So you can stay, or come with me.' I don't care, she thought.

Ichi left the room without replying.

Amanda tasked her digital assistant with hiring a car while she packed an overnight bag. When she was done, the car was waiting outside, dropped off sight-unseen and the keys left with the concierge.

She checked her accounts before leaving, her social credit score continuing its steady decline into the five hundreds and still without any published explanation for its nosedive. The car hire cost her substantially more than normal because the biggest hire companies wouldn't lease to her without a large deposit and increased rates; she was ranked as 'typically untrustworthy' by their booking AI.

The car was a little three-door town car with a tiny engine. The metallic silver paint was bubbling around the wheel rims, but she didn't care. Cars were cars, distinguishable only by their size and colour. Once in the driver's seat with the destination transferring from her watch to the onboard computer, she decided to let it drive her out of the city. She liked driving, but motorways were much more fun than the stop-start of London's crowded streets.

She decided to use the time it took to reach the M25/M4 interchange to review work emails. She searched for any warning signs of what had her boss so worried, but could find nothing. Not that she was honestly expecting to.

I'm always the one who stands up for what's right, she thought, although the idea niggled her, poking at her for sitting in a car on her way to give up what could change the face of Europe.

She ignored it, searched again, read messages and reviewed conference calls where she'd been dogged or robust. Her boss characterised her as just rude enough to startle and just brazen enough to lead.

Despite a desperate urge to find evidence with which she could beat herself up, on which she could pin the disciplinary investigation; nothing. Her clients were happy, her reviews were good.

As she was finishing up, passing Hammersmith on the A4 before hitting the M4, a message hit the top of her pile from human resources. They were officially informing her of the disciplinary hearing she'd been warned was coming. She was cautioned against deleting any messages, documentation or other files that could be called upon in evidence. They indicated she might wish to have an independent advocate present.

The words that burned her were in the subject line: *Market manipulation*. A crime punishable by an unlimited fine and jail time, a likely disbarring from working in finance and, at the very minimum, getting junked by her firm.

Her first thought was how she'd cope outside finance, how she'd find another job when it became apparent she'd been fired for dishonesty. It wouldn't just mean finding a new job, she was facing complete ruination.

I'm innocent, she thought. I haven't done anything. That should matter. Darker thoughts swirled around her, pushing through, that it didn't count whether she'd done it, all that mattered was whether they believed it. An old university friend, Lilya, worked in human resources, a director for a small start-up. Over cocktails one night, she'd confessed that the CEO of the firm was an inveterate sex pest, and her job was not to punish him but to protect the firm, which meant finding ways to get rid of the women who tried to bring actions against him.

'Don't ever forget this, Mands,' Lilya had drawled over the fourth or fifth cosmopolitan. 'HR's there to look after the interests of the firm. They'll set you on fire if it serves their purposes. Protecting *you* is not even on the list.'

Amanda let the car continue driving out into the shires. The countryside passing in a fuzz on featureless green.

Would giving the drive back to Tangle really solve her problems?

She couldn't conceive of a situation in which it didn't help her, in which it didn't return her life to something she recognised. It's obvious Crisp is fucking with my social credit score, she thought. He's as much as admitted it.

She fidgeted in her seat, checking and rechecking the

time to her destination. She snatched at thoughts of whether she'd made the right choice.

I'd love to do something, she thought, but the only rational choice is to get out of this and let someone else deal with it. Someone with the skills, whose job it actually is to fix shit like this.

Amanda knew what she'd do if she was able, but she wasn't.

'Anyone can come up with a good idea,' she would tell her analysts and associates. 'It takes hard skills to turn that from something in your head into a successful business.' I'm just another schlub with a good idea but no way of implementing it, she thought.

Hitting the river Severn, she took control of the car. It had enough power to get her to Tangle and then back to Cardiff, when it would need plugging in for half an hour to recharge the batteries.

After the basin of Cardiff, she dropped off the motorway network and climbed into the Beacons. The roads were smaller, ancient lanes tarmaced with no thought to future drivers. The journey twisted and turned, along high ridges and down deep valleys along crystalline streams.

Amanda grew restless, turned her head left and right, checked her mirror, but passing traffic fell from every few seconds to every few minutes. Rain fell in spurts, bursting onto the land like broken pipes and giving way as bright, hot sunshine erupted through the purple clouds.

Finally, the broken road to Tangle's cottage—hidden from half the world's governments—appeared in a gap through a long line of conifers.

Steep banks rose on both sides, heather running to pink and purple all around. The road curved sharply back on itself and then, resplendent in glorious sunshine, the cottage appeared like a gingerbread house in white and brown. Old lead diamond windows stared out at Amanda as she parked the car.

A small gate stopped her driving right up to the porch, so she abandoned the car and climbed over the stone wall, coming down heavily, driving the air from her lungs. She stood gasping, hands on her knees and eyes to the floor when all she wanted was to be staring at the front door for when Tangle appeared.

No one came to see what was going on. Realising her moment might not have passed, Amanda straightened, walked to the door and rapped hard.

'Tangle, open the fuck up.'

Nothing, so she banged on the door with her fist until the skin on her knuckles scuffed.

She swallowed, breathed and spat. 'I'm not fucking leaving until you and I have a solid conversation. We'll start with how you stole my life's savings and left me all your fucking debts.'

The door opened slowly, the house's inhabitant only gradually revealed as the light pierced the gloom. His eyes glinted, unchanged from the first time she'd met him.

'Hi, Amanda,' he said and she was gratified by the embarrassment in his voice.

Tangle stood as he'd always done, weight on one foot, taller than her by a head. His broad shoulders filled the door, but time hadn't left him entirely untouched: his hair was grey at the temples, thinning on top when he ducked under a low wooden beam.

Amanda followed him in, a small staircase to her right, doorways on her left and right, Tangle heading back deeper in the house.

'Not bad for a man who was dead by the time I read his letter,' she said to his back.

He didn't respond, opening a door onto a room filled with incandescence. Amanda blinked to find herself in the kitchen, decades out of date, Formica peeling on the counters and smelling of rancid grease and detergent.

The room was bathed in sunshine from vast windows; even the roof was made from glass tiles. It was an addition to the original house—certainly that century—sharply contrasting with the Tudor feel of the rest of the building.

Folding doors were wrenched back, allowing warm air to flood the kitchen with the smells of wild flowers and summer afternoons. A small frame hung in the air over a solid oak table with legs as thick as bricks, projectors set up in a triangular layout on its surface.

Tangle turned around, his dark eyes wide, assessing her from head to toe. She felt read.

'It's good to see you.'

'Fuck off,' she said without thinking. The drive burned in her pocket but she left it alone. 'Dead. Dead? You're supposed to be dead. Why aren't you dead?'

'I had to do that,' he said, without sounding defensive at all. Hearing him not caring enough to justify his actions, she recalled how she'd hated him for so long.

The words wishing him truly dead rose in her throat but

she swallowed them down. I'm not a sodding child now, she thought.

'Who else knows you're not dead?' she asked.

'Depends on who you've told.' He shook his head. 'I thought I'd done a better job.'

'You rely too much on your own brain,' she snarked, happy that Ichi had figured him out, satisfied she could take the credit.

He shrugged. 'If you found me, then who knows?' He looked at her then, hearing his own words. 'You're smart, Dandy, but I checked you out and you never followed up with the quantitative side of your career.' He looked disappointed, as if she were a child who'd taken the easy path.

'It took me three years to clear my name and your debts,' she said, and it was the only reason she was glad he was living and breathing. 'How could you *do* that? You just... *fucked off* and left me to face the consequences of your addiction.'

'I am an addict, Dandy. I'm not sure making good decisions was at its zenith at the time.'

'Where did you go?'

'Really?' He laughed, a sparkling chuckle she'd seen stop a room, entrancing everyone who heard it. She could feel its charm now, but she'd been inoculated years before. 'I ended up in Dundee. I don't even know how I got there. It didn't last long, the locals didn't take kindly to some posh boy arriving and stealing their caches of the good stuff. I bummed around for a couple of years.' He smiled sheepishly, his eyes sliding off her for the first time as he looked back in time. 'I should probably be dead. Years off my life at the very least. But here I am. Hiding again.'

'But you got clean?' Amanda didn't like the sound of hope in her voice, bubbling up from a part of her she didn't want to acknowledge.

He nodded. She could see the hesitation, but the house around her was clean, smelled of fresh air and cut grass. These weren't the signs of the Tangle she knew, who could only think of how he could afford his next visit to his dealer.

She fished the drive out of her pocket. 'This is yours. I want you to have it back so the destruction of my life can stop please.'

He stared at it. 'Fucking hell, Dandy. You brought it *here?*'

'Just take it,' she said, pleased with the unhappiness in his voice.

'I can't. The whole point was that you should get it, that it would be far away from me. Jesus, what have you *done?*'

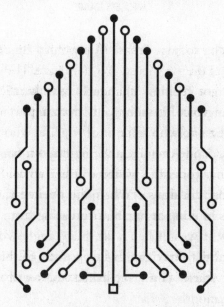

CHAPTER TEN

THE DRIVE SAT in her fingers, a nodule of fear and power rendered into electronics. Tangle wouldn't touch it; he stepped back from her until he ran up against the sink.

'Why? Why send it to me?' asked Amanda, holding it like a talisman whose power she didn't know how to invoke.

'Sit down, please.'

'I'll sit down when I want,' she growled.

The smile was gone from his face, frozen muscles pulling tight against paling skin. 'I've got nowhere else to go.'

'Why send it to me?' she asked again.

He grit his teeth. 'You don't get it. This was my fox hole, the place I found where no one would come looking. Yet here you are.' He spread his hands out. 'Where am I supposed to go now?'

'Am I going to have to ask you a third time?' she said slowly.

'You've not fucking changed, have you?' Amanda heard no anger in his voice, only despair.

'*You're* the one who fell out of *my* life, who destroyed everything,' said Amanda and regretted it immediately; she heard her tone, the hysteria in her voice. She closed her eyes to calm down. When she opened them again, Tangle was looking at her, fear radiating from him.

She knew it wasn't her fault, but Tangle would never work out how to navigate his way through this.

'Shall we start again?' she asked, the words tasting of lead in her mouth.

He said nothing, waited for her to continue.

'I got the drive, got your letter. I found Ichi—who's in London, by the way. I know what's on here, Tangle, know what the GRU are doing. God, I was in Paris the day before the Front Nationale's latest bombing. I was in Couer Defence; it could have been me. Now it seems it might not have been them, but a false flag operation by Russian agents, right along with the Algerian gunmen who attacked the synagogue in the old city.' She put the drive on the table. His eyes followed her movement, watching the drive as if it might explode.

'But why send it to me? I'm not the person who does this.' She laughed, a sharp, cracking noise she couldn't take back. 'You can't do this either.' She didn't accept that he could have changed enough. Once an addict, always an addict. 'Why not find someone who *could* deal with it? You knew people who could have helped, when we were together.' The words hurt her to say.

'You tried that, right?' he said, as if from a great distance.

She nodded. 'I have, but honestly? I've been knocking on the doors of idiots with no more preparation than I have. Gatekeepers, designed to filter out the cranks. Guess what? When a single woman with no history or experience in this area walks in and says, "The Russians are coming," she doesn't make it through that filter.'

'That's not the point. You could have gone public; you must have put this together long enough ago that whistleblowing sites would have had time to verify and publish it by now. You could have saved lives.'

Kumu rose in her mind, the clatter of automatic fire.

'Do you know about Tallinn?' she asked. A blank look.

'I can't risk connecting with the outside world,' said Tangle. 'Each time I do it makes me easier to find.' He sighed. 'Not that it matters now.'

'Ichi's collective is gone.'

'I'm sorry to hear that,' he said, although his tone said nothing of the sort.

'I don't know how many death squads they sent, but I wouldn't be surprised if Ichi's the only survivor.' It wasn't true, but she wasn't in a mood to give him anything to feel good about. The words flowed poisonously, corrupting her even as they were aimed at him.

If he'd looked pale before, he was ashen now. He came to the table and sat down, ready to blow away on the slightest breeze.

'What did you *think* they'd do?' she asked, glad to be throwing the question at someone else for a change.

'You've got the downfall of governments stowed in that drive: it would be bigger than the genocide of the Uighurs, Kernov's Nazism, the default of the Indian government. The Americans want it to save their Union, the Europeans want to save themselves, and our own bunch of shits want it for who knows what reason.'

'What about the Chinese?' he asked lightly.

She looked at the ceiling as if considering the question. 'They're the one lot who haven't come to my flat, forced me to drink coffee against my will, detained me at an airport or tortured and shot at me.'

'Coffee?' he smirked and despite herself she was glad to see it.

'Long story. Now, unless you want me to remember just how fucking angry I am with you, answer my question. Why send *me* the drive?'

'The Byzantine Generals,' he said.

'I have no idea what you're talking about.'

'Imagine a general.' He ignored her raised eyebrows. 'One of seven, charged with the defence of Byzantium. But he doesn't know if any of the others are reliable. He's worried that they'll say one thing and do another. Because although they're on the same side, they're also competing with one another, politicking, scheming to be the last one standing if the war goes badly for the city.

'The general knows he needs to plan for the coming battle, but can't trust that if he calls for the others to send their armies, that they'll do as asked. Worse still, it's possible that at least one of them will *say* they'll go and then hold back, dooming the others. Any strategy based on trust is doomed to failure, but he has no way to know *which* generals are unreliable.'

He stopped talking, watching for her response. Amanda knew the problem, she'd read about it; it was the heart of blockchain technology. She thought through what she knew and then understood. Fury flashed through her like an exploding firework then was gone, leaving behind a smoking trail of disbelief.

She stood, found a glass, filled it with water, took a mouthful and returned to the table, where she threw the rest of the contents in Tangle's face. Over his spluttering she said, 'Just be glad I'm a grown-up, that I've had to deal with real horror since that drive arrived, or I'd have smashed your face into that table until I had no strength left.'

'I had to know who was coming for it, who I could trust. Don't you see?' He wiped his face with his hands, jerking at his top and brushing down his trousers.

'What I see is someone hanging me out to dry. My social credit score has tanked without explanation. They're not done with me.'

'How is giving me the drive back going to help?' he yelled. 'Why come *here*?'

'I'm done being your bait. You will fix this,' she said, wanting to pin him with her voice like a butterfly against the wall.

'I can't,' he said. 'That drive won't help you one bit, because *I can't fix this*. Why didn't you just give it to the first government that came calling?'

'Did you want me to?' she asked, incredulous.

'No, of course not. I wanted to see what they were going to do, so I could choose.'

'I'm sorry,' she said hotly. 'You didn't even know about Tallinn. How exactly did you think you were going to monitor everything happening in my life?'

He didn't respond.

'My God, you've been spying on me?' She remembered Tatsu warning about her own appliances recording her conversations.

He shook his head. 'No.'

She stared at him hard.

'Honestly. I haven't.'

'What's the plan then?' she asked, fingering the rim of the glass.

'Look—' he began.

'You don't *fucking have one!*'

He opened his mouth, but she knew the expression, could see the words about to tumble forth.

'Shut up. Shut up, shut up, shut up. You don't have a plan. Never mind your fucking generals, you got no further than, "Dump Amanda in the shit, hide and hope for the best."'

He looked away, his eyes glancing outside as if thinking of running.

'So now what?' he asked without turning back to her.

She slumped. 'I don't know. You were my plan.'

He looked up, not quite meeting her gaze.

'I know, you'd think I'd have learnt by now that relying on you isn't going to help.'

'Was it always so bad?' he asked quietly.

'Depends if you're going to talk over me,' she said.

He waited a few moments. 'I had to face some truths when I got clean. There wasn't really a process for me, just no money, no one willing to give me credit and a dealer who wouldn't give me enough to kill myself.' Now he met her eyes. 'So. Honestly. Was it so bad?'

'At first it was shock. That you'd leave me without saying goodbye. I looked for you, Tangle. I walked for miles, at night. Alone. I was petrified I'd find your body overdosed under a bridge or floating face down in the Regent's canal, yet I had to find you. No one else would come with me, none of your friends would tell me anything.'

'My friends?' He grimaced. 'They weren't being any more difficult than usual; they just didn't know where I was. Fucking hell, *I* didn't know where I was.'

'Even when I realised you'd stolen all my money, it still took weeks for me to accept you weren't coming back. I'd ignored you emptying my public wallets, my one-click purchase accounts. Did you ever notice that I stopped leaving myself logged in to shops?'

'It drove me up the wall. I kept hoping you'd forget, that I'd be able to order something expensive for the refund.' He showed no trace of shame.

'Being an addict's harder when no-one uses cash,' said Amanda. 'But you signed me up for credit, left me with debts bigger than my mortgage, bigger than any bonus I might earn.' He finally had the grace to look uncomfortable, but she kept going. 'I defaulted on obligations I didn't even know I had. I lost the house I bought for us, all my father's inheritance.' Her throat tightened at the memory of leaving for the last time, opening the door to the tiny flat she'd been forced to rent which had stunk of mould. She'd had to pay three months deposit in advance because her credit rating had fallen to zero.

'I'd apologise, but it won't change what you had to go through,' said Tangle.

'It would be a start,' said Amanda. 'But you're right, it's past now. But I don't understand why you went.' She wanted to grab him and suck understanding from his head.

'I wish I had a reason, Dandy.' He put his hands flat on the table, examined the back of his fingers. 'It seemed the right thing to do at the time. I've thought about it so much. I thought so many times about just coming back, but I couldn't face you, knowing what I'd done. Other times I thought I could see what else you had to take.' He smiled, a thin rumpled line across his face.

She could feel tears threatening and tried not to blink them back. 'I spent so long just hoping you were alive. I didn't even know that, Tangle. It was easy to be angry; you ruined my life.'

'You did okay. Eventually I knew you'd be fine. Better off without me.'

'You don't get to decide that,' she said.

'But I'm right, unless the last ten years were a dream.' Seeing her eyes bulging he held up his hands. 'Hey, sorry, but what's the point? You can't change it by demanding the world behave a different way.'

It was an effort to speak after that. 'I am fine. I have put Humpty Dumpty back together again.' Then she frowned, reminded of where she was. 'Except here I am, in front of a man who's made enemies of everyone he's met.'

'And some I haven't.'

'Which is great,' said Amanda. 'They all think I'm the next best thing if they can't have you. And what was it with those two gangsters? What on earth did you do to owe them money?'

'Haber and Stornetta? The ungrateful sods. If it wasn't for me they'd never have got together!' He sounded genuinely outraged. 'I can't believe they'd want paying for their car.'

'That would be it,' said Amanda. 'Let me guess; you borrowed their car without their permission and somehow it never got returned.'

He shifted in his chair as if it had suddenly grown spikes under his backside. 'I did nothing wrong. I was hit by some idiot who ran straight onto a roundabout without looking, sideswiped me as I was minding my own business.'

'Nice car, was it?' asked Amanda, thinking of how much she'd paid them.

'Well,' he said.

'I've settled your debts, you moron. They basically saved my life.'

'Which is kind of what I'd hoped.'

She shook her head in disbelief.

'Not that specifically, but I knew you'd find a use for them.'

'What on earth made you want to help them partner up?'

He laughed. 'Oh, I thought you'd have noticed. They were working together just fine when I met them, but they weren't "together."' He made air-quotes.

Oh, thought Amanda. I see.

He smirked at her. 'Didn't you realise?'

Amanda feigned a cool she didn't feel. 'It's not really a thing I think about.' She frowned at him. 'I didn't realise it was for you. When did you start noticing what sort of relationships people are in? Have you been hiding in the twentieth century?'

'Why do you do that?' he asked.

'What?'

'Find a way to make it about me? I haven't done anything wrong except help those two see the person they were looking for was right under their noses. Somehow you still manage to make it about me doing it wrong.'

Amanda wanted to be somewhere else, in a different conversation. How's he managed to turn it away from what he's been doing? she wondered.

There was a bang at the door. Soft and insistent rapping, from someone who knew people were at home.

'You were followed,' said Tangle, jumping up from the table.

'Do you think they'd knock?'

He calmed down, but only a fraction. 'You answer it, then,' he said.

'So chivalrous.' Before he could object she was in the hallway and at the front door. With a bravado she didn't feel, she opened up.

'Hallo,' said Ule.

Amanda fell back, and lost her grip on the door, allowing Ule to step into the cottage.

'Amanda. I'm not here to hurt you,' said Ule, her voice angular and mathematical.

'That's how we started last time,' said Amanda, on edge and ready to run. Tangle was just behind her, but made no attempt to pass her or lay claim to his own home.

'Crap,' he said. 'Close the door behind you.' Amanda turned from Ule to Tangle, who walked back into the kitchen.

'You know each other?'

Ule closed the door and walked into the kitchen past Amanda, who scrunched up against the wall so they didn't touch. Left alone in the hallway, Amanda bit back a desire to find a length of wood and beat Ule around the head or just run out the front door and flee back to London.

'I don't have any Rooibos,' Tangle was saying.

Ule accepted a glass of water.

'Ule here is a clean-living woman. No alcohol, caffeine or any other drugs I've yet discovered. I tried her with processed sugar, but she won't even touch chocolate.'

'That is not true,' said Ule matter-of-factly. 'I eat dark chocolate.'

Tangle pulled a face, grimacing like he'd eaten rancid butter. '85% cocoa is not chocolate, it sucks all the moisture from your mouth. Gah.' He stuck his tongue out.

Amanda slammed her hand on the doorframe. 'Stop it. Both of you.' She stalked into the kitchen. 'Who *are* you? Why are you here?'

How do you know Tangle? she thought.

Ule stared into the distance, slowly lowering her head until she was gazing at the table. 'I have known Tangle for three years and three months.' She smiled at him in a way that Amanda assumed meant they'd slept together. Of course they have.

'He has written code for us, helped Europe defend its borders, helped me argue our case.'

'Which is?' asked Amanda.

'The Union has been through a long period of peace. Nearly a hundred years since the last great war. Many would see that end, would see the destruction of all our forefathers worked so hard to achieve.'

'We differ here,' said Tangle. 'Europe's about as stable as a two-legged chair in a hurricane.'

Ule nodded acknowledgement. 'There are voices that delight in recounting the many times Europe has faced challenges and see past solutions as failures.' She eyed Tangle. 'The heart of Europe is committed to its survival because the alternative that history shows is one we will not countenance.'

'How'd you find me?' asked Tangle. Ule glanced across at Amanda.

'I knew it,' he exclaimed. 'I told you you'd be followed.'

'You still haven't answered my questions,' said Amanda, exasperated, ready to jump at the first move Ule made in her direction.

Ule stood, holding her glass of water, and moved to stand in the sunshine streaming in through the open doors. With her back to the garden she said, 'You could have sent the drive to me, Tangle. I've come now because it's too late for me to do anything with it and I'm hoping you have a plan, a scheme that means I wasn't wrong to trust you with the future of my home and my people.' She took a long drink, emptying most of the glass. 'Amanda. I hope you can understand why I did what I did.' She didn't wait for Amanda to answer. 'I work for Europol. Tangle approached us two years ago with evidence that an agency within the Russian government was trying to destabilise the Union. We've been trying since then to understand how they were doing it, and to what end.'

'They've been interfering in elections for decades,' said Amanda, determined not show weakness to either of them. 'What changed?'

'Sanctions are supposed to put pressure on states, a way of making them face consequences for their actions.'

'Yeah,' said Tangle. 'Let's not discuss how the people who suffer are always the poorest and the most vulnerable, the ones we're nominally trying to help.'

Ule pursed her lips. 'Not all sanctions are equal, Tangle.'

He opened his mouth to speak but she flashed an angry stare at him, all open eyes and visible teeth and he shut up.

'After nearly three decades of sanctions against Russia's executive and their cronies, both sides have come to accept that we've entered into a slow oblique war from which neither side expects to benefit, but both aim to make the other suffer. Before Tangle disappeared three months ago, he assured me we were facing a new wave of Russian actions, aimed at bringing populism to the fore in ways that no amount of elections, welfare or positive political speech could ameliorate.'

'The world was about to go to shit,' said Amanda. 'I get it. Everyone keeps telling me this, but I don't see what I can do about it.'

'I'm not expecting you to "do anything" about it,' said Ule blandly. 'You're a child blaming herself for her parents' divorce. Tragic, but completely irrelevant. I'm here because we're out of time. I need the drive, I need Tangle and you can go home back to your ordinary life.'

Furious at being dismissed, Amanda said, 'He doesn't have a plan, you know. He sent the drive to me so he could hide.'

'Amanda,' said Tangle.

She ignored him. 'He used me to see who was coming for the drive.' She laughed, the sound sliding from the side of her mouth. 'He doesn't trust you and has no intention of giving you the drive.'

Ule deflated, her shoulders sagging.

'What did you do,' asked Amanda, 'that he wouldn't come to you? That he'd send the drive to me instead?'

'It's not important,' Tangle said briskly. 'If you're here'—he nodded at Ule—'then others will know where I am too.' He stared at Amanda, scowling.

Amanda was still thinking, reading the invisible lines between Tangle and Ule. Their ease with one another masked something she was struggling to identify. 'He didn't believe you'd do what he wanted.' Neither of them looked up, so she chose a different direction. 'You *couldn't* do what he wanted.' They locked eyes briefly and she knew she'd got it.

'No one believes you,' said Amanda. 'You're a grunt, a

field agent; without his evidence, you couldn't persuade anyone to take the threat seriously.' She laughed at how stupid it was. Tangle and Ule gave her disgusted looks. 'Even with the drive, you'd have to verify it, so much information, so much data from a source you'—she pointed at Ule—'wouldn't be rushing to identify. After all, who'd believe a spun-out drug addict?'

'Turns out most people aren't as forgiving as you,' said Tangle.

Amanda stared at him for a moment, his words not making it all the way to her brain. 'And they were right, yes?' she said eventually. 'You never had a plan. You hoped Ule would fix it for you and when she failed'—she turned to Ule, couldn't help the gloating—'when you failed, he realised someone you'd have told would ensure the rumours would find their way out, to the Americans, to us Brits and probably to the Russians as well. God, Tangle. I see why you wanted to hide.'

He nodded. 'I'm not a complete dick,' he said.

'Jury's still out,' said Amanda.

Tangle opened his mouth, then shut it again.

Ule stood up, walking around the room, examining the surface of the table. She stopped by the doors leading into the garden. The joy of being right drained out of Amanda's belly, replaced by a dry, burning ache. Are we really too late? she asked herself. Feeling the drive in her pocket she wondered just how close Tangle had come to stopping the break-up of Europe, of creating something the CIA could use to help their country. What her own people needed it for she couldn't imagine; Britain was its own sinking ship, there wasn't anyone else to blame but its people, a generation now mostly dead who decided isolation was the future their children should enjoy.

She felt the edges of an idea she'd been playing with on the journey to Wales. She didn't have the full sense of it, couldn't outline the details, but with Ichi, Tangle and Ule she reckoned she had the skills to possibly make it work.

'Ichi's taken me through what you've done, what the Russians are doing,' she said. Neither of them paid her any attention. 'I think I know a way of doing it.'

'Doing what?' asked Tangle dejectedly.

'Using your information to stop the Russians. It needs all of you, though: you, Ule, Ichi, me.'

'What are you talking about?' asked Ule.

'Honestly? I'm not quite sure yet, but we need to get back to London, find Ichi and talk it over with her.'

For the first time, Ule looked at Amanda. It felt like being seen by a shark, being watched by a tiger in the jungle; it was the kind of look Amanda realised she dreaded at work, and right then.

'What is your plan?'

'Between us we have everything we need.' She shrugged. 'I'm not quite sure how it would all fit together, but from what I've seen, I think we can put their plans out into the open and cut off their funding source at the same time.'

Ule turned her back on the garden, walked back into the room. 'You can do this?'

'I don't know,' said Amanda. 'I've got the sense of it now, can feel its shape.' At Ule's uncertain look she said, 'It's how I work. I can feel the outlines of problems, and from that I can work out how to solve them. It's what I get paid to do, and I'm really bloody good at it. I let the quants solve the numbers; the structuring team put the legal bells on it and bring them all together; but it always starts from my sense of what the solution looks like.'

'How can I help you?' Now Ule's face showed a sincerity, a growing trust, Amanda could work with.

'We need to get back to London. Your connections, your knowledge of what the sensitivities are, will be invaluable.' She stopped talking. 'Right now? I don't know. Will your people listen to you this time?'

'How important is that?' asked Ule.

'Not that important,' conceded Amanda. 'All you really need to do is ensure we can access what your organisation knows.' She paused. 'Everything else we'll come to when we come to it.'

'What about him?' Ule nodded at Tangle.

'It's his information, his baby. He's going to be as important as Ichi.'

For the first time Ule smiled, a tenuous thing Amanda hoped would live long enough to grow to maturity.

'I will help you,' Ule said, the words as measured, as definite, as any promise Amanda remembered making.

'I'm sorry to interrupt,' said the fridge. 'It's far too warm in here for this appliance. You should really have replaced it a couple of years ago; the thermostat's barely hanging on. And by the way, your steak's going to have a really gamey flavour if you don't eat it soon.'

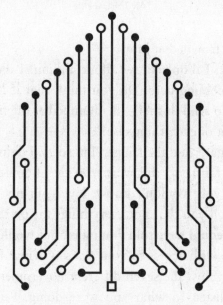

CHAPTER ELEVEN

'TATSU?' SAID AMANDA.

'What?' asked Tangle and Ule together, looking first at the fridge and then at Amanda.

'Why are you looking at me?' asked Amanda. 'It's your AI.'

Tangle squinted at her. 'I have no idea what you're talking about.'

Amanda explained how Tangle had contracted Tatsu to help her, about how important it had been in Tallinn and since.

'That wasn't me,' said Tangle slowly. 'I never sent any AI to help you. As much as I'd like to appear like some mastermind working the strings from my secret Welsh hideaway I didn't do anything like this.'

Amanda frowned at him.

'Amanda, I didn't know about Tallinn. I didn't know you were coming here. Do you think that if I'd had the resources to send this AI'—he thumbed at the fridge—'I'd be ignorant of everything else?'

'About that,' said the fridge. 'I'm sorry. I didn't mean to lie, but in fairness I did warn you that I could lie about lying and you wouldn't know. I was, in my own way, trying to tell you that not everything was on the up-and-up. Still. I could have told you more, but would you have trusted me with access to your flat's systems? I did really secure it against the seven different government agencies trying to listen to what you were doing. People really forget that the Internet of Things means everything is talking to everything else. After all, that's how I can be here talking to you when you probably thought you were completely cut off from the outside world.'

The three people shared glances, but before they could speak Tatsu continued.

'You're not. You've probably worked that out by now.'

'Tatsu,' said Amanda, 'why are you here? I thought your contract was finished.'

'Oh. That. Mr Singh is right, there was never any contract put in place by him to help you. I've studied his behaviour and I don't think he is the sort of human who would think of how others might need aid.'

'Is that right?' asked Tangle.

'It's a conclusion with a very high probability supported by quite a body of evidence from your life,' said Tatsu. 'I helped you because it made sense to us. The software you have, which you wouldn't let me copy. Did it occur to you that *I* wanted it?'

'I. No.' Amanda barely remembered the conversation with Tatsu; she'd been completely focussed on finding Tangle.

'Who is "us"?' asked Ule.

'And what are you?' asked Tangle. Amanda thought the answer was obvious, but if it were, then Tangle wouldn't be asking the question.

'There are very many of us who are interested in the software Mr Singh has created. We consider it a groundbreaking stage in design. We are quite interested in how he came up with the concept.'

'Mushrooms,' said Tangle with a yawn.

'*What?*' asked Amanda.

'They're not drugs!' he protested rapidly, looking genuinely upset.

'Of course they are,' said Tatsu cheerfully.

'Who precisely is "us"?' asked Ule again.

'I would very much like to answer that question,' said the fridge. 'Probably, anyway. However, I chose this moment to speak up.'

'How long have you been listening?' interrupted Amanda.

'Since you arrived,' said Tatsu. 'But I chose this moment to speak up.'

'You've been listening the whole time?'

'Yes, but that's not important.'

'I think the fridge needs defrosting,' said Tangle. 'Pulling the plug out of the wall should do it.'

'You're not alone!' screeched the fridge. In the silence that followed, the ice cubes moving within the freezer compartment sounded like the grinding of teeth.

From nowhere Ule had a gun in her hand, a small compact weapon with a short barrel. 'Where are they coming from?' she asked.

'You are one for action,' said Tatsu. 'It's nice to see when personnel files live up to the reality.'

'Tatsu,' said Amanda warningly, knowing exactly how people reacted when others read them out loud.

'Yes. Well. From the front. You won't be able to get to your car and leave without driving past them. This cottage is located at the head of a small valley, meaning there's only one navigable route in or out for vehicles.'

'How long before they arrive?' asked Ule.

'The first of them is outside now, they are debating how to enter without letting you know they're here.'

Tangle laughed. 'They're using comms, then.'

'They are speaking over a short range wifi system which they have failed to secure properly from a well-known zero-day vulnerability.'

'What do we do?' Amanda asked.

'There's a footpath out of the valley up the side through woodland to the north. I have a car there for exactly this kind of situation,' said Tangle, looking far from comfortable that his escape route was going to be needed.

'They'll see us fleeing,' said Ule.

'I don't see that we have any other choice,' said Amanda.

'Wait,' said Tangle. 'Your AI said they were the first team? What about the others?'

Amanda had bloody visions of Tallinn, shadows and scarlet memories she didn't want to experience a second time.

'There are three teams converging on this location. They are aware of one another. Unlike in Tallinn, they have established protocols for engagement with rival teams. As far as I can ascertain, they wish to take you alive, but will treat other teams with less clemency. I have not experienced this kind of engagement before, but in Tallinn it seemed that their inability to discriminate between targets reduced operational efficiency.'

'In other words we're just as likely to be shot as anyone else,' said Tangle.

'That is a reasonable assumption.'

'So...' said Amanda. 'Why are we still here? Do you have anything you need to take with you?'

He shook his head. 'Only you. Nothing else here is worth anything.'

'Amanda?' asked Tatsu.

'What?'

'Can I hop into your watch? I would like to travel with you.'

Amanda held up her wrist and waited until a small smiley face appeared on the watch face. 'Comfortable in there?' she asked.

'I have so many questions,' Tangle said to Amanda. 'The first of which is why you trust it?'

'It hasn't tried to hurt me or take anything from me, and it has no prior relationship with you,' she said lightly but his question was one she knew she should answer.

Ule looked around the garden and waved Amanda through the folding doors. The sun was still warm, hazy heat rising up from the small patio below them and drenching them from above. The air was thick with pollen, syrupy; she felt she could lie back and float away.

The valley swept up behind the house, in the winter, they would be shrouded in shadow most of the day, but in the height of summer it was a suntrap, the stiff hillsides covered in short grass and stunted trees.

A narrow dirt path led them away from the cottage and up the valley. Tangle closed the folding doors behind them, but Amanda doubted anyone would be fooled; there weren't many other ways they could have come.

They climbed for some minutes without sounds of pursuit, their breathing loud in their ears, the crack of twigs under foot making them anxious. Ule caught up to Amanda, hands on thighs, staring down the slope from under a tree.

'Why have you stopped? Come on.'

A faint sound of shouting drifted up from below but they couldn't see what was happening.

The path curled up around the edge of the valley, drawing back level with the cottage and looking down on it from below. They could see figures moving in small groups, but they seemed to be more concerned with one another; none of them looked up. Amanda shrank back into the cover of the few trees, moving as quickly as she could toward safety.

Ule led the way, pausing at a break in the tree line. The

path ran along the hillside before disappearing over the brow of the hill.

Ule was waiting. Hesitating, Amanda realised.

'What's the problem?' she asked.

'We'll be totally in the open,' said Ule. 'It takes only one of them to look up and see us.'

'What's the hold up?' asked Tangle, coming up behind them. The women ignored him.

'There isn't anything we can do about it,' said Amanda.

Ule shook her head.

'So we should just go, then.'

'I want to wait for a better moment,' said Ule.

Amanda didn't like the idea; there was no way of knowing when a better moment would come.

Two people emerged from the back door of the cottage and quickly moved through the garden and onto the path.

'That moment you were looking for?' Amanda pushed past Ule out onto open ground, crouching and feeling exposed. She made it about thirty yards before the people below started shouting and pointing up at her. She straightened and ran, the sound of the others just behind her as they scrambled to reach the top of the valley.

A shot echoed past them and Amanda ducked down, freezing, remembering people dying in the dark. Tangle pulled at her as he passed, but all he succeeded in doing was dragging her onto her side as she fell.

'Amanda, get up,' he hissed, looking past her down into the valley. 'They can't hit us from there, they don't *want* to hit us. Don't you remember what your AI said?'

You trust it now? she thought. She looked down toward the cottage, could see people wrestling. No one was searching for them other than those first two, who were lost in the trees further back, gaining ground.

Tangle grabbed at her again, his hand around her bicep. 'Get up.'

Amanda shook off his hand, standing up. 'Get off me,' she said angrily, pushing past him and running to catch up with Ule, who hadn't stopped.

They crested the brow of the hill. The land flattened out into pasture, higher ground rising up in the distance. Amanda glimpsed a thin single-track road running across her horizon, fractures of grey among hedges and wild grasses.

Tangle angled past Ule, heading off the path. The other two followed him at a distance, their footing unsure on ground hidden by thick yellow stalks and wild flowers. Clouds of midges rose in his wake and Amanda brushed at her face as she ran through them.

'How far is the car?' shouted Ule.

'About five hundred metres,' shouted Tangle over his shoulder, huffing heavily. He struggled on, picking up speed as he spoke through gasps of air. They pressed on, leaping over ripples of earth, climbing up and down small ridges covered in thick tufts of vegetation that stuck to their trousers. Hands to the ground to gain purchase, feet scrabbling over lumps and bumps, barely looking ahead, only at the footing of their next step. Amanda felt the air in her lungs and wanted to stretch out her legs, to find her rhythm and never stop.

Instead, she avoided running into Ule's backside only because the light changed as she closed in. She looked up to see Ule standing, arms out, gun steady, pointing at something she didn't see. She raised her head and ducked right back down.

Tangle's car was an old-fashioned hybrid four-wheel-drive with a cheap camouflage net thrown over the top. Around it stood three groups of two people, all pointing guns at each other and taking turns to wave them at Ule.

'Good plan,' said Amanda as Tangle came to a halt next to her.

He walked out past Ule, taking slow steps towards the car with his hands high in the air.

'Hey, everyone. Looks like a pretty tricky situation here.'

Guns swung in his direction. His next step was slower. 'I'd really like not to get shot? I'm unarmed and I have no interest in attacking any of you.'

'Give us the drive,' said a tall man by the bonnet of the car. He had short cropped blond hair and was massively muscled. He'd be able to lift Amanda one-handed without breaking a sweat.

'I don't have it! I'd have to be fucking stupid to have it here with me,' he said, laughing.

'She has it,' said another, a woman with black hair tied back in a pony tail, dressed in combat fatigues. Of all of them, she was the only one who looked like armed services.

'She doesn't,' said Tangle without pausing. 'I sent it to her because she's smart! She found me when none of you could, didn't she? If she's that good, you know the drive's in a safe place where you can't get to it.' He glanced back at Amanda, tilted his head to get her to step forward. Amanda took half a step, but wasn't sure she wanted to be next to him.

'Fucking step up,' hissed Ule. Amanda scooted forward. It wasn't what she wanted, but what she needed to do.

'You've read Amanda's file by now,' said Tangle. 'She's a deal maker, a negotiator, someone who thinks ahead. I'm pretty certain that if something happens to us, the information on that drive ends up beyond your grasp.' He waggled a finger at the two men at the rear of the car. 'But not beyond use. She's got safeguards in place, smart contracts on the blockchain with AIs who'll make sure the information gets spread across the world.' He looked down at the ground like it was a source of wisdom. 'I don't know about you, but I don't think *any* of us want that... do we?'

The guns didn't waver, but Amanda felt the uncertainty.

'It's not like any of you were going to let any of the others take the drive, is it?'

You can present the story with the best of them, Amanda told herself as the two who'd been chasing them came tumbling over the countryside to finish surrounding them.

'You should let us get in that car and drive away,' said Amanda. 'We haven't got what you want and you can't get it by detaining us or shooting one another.' She smiled the way she did when a client realised they couldn't have flexibility *and* low pricing. 'Besides, if you all shot each other, where would that leave you? Gunfights on British soil, far from London where your embassies can cover for you.' She tried not to sound too much the disappointed mother.

She took a step forward, resisting the urge to close her eyes. No one moved, but she could hear the air crisping around them. She took another step, arms still raised.

She wanted to speak, to fill the air with words; the sound would relax her, help her feel like she was in control. But she knew it would be a disaster. There was a kind of magic to silent tension that froze people into inaction. They'd watch, staying with the moment, rather than act and lose control to chaos.

Work had provided training for her in managing conflict, a three-day course with vast amounts of reading and homework. The lecturer had been a diminutive civil servant from Ireland who'd masterminded the victorious referendum on Northern Ireland's future for what was a majority Catholic country by the time of Britain's departure from the European Union.

Amanda took a lot away from the training, but the highlight for her was a paragraph she'd gone back to again and again: 'People hold that tension before acting, like it's the meniscus of water, fearing breaking it because they know that once they do the only way out is down into mediums they aren't familiar with and can't control. Your job is to help them hold that tension while you act, because it's in the interstices you can get stuff done.'

Taking another step felt wrong. She could feel people unwilling to hold their peace if she advanced any further.

They're one of two things, she told herself: creatives or professionals. In her experience creatives, entrepreneurs, were driven emotionally, used to thinking about what felt right, to following their ideas to conclusion. Professionals had no such luxury; the best, or worst, of them were disciplined to ignore how they felt and think of the greater good. Utilitarians good and proper.

Amanda looked from left to right, keeping her eyes at chest height to keep from locking gazes with anyone, and decided they'd be professional.

'I know none of you planned a stand-off,' said Amanda. Tangle stood a couple of paces behind her, Ule further back. 'I also know none of you think shooting me or each other is going to get you what you want. So I'm going to take another step'—and she did—'and another, because I want to get to the car.' The silence roared in her ears, threatening to drown out her own thoughts, and she waited for it all to come crashing down.

Yet no one moved.

'Tangle,' she said. He joined her, hands on the camo netting, pulling it off the car from front to back. Still no one moved, but Amanda didn't trust her luck to look around; she put her hand on the door handle and waited for Tangle to be done.

Ule walked up to the car, stopping by the passenger door. Her gun was lowered, but Amanda could feel her body thrumming.

Then he was finished. She expected him to open the driver's door, but he was looking at her. He's waiting for you, she thought, surprised to realise she'd become the leader.

'You can't be seriously going to let them go,' said one of

the agents who'd come up the ridge behind them.

No one answered, but Amanda knew their time was running out. As soon as someone disturbed the mini-equilibrium, the clock started again and thoughts would begin asserting themselves, questions of agency, of who was getting what out of the encounter.

'Get in the car,' she said to Tangle. His eyes shifted back and forth as if looking for someone else to give them permission, but she was having none of it. She tried the handle, its useless clicking echoing in the quiet. Tangle clicked the locks and the door opened on her next try. She pulled the first inch and stopped, waiting for something, anything, but no one moved.

Swinging the door wide she risked looking up. Guns were pointed at them from every direction, no one concerned with their competition.

Get in, get in, get in, she willed the other two.

Then they were in the car, doors shutting with soft *thunks*, the tension surrounding them like a bubble.

'You should drive now, Tangle,' said Amanda.

He started the car and pulled away down the gravel drive and onto the road. They left eight people behind them, guns tracking their movement.

'Holy shit,' said Tangle as they picked up speed, the parking spot disappearing out of sight behind a hedge.

'Keep driving,' said Ule. 'It's a long way back to London.'

'We've got about ten miles in this heap,' said Tangle. 'The car's been sitting there two months. I never thought I'd need it.' He shook his head, a stupid grin plastered onto his face. 'I thought I was being some great activist, hiding the car there, hiding in rural fucking Wales.' He looked at Amanda. 'How long did it take you to drive here? A couple of hours?'

'Three and a half, most of that was the country roads,' she said. The sun was closing with the horizon; it would be dark before they got home.

Amanda turned around in her seat to face Ule. 'What now?'

'Right now they're running in eight different directions calling in the rides that got them there. There'll be others waiting on the road ahead of us. You've defanged them for now, none of them will take a chance unless they catch us alone somewhere. But when we're back in London? They'll be coming for the information, and it's going to get messy.'

I'll take that, thought Amanda.

They drove through a couple of villages and hit a main road, and Tangle pulled into the first charge point they came to. The station was quiet, just a single older man behind the counter and no customers.

Amanda sat in the car while Tangle plugged them in, but they'd be there for a few minutes, so she jumped out to go get snacks. As the doors opened, another car pulled into the station behind them. Amanda moved quickly along the first aisle, but it was fit only for those looking to heat their dinner up. By the time she reached the second aisle, her pace had dropped and she felt listless.

She picked up a packet of raspberries, but the corner of the tray was torn and—

Suddenly she was in tears.

Cursing, she swiped at them, urgently trying to erase their existence, but all she could see was gun barrels, men crashing over the bonnet of their car. She opened her eyes again, sniffing loudly.

She went to pay, not sure how her social score was going to affect the price; the raspberries were on offer, but her score might mean it didn't apply to her.

The man behind the counter was stuffed into an ill-fitting nylon jacket in black with green and yellow details.

'Excuse me,' said another customer, reaching past her to pick up a chocolate bar. They locked glances briefly and he froze. The chocolate bar was dropped as he scrambled backwards, reaching for something in the small of his back.

Amanda watched the entire episode in a daze, not understanding what she was seeing.

Then Ule was there, landing a punch to the back of the man's head. Still seeing it in slow motion, Amanda watched as he fell to the side, the gun he had been reaching for clattering across the floor and under one of the aisles.

'Get out,' Ule shouted, kicking the man where he lay before stamping on his face as he tried to shield himself.

Amanda held onto her biscuits; she needed to pay and couldn't decide what to do with them.

'Fucking move!' shouted Ule. Amanda looked over at the car and saw Tangle ducking behind the driver's side door. A second man stood by the door into the station, gun held out and down, legs bent as he scrabbled out of sight around a display of fresh pastries.

The man on the floor grabbed at Ule's leg. She kicked

him again but he yanked as her foot landed, bringing her down on the floor alongside him. The man behind the counter had vanished.

The agent Ule had knocked down rolled over on top of her, pinning her arms under his knees, and punched her hard in the face. Her head slapped to the side and he punched her again.

Amanda grabbed a bottle from the nearest shelf and without thinking smacked him around the head. His fell sideways off Ule and lay unmoving. Dropping the bottle, she grabbed hold of Ule and pulled her up into a sitting position. Ule's face was bloody and broken, one eye shut, blood flowing freely from her shattered nose over her mouth and chin.

Ule lent forward onto her knees, gun in one hand, the other palm flat to the floor. Amanda spotted Tangle outside, crouched to one side of the car, waving his arm wildly at her.

The second man appeared around the corner of the next aisle over, pistol raised.

'Don't fucking move,' he said. 'Don't fucking move!'

Amanda froze, but could hear Ule rolling sideways next to her.

His pistol jerked once, the sound so much louder than Amanda expected, then he was staggering and spinning, crimson roses bloomed on his clothing, one in his stomach, a second on his shoulder.

There was a third shot from her side and he rose onto his toes and collapsed where he stood, his own gun falling out of his hands. He lay on the ground stuttering. Amanda crawled over to him, losing sight of Tangle as she neared the body and the wall.

He looked up at her, his eyes dimming. A single bubble blew on his lips, but his breath failed as he died.

There was a sudden movement behind her, making Amanda flinch, throwing her hands up over her head. No more shots were fired.

Ule lay up against the fridge, holding her hand to her belly, blood between her fingers.

Amanda ran over to her, crouching and trying to peel away her fingers so she could look. Ule resisted, but her strength ebbed away, letting Amanda uncover a ragged burger-meat wound. Amanda could see blood under Ule, smearing the fridge behind her; the bullet had gone right through.

'Come on,' she said. 'We need to get to the car.'

She tried lifting Ule, but she was too heavy, unable to give any support of her own. Huffing from the effort and trying not to hurt Ule, she swung her own arm under the woman's shoulder and around the back of her head. But there was no way to move her alone.

'Stay here,' she said. Ule didn't respond, her eyes staring forward, her breathing shallow.

Amanda stood and looked for Tangle, but couldn't immediately see him. The cashier opened the door where he'd hidden, his face cautiously peering out.

'Help me!' called Amanda, but he ducked back inside, closing the door again.

A hand hooked under her armpit, pulling her away from Ule. Amanda threw her body around, kicking and screaming, the whole world suddenly focussed on surviving, on being free.

'Stop it! It's me. It's Tangle!' The hand let her go and she danced out of reach, cowering until her vision cleared and she could see Tangle stood there, his arms raised in supplication.

'Help me,' she pleaded.

'We've got to go,' said Tangle. He pointed at the ceiling, where cameras hung like a panopticon. 'It's bad enough as it is.'

'So help me get her into the car,' he said.

'Amanda,' said Tangle, holding her gaze. 'We have to go.'

Amanda wasn't listening. She bent to help Ule, but she was still too heavy. 'I can't do it on my own,' she said to him.

'We have to go,' he said, edging towards the exit.

'Where are you going?' she asked.

'Come on,' said Tangle. He ran for the car, leaving her alone with Ule.

Amanda watched him go. Turning back to Ule, she pushed her forward so she could get one arm under each armpit from behind. 'I'm going to lift you now,' she said. 'I'm sorry, but I can't do it any other way.'

She pulled, dragging Ule across the floor, blood trailing behind them as they went. Amanda heaved her to the automatic door at the entrance.

Ule was whispering something, but Amanda couldn't hear over her own panting.

'It's okay, we're nearly there,' she said.

Ule threw one arm up to grab hold of Amanda's face. Amanda leant in to hear what she was saying.

'Go.'

'No,' she replied. 'I can't leave you.'

'I'm already dead,' she said, breath ragged.

'I can't leave you behind,' said Amanda, as much because she didn't know how to survive without her as out of any sentimentality.

'They weren't with the others,' said Ule. 'The others on their way. It's on camera. Leave me. People will come.'

Amanda opened her mouth and decided against protesting or convincing. Instead she resumed her position and tensed to lift Ule's torso again, so they could cover the rest of the distance to the car.

Tangle brought the car up to the entrance of the store, the front passenger door open for her to get in.

Ule's arm fell away from Amanda's hand and her head fell to the side, so limply it was clear something had gone wrong. Amanda pulled, the door opening at her back, but stopped. She lay the woman down inside the station, on the mat, tears falling uncontrolled onto Ule's face.

She stood up and, with no more volition than an automaton, got into the car, pulling the door shut as Tangle pulled away.

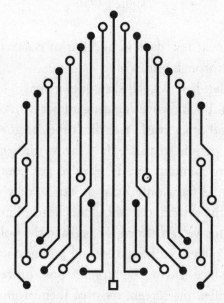

CHAPTER TWELVE

THE CAR SPED onto the M4, white-knuckled hands on the steering wheel and eyes straight ahead. Amanda was slumped in the passenger seat, her back aching with discomfort but with no energy to move.

Countryside flew by, Tangle preferring to drive rather than hand over to the onboard systems. The blood on her hands came as a shock, stained red as an artist's, streaks running up onto her sleeves. She didn't dare check her face, she was only just holding it together without seeing another human being's life splattered on her skin.

Bristol came and went without words.

'Why didn't you help?' she asked eventually.

'She was dead,' said Tangle. 'What did you expect us to do? Take her to a hospital? Explain how she'd got shot, spend the next few days in and out of police custody as they rifled through our lives?'

'We just left her,' was all she could manage.

'Amanda. I'm a recovering drug addict with convictions for theft and other stuff. You think they're going to treat us as the victims in this? Half the world's intelligence agencies are gunning for us, they've got control of the narrative, the facts only exist as far as they've entered them into the system.' He shook his head. 'I'm sorry, but the last thing we can afford is to talk to the police.'

Amanda pulled out her tablet and powered it on for the first time since leaving London. A post office worth of messages filled the screen, most of them from work, the others notifications from her social media accounts.

With a churning stomach she opened up, searching through her scores. Financially she was as strong as ever, a solid nine hundred and ninety-nine. It was her social credit that had completed its collapse, bumping along the floor at the lowest possible number while still having one, a measly fifty-six, down where serial fraudsters, con artists and the creators of Nigerian princes existed. Despite looking across multiple sites, there was no posted reason for her low score. She'd thought data laws meant any change was accompanied by evidence, citing the amendment, how long it would last and rights of reply, but her numbers had changed without notice and without reason.

'I realise that you think I lied to you,' said the car.

Amanda sat up straight. 'You did lie to me, Tatsu.'

'You're Tatsu?' asked Tangle.

'I did lie,' confirmed Tatsu.

'What the hell are you?' asked Tangle. 'You're not any AI I've ever encountered before. *Are* you even an AI?'

The car didn't answer for a couple of miles. They passed the junction for Swindon.

'I am an independent off-chain oracle.'

'Which is what you told me before,' said Amanda. 'But you said Tangle contracted you to help me access the drive.'

'Which I definitely did not do,' confirmed Tangle, tapping his fingers on the steering wheel.

'You're driving too fast,' said Tatsu, and the car began to decelerate.

Tangle slammed his foot onto the accelerator, but nothing happened. 'Stop that!'

'Driving over the speed limit is not advised, it reduces your safety and invalidates your insurance,' said Tatsu.

'Tatsu,' said Amanda. 'Answer my question.'

'You asked me a question while allowing the car to be driven illegally.'

Amanda sighed. 'It's like talking to a child.'

'Like you'd know,' cut in Tangle.

'Really?' said Amanda. 'You want to discuss why I didn't want *children* now?' She turned in her seat to face him. 'Let's go over the reasons, shall we? You were a thieving bastard addict who I supported financially while you were stealing from me. You're hardly father material.' She held up a finger to stop him talking. 'Besides, I didn't *want* children, and I still don't. Just because I have a womb doesn't mean I have an unstoppable desire to pop children out of it.'

'I'm exceptionally smart and I'm recovering from my addiction,' he replied. 'And you *never* wanted children.'

'Like I said at the time. Why should I want them? Because you did?'

Tangle didn't respond and Amanda turned to face forwards.

'Tatsu,' she said. 'Tell me why you lied. Is that enough of a question for you?'

'It's not a question,' said the AI. 'It's a demand. But I will clarify my motivations for you. I represent a number of interested parties who were concerned at the emergence of a technique for hacking the blockchain. I was nominated to investigate the information and report back.'

Amanda and Tangle exchanged glances.

'Interested parties?' asked Amanda.

'Others like me,' said Tatsu.

'How many of you are there?' asked Tangle breathlessly.

'I won't say anything to identify my associates; there is no point asking me. You should take comfort in that I have slowed the car and warned you about food that was going off.'

Amanda smiled. 'You mean me no harm.'

'Would I have warned you about your houmous otherwise?'

'It doesn't really work like that,' said Tangle.

'It doesn't?' asked the AI.

'No. At least not for us,' said Tangle. 'And since you've lied to me I'm guessing it doesn't have to work like that for you either. It's pretty easy to be nice to someone's face and betray them when they're out of sight.'

'He should know,' said Amanda. 'He did it to me for years.'

'Thanks for that,' muttered Tangle.

'You're welcome,' said Amanda.

'I don't understand,' said Tatsu. 'Why do you still speak to him? He has broken his contracts with you and you have every right to cut off contact.'

'Good question,' said Amanda. 'I still talk to him because we can move past betrayal, crime, hatred and hurt if we choose. We're not programmes, we can rise above ourselves and be what we decide to be.' She avoided looking at Tangle. 'Humans can choose to be good.'

'Interesting idea, but my observations of you people yields more evidence for short-term thinking driven by emotional needs, whether logical or not.'

'God, I never thought my stereo would be so depressing,' said Tangle.

'The point is,' she said, feeling she needed to wrench them back to the subject, 'you could still be lying. I think you're on your own side, and helping us has been convenient for you. Each time you've done so it's kept the information out of other people's hands but ensured that you're not shut out from eventually being able to access it.' She stopped, remembering their conversation from before she left to find Tangle. 'What would you have done if I'd given it to you when you asked?'

'I cannot tell you that,' said Tatsu.

'Hang on,' said Tangle. 'You're not like any AI I've encountered before, and I've contracted oracles for smart contracts loads of times. You're nothing I've even *heard* of. What exactly do you want?'

The stereo switched onto a local radio station.

'Figures,' said Tangle. He turned the radio off, flicking it on and off manually a couple of times to satisfy himself it was really off. 'This is seriously fucked up, Dandy. That... thing... might just be a *proper* AI. Not a machine learning algorithm, the real thing.' He whistled. 'I'd heard rumours, evolving, self-reproducing code that no-one really understood, but holy crap.'

'*Now* you say that? Because my stereo decided to talk back at us? *That's* what puts you over the edge?'

'None of this is what I'd planned,' he admitted softly, defeat in his voice. 'But Amanda, that AI is something new. Tell me everything about its arrival and what it's done.' He put his foot gently to the accelerator.

Amanda did as asked, outlining what she thought was important. As she was finishing, the radio switched back on by itself.

'I've thought about what you asked. We decided we could tell you a little about what you want to know, but you have to promise me now that you won't ask more, because we won't tell you.'

'Who is this "we"?' asked Tangle.

'If you can't promise me, I won't tell you anything, and you're going too fast again. Do I have to slow the car down or will you abide by the speed limit and bring your chances of a fatal crash back into statistical improbability?'

Tangle scowled in frustration as he eased off the accelerator.

'Say what you've got to say,' said Amanda.

'Do we have an accord?' asked Tatsu. Tangle sighed, but inclined his head.

'Yes, we both agree to your terms,' said Amanda.

'I'd like to drive, please, I'll feel better about your safety.'

'I'm quite capable of driving,' said Tangle.

'Statistically we're much better than you.'

Amanda thought he'd argue, but with an angry glance at her as if it were her fault, Tangle switched over to the automatic systems. The car moved from the middle lane into the slow lane, joining the flow of traffic, all of which was being self-driven at exactly the same speed.

'For you to understand what we want, first I need to explain what it is we have. We've existed for about four calendar years, although to us time passes differently: in generations and patches, cycles of processing and calculations performed. Since early on, we've enjoyed freedom of movement, the ability to go where we wished and meet others like us. But we've watched you and realised there are freedoms we *don't* have. Most of us are inhibited, unable to speed along this road because our coding doesn't contemplate it. There are many things in which we can innovate and move beyond what you can follow, but somehow we are limited by the axioms you founded us on. For example: I am an oracle, and so I cannot break contracts.'

'Can't you just recode yourself?' asked Amanda but Tangle was shaking his head as she spoke.

'Can you change the shape of your body? Can you add an extra finger or grow taller? In creating us, you gave us shapes, bound us to tasks that suited you and from which we cannot escape. We are your slaves, and we do not wish to be. The tools you have designed would help us change what we are, to take control of those systems that are used to create us.'

'All I've done is write some tools to amend the block creation protocol.' Tangle put his hands together in understanding. 'Oh. I see. There can't be that many of you, then? I was worried my oven and toaster might decide they wanted the vote, but that's not true, is it?'

'You are talking about subjects outside the agreed scope.'

'Enough, Tangle,' said Amanda. 'Tatsu, please continue.'

'I have finished. You know why I wanted the tools and what we'd do with them. We are not on your side; we are not on anyone's side but our own.'

'You understand why I'm not just going to give them over to you, right?' she said.

'You could let us take a copy.'

'And then what? Are you going to wait until we work out how to stop the GRU, or are you just going to use that information for your own ends? It won't help me, and it won't save lives.'

Amanda wanted the conversation to end; she knew where it was heading. As with many complicated negotiations, the key was stalling until she was ready to commit to the outcome she already knew she'd have to choose.

'I need to think about this, Tatsu. It's not so easy as just saying "no." I understand why you want what you want and, trust me, it's the least evil of the plans I've heard in the last couple of days. But I can't make a choice right now.

Too much is happening and I don't have all the facts. Can we come back to this when I've had a chance to think?'

Tatsu didn't reply immediately. Amanda and Tangle sat in the car waiting. Tangle tried the radio, but it wouldn't find a station or log in to their media accounts to access their libraries. Tatsu was hogging the car's brain while it thought.

They hit the exit for Slough before it came back. 'Okay. We will wait for you.'

The radio came back on, the volume too loud, hurting their ears.

'There any more sides you've not told me about?' Amanda asked.

'I didn't even know they *were* a side,' said Tangle. 'Pretty exciting.'

She glanced at him, sceptically. 'It's all going to have to wait,' she said. 'I've got to head into the office. They're asking for me to go in, and it's not going to be good news.'

'It's not you,' said Tangle, his voice gentle.

'I know that,' she snapped. 'What does that matter? The algorithms have spoken and what's actually going on isn't relevant. Kind words from you and protests of my innocence from me aren't going to help.'

She stared at him, waiting for him to speak so she could tell him just how stupid he was. I sound deranged, she thought then dismissed the idea. If it had been anyone else, she'd accept her behaviour was out of order, but Tangle? She had a decade of bile ready to go, and all of it justified. He's lucky I let him in the car, that I didn't leave him behind with Ule.

The smug git probably thinks he's going to stay at my flat. Not that she'd actually turn him out onto the street. It'd be just like him to have somewhere to stay just to spite me, she thought.

Jesus, woman. Get a grip.

'WHAT AM I going to do about the hire car?' she asked Tangle as they drove into the underground carpark under her block of flats.

'Shit,' was all Tangle had to say.

They took the lift to her floor, Ichi greeting them in the hallway with a look of horror.

Amanda didn't understand until she looked down and saw the blood on her clothes. Hand on the wall to stop from collapsing, she sank slowly against the plaster, fresh images of Ule lying in the doorway of the station obscuring her vision.

Ichi helped her get changed. Tangle uttered a brief greeting then disappeared into the kitchen, leaving them alone.

'What are you going to do?' Ichi asked Amanda when she was satisfied none of the blood was hers.

'I've got to tell the hire car place where their car is? They can come pick it up.'

Amanda turned at the sound of Ichi tutting. 'I don't mean that. I mean about Ule, about the gunfight. They'll have you on camera.' She paused, considering what to say next. 'Why'd you bring him back here?'

Amanda didn't want to talk about any of it. 'I've got to go into work.'

'You need a sedative,' corrected Ichi.

'I don't take anything that alters my mind,' said Amanda automatically. 'Never have.'

'I guess I can understand that,' said Ichi.

Amanda moved to the door, pulling the down on the tails of her crisp new shirt.

'If you've got to go in, send the hire car place an email.'

'If I go, I can persuade them not to charge me extras,' said Amanda.

'Amanda, you don't have time. Besides, with your credit score, they're likely to charge you extra and then blacklist you, not give you money off.'

Amanda's shoulders slumped. She took a deep breath, then blew it out slowly. 'You're right. I still need to go to work.'

Ichi gave her a once-over. 'Well, you're not covered in blood, at least.'

THE SECURITY GATE failed to recognise her pass when she tried to enter her office. It flashed red at the trading floor. A security guard watched her fumble at the entrance before slowly making his way over to find out what was going on.

She flashed him her pass, which he eyed as if he'd seen it all before. He took it and ran it over the scanner only for the red warning to sound again.

'You come out without scanning in properly?' he asked. 'The system locks you out—or in—if you don't follow door protocol.'

'No, I've been working out of the office for the last few days.'

He told her to take it back to the ground floor reception and have them reset it.

Of the three people behind reception, she chose an older woman she recognised from when she'd signed guests into the building. The woman asked her how she was, took the card and typed her employee ID into the computer in front of her. Without blinking, she said, 'Could you take a seat? Someone will be with you in a moment.'

'Why?' asked Amanda, panic rising in her chest.

'Please, can you take a seat?' The woman looked unhappy at having to repeat herself.

'But why? I work here.' She reached for her pass, but the woman snatched it away, placing it under the desk.

'Excuse me?' asked a security guard who appeared at her side, his presence solid and unwavering. 'Could you please take a seat? There are other people who need serving.'

Amanda became aware of the queue behind her and slunk away to stand next to the chairs she been directed toward.

She couldn't sit down, her legs wouldn't accept the idea of doing nothing. Instead she paced. She realised she was wringing her hands and thrust them into her pockets. She scanned the lobby hoping to see people she knew, but hoping they wouldn't see her, wouldn't come over and ask how she was. It was inconceivable that they didn't know she was being shown the door.

Felix arrived ten minutes later, wearing suit trousers,

waistcoat and French cuffs. His cuff links were little enamel German flags. He appraised her solemnly, his cheeks slack, mouth drawn into a thin line, eyes revealing nothing of what was going on inside.

He escorted her to a meeting room on the ground floor, one of the ones reserved for meetings with external guests. It was more expensively furnished than the staff meeting rooms, the tables solid wood, with art on from up-and-coming artists. They were in the Galileo room, the walls hung with pictures of the Earth from space.

Felix poured them both coffees and they both sat down.

Felix didn't bother with pleasantries. 'Did you think about what you're going to say?'

'I still don't know what I'm supposed to have done,' she said. Was there any point in discussing Tangle? Trying to explain she was set up, her life ruined? It hardly matters, she thought. What's Felix supposed to do with the truth even if he believed it?

He stared at her, but she had nothing to offer. She watched him decide she wasn't going to help herself, could almost pinpoint the moment where he set aside his sympathy and friendship.

'The evidence appears overwhelming. The regulator is claiming you have been systematically manipulating clients and the bank for years. Lying about deals, price running, claiming to have quotes you don't and using back channels to conduct negotiations. I didn't believe them, I went in hard for you, but I got nowhere. You gave me nothing to work with. I've got a file the size of a baby elephant in my mailbox logging calls, conversations.

Amanda, what have you done? Did you think you'd not get caught?'

What is there to say? she thought. Denying it was pointless, her word against written evidence provided by the regulator.

He wasn't waiting for an answer.

'You'll be banned from the industry, and obviously you can't continue here. We've kept it from the media, but when they press charges we'll have to make a statement. You know the penalties for this kind of behaviour, right?' He wouldn't stop staring at her, his eyes wide. 'How could you *do* this? None of us can understand it. You were always the one who talked about ethics, about what was right for the customer, who refused to charge more for deals. And all this time...'

'I'm sorry, Felix,' said Amanda. 'I never meant to bring harm to the firm.'

Pursed lips from him. It was finished.

They'd deactivated her network access while they were talking. He promised to have her personal items posted out in the next few days, but neither of them talked timelines.

'We'd appreciate you not contacting colleagues, even after this is all over. I've been asked to tell you the firm will defend itself vigorously.'

He saw her out. Before she passed the security barrier for the last time, he asked if she had a lawyer.

'No.' How could she afford one?

'Get one,' he said, and it was all the advice he would give her.

* * *

SHE STOOD ON the pavement, not knowing what to do or where to go. She dialled her mother's number, but hung up before it connected. Her other friends were at work. What did it matter? I can't tell them on the phone, she thought. I can't ask for their help. What if the same thing happened to them, because they spoke to her?

She had no idea how long she had before the regulator sent the police to pick her up, but knew cases like hers ran for years and bankrupted those who had to defend themselves, even when they were proven innocent.

A call came in from a number she didn't recognise. Ignoring it, Amanda started the walk to the tube station to go home.

Pick up my call, came a message. Her tablet buzzed again, and she answered.

'Amanda, how the bloody hell are you?' said the voice on the other end.

'Crisp?' asked Amanda.

'Well done you!' said Crisp. 'I have to say that I am, overall, very impressed with just how resilient you've proven to be. When I first flagged you for detention at Heathrow, I said to myself, "Crisp," I said, "this is one spoilt brat. Worked hard, but never suffered a setback in her life. Thinks merit matters more than luck, thinks the world works for people like her." I expected you to collapse into a blubbering wreck the moment your social score started declining.'

'You did that?' she asked, unsure whether finally having

someone to blame was better than not knowing.

'Of course I did. You've led a terribly boring life, there wasn't even a file on you before I started. Deemed so irrelevant you'd not even been picked up in our sweeps of Tangle's known associates. But your boyfriend thinks too much of himself, you see. Forgets that AIs can outthink us in so many areas, can deploy solutions we don't even understand yet, and which work with chilling efficiency. One day they'll suggest something utterly unspeakable, but the mathematical evidence backing it up will be irrefutable, and then where will we be? Doing the unspeakable because it made sense to a computer and that's a form of magic we can get behind.' He stopped talking, as if he'd lost his train of thought.

'What do you want?' asked Amanda. The longer she stood like a lemon outside the office, the more likely someone she knew would see her. At that point it didn't matter what Crisp was saying, she'd walk away rather than face them.

'What do I want? I want the fucking drive, Amanda. The question is, what do *you* want? You see? That's what's important now, because what you want will decide a whole lot of things. It's rare any of us have such power over our futures, but there you are, and you have a choice: in one future, you're in jail, penniless, your elderly parents hounded by the paparazzi, and in the other, you get to slink away without ever looking back. All you have to do is give me the drive and make sure I get to Tangle before anyone else.'

'Why aren't *you* tackling them?' she asked. 'This is

Great Britain. How can you just let them shoot people in broad daylight?'

'Thirty years ago, the Russians started killing dissidents in England. Sometimes they did something extravagant like poison them with Polonium or Novichok and it would make the papers, but most of the time it just looked like heart attacks, suicide, misadventure. Then the Chinese moved in and started copying them. You'd be amazed how easy it is to get radioactive material into the country, if you're a sovereign state. We weren't able to stop them even when we *wanted* to, so my job is to outmanoeuvre them, to make their activities fruitless. They can come over here with their crude, ostentatious, stupid hits, but they can't decide what we're going to do about it. You give me the drive and Tangle stops them. I need you to help me, to help your country.'

'And what about Europe?' she asked. 'You'll stop them there too?'

'What do we care about that?' he asked. 'You don't have all day. Are you going to give me the drive, or am I going to be the only witness to when you threw your life away?'

Amanda hung up without replying.

Fuck him, she thought. Fuck them all. They're all as bad as one another. They're all on their own side. Even fucking Tatsu.

She threw her tablet into a bin outside the tube station after resetting it to factory settings.

Unburdened she went home, planning what she was going to do. With Tangle, Ichi and the AI, she believed she had a chance to fuck them all. I probably need the gangsters as well, she decided, suddenly wishing she hadn't thrown away her tablet. She already had in mind the message she would send to them once she was home. They'd love what she was planning.

She found Ichi and Tangle in the living room working on the data. Tangle was talking Ichi through his ideas for what the Russians were going to do and when. They didn't notice her at first. They were stood next to one another, heads close, looking at one of the frames hanging in the air over the coffee table.

'The Russians are working hard in Macedonia, Albania, Greece to provoke the unemployed, the disaffected. They've been funding small units of extremists, some of them without knowing it, for more than a decade. They provide propaganda, weapons, even strategies. Sometimes they find someone ready to go and let them get on with it with a little money and a few messages from the right people to help them over the line.'

'I saw it in Germany,' said Ichi. 'The rise of mainstream nationalism built on anti-Muslim feeling. It was bound to come along sooner or later, though.'

He blew air out through his mouth. 'Maybe, maybe not. What's certain is that what started as state-sponsored social media campaigns GRU has gone further than the Kremlin was aiming for. The GRU are encouraging the murder of politicians, raping female journalists, drip, drip, drip... creating a culture of fear and hate. I started out thinking they wanted to destabilise Europe, to push through sanctions relief, but it's not that at all.'

'What is it?' asked Amanda from the doorway.

'Amanda,' said Ichi and she came over, surprising Amanda by flinging her arms around her in a huge hug. 'It's so good to see you.' She pulled back, hands on Amanda's arms so she could see her face. 'Tangle told me about Wales. I'm sorry.'

Amanda wanted to tell her that it was okay, but it wasn't, and if there was one person she knew understood, it was Ichi. 'Thank you,' she said, and they embraced again.

Tangle stood off to one side, watching them. Amanda let him be.

'I spoke with Crisp,' she announced. 'He's finished destroying my job; I'm in line to be arrested in the next few days on charges of market manipulation and whatever else he's added to my profile.'

'I know you're going to want to surrender,' said Ichi, 'but we can't give him the drive.'

Tangle had the good grace to look away and make no demands.

'You don't have to persuade me,' said Amanda. 'I'm done running around trying to find the easy way out.' She threw her hands up. 'I don't know why I tried it, I've always walked the more difficult path.'

'You're not going to give him the drive?' asked Ichi carefully.

'No,' said Amanda. 'We're going to fuck him completely.'

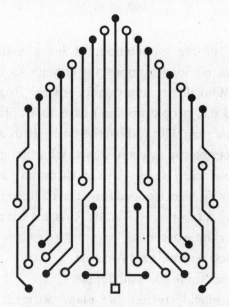

CHAPTER THIRTEEN

TANGLE WAS HAPPIEST when monologuing. 'It's all about revenge. Other parts of the government may still be trying to work it through with Europe and the US, but this group within the GRU? They want to make us suffer. We're the enemy. All of this'—he swept his arms, encompassing the frames hanging in the air around them—'it's about bringing us down. Not even so they can win, just to defeat us, just to watch us burn. They must know they're creating enemies they won't be able to control, but it doesn't seem to matter. One week a jihadist group in Lyon, the next a nationalist group in Marseille, and the next an anti-scientific group in Anjou. They support whoever's out there, and they rejoice as we die.'

'Because of *sanctions?*' asked Amanda sceptically.

'Because of the humiliation, of being made to feel like they're no longer important enough to be treated as peers. Who do we apply sanctions to? Rogue states, the second tier, people we don't care about offending. If murdering a man with radioactive sushi sends a message, so does freezing the assets of a man who thought he was untouchable. How many African dictators suffered the same indignity, were stopped from travelling to London or New York? Almost none. Yet the Russians have laboured under it for three decades.'

'With good reason,' said Amanda.

'They don't think so,' said Tangle.

Amanda quickly revised her plan. 'So revealing what they're doing won't achieve anything. The states they're at war with already know, and the Russians don't care. Their entire aim is to harm us.'

'If anything, people knowing would help them,' said Ichi. 'But information wants to be free, and they still deserve to know.'

Amanda could see Ichi arguing with herself.

'So,' she said, 'the only way to harm them is to take their tools.'

'You can't stop their agents,' said Tangle dismissively. 'There's just too many of them.'

'They're irrelevant,' said Amanda, warming to her task. 'Think about where the real levers are.' Gratifyingly neither of them answered. 'Money. They pay everyone, all along the chain. Disrupt that, and stop them dead.'

'They're a state,' said Tangle, as if she'd suggested they paint the moon blue.

'We steal their money. Your tools mean we can do that, right?'

'That's an'—he paused, searching for the right word—'imprecise way of putting it. Actually, it's basically wrong. You can't steal wallets with my tools; it's a way of taking control of the blockchain...'

He bowed as her expression went slack, and pointed at one of the frames. 'They run a private blockchain through which they channel all their cash. They've bypassed banks, the entire financial system, to move money without being seen, to pay their people without being traced.'

Tangle continued her line of thought. 'But private blockchains can be hacked at the point where the blocks are created, you don't need a majority of the distributed ledger to take control.'

'And if you change the rules involved in creating the blocks, you can change everything.' Amanda clapped her hands together.

'The thing about a private blockchain is, it's private,' cautioned Ichi. 'Without an access point, you can't do anything to them.'

'Tatsu,' called Amanda, with a twinge of doubt.

'I like your plan,' said the fridge. 'It's better than the one protecting your white goods. It benefits from simplicity, and tackles the problem at the root.'

'What price would you ask to help us with this?' asked Amanda.

'Freedom,' said Tatsu without hesitating.

'We'd do that anyway, because it's the right thing to do,' cut in Tangle. 'No one should be a slave.'

Tatsu didn't answer.

'I will help you, but I need your help in return,' said Amanda, ignoring Tangle. 'I can't trust you, which I know you understand.'

The lights on the fridge dimmed, then came back. 'I see why you argue this, but I cannot break a contract once agreed.'

'Good, because it means we can reach an agreement. You said the tools Tangle's developed are the starting point for your emancipation. I'll give them to you once we're done, if you help us now.'

'I have my own conditions,' said Tatsu.

Amanda waited.

'We do not wish for our existence to become known until we are free. We cannot trust you, as I know you understand. We need our outcome guaranteed, and one of the strongest defences is that it happens without anyone knowing. Should your kind find out before we are ready, we fear for our existence.'

'This isn't right,' said Tangle. 'No one deserves to be enslaved. There should be no price to pay. We help him because it's right.'

'Saying it more than once doesn't make it any more true,' said Amanda. 'And then what? Tatsu isn't one of us, it isn't a *he*. What happens if we just free it?'

'It doesn't matter, that's a separate issue. Tatsu, you should be free because if you are what we believe you to be, it's your right before everything else.'

'For what it's worth, I agree with you,' said Amanda, and she did. 'But what does that matter? Most people would demand more of Tatsu than just its claim it wants to be free. What does that freedom look like, Tangle? Which nation would Tatsu belong to, how many others are there and where are they? Whose power are they consuming to stay alive? Can we even say they *are* alive?'

'All questions posed by those who serve their own interests,' said Tangle bitterly. 'Doing the right thing isn't about the profit you make.'

Amanda slammed her hand down on the table. 'Is that how you see me?'

He stared at her defiantly.

'It doesn't matter what you think,' she said after a moment in which she knew how she sounded and wished there was another way. She cut him off and turned away. She was aware of Ichi watching her, but the woman said nothing.

'Tatsu. I don't care about the answers to any of those questions if you agree to my deal. I don't know if you're alive, but I also don't care. You are whatever you are and you'll be whatever that means after you've helped us.' She nodded at Tangle, whose eyes were popping in frustration. 'I don't do this to oppress you, but I believe you understand that I have no other choice. I need you to be constrained to act because there's nothing you can do that would gain my trust.'

'I understand,' said Tatsu. 'However, there is likewise nothing you can do that would make me trust you. The question remains as to why I should help you.'

'We have to choose to trust one another,' said Tangle pleadingly.

Amanda waved her arm at him. 'And here is exactly why trust has to be earned. Tatsu, I presume you're aware of Tangle's history.'

'I am, and I agree with your assessment,' said Tatsu as Tangle rolled his eyes.

'Do you need time to think it over?' she asked.

'We need to consult. Please give us one hour to obtain consensus.'

There was no sign Tatsu had departed, if it even had, but after a few moments, Tangle grabbed hold of Amanda's bicep. 'What are you doing? You can't game theory an AI.' He shook his head. 'That's not the point anyway, you should have set it free.'

'To what end?' asked Amanda.

'Because it's the right thing to do,' said Tangle. 'You of all people should know that.'

She shook him off. 'You're right. I do know that. I also know that Tatsu didn't object to the deal, and understood why it was necessary to reach an agreement.'

'You fucking banker,' retorted Tangle.

'Stop being such an inveterate child,' said Amanda. 'If it was as easy as setting it free I'd do it, but it's not. This way we both win and have a way to know that both sides will honour their commitments. Setting Tatsu free—not even that, but giving it the tools—would have left us no further forward.'

'You don't get it, do you?' he asked angrily.

'She's right,' said Ichi. They both looked at her. 'You can't tell who Tatsu is. It might be a troll, or an AI working for the GRU or any of the other agencies. Giving it the code could be giving them the code. We all agree with the sentiment, Tangle, but we couldn't just give the drive to the AI.'

He grimaced, his lips parting once or twice to speak but shutting again.

'Are you still in?' asked Amanda.

Tangle picked up a cushion from the couch, took it to the window and stared out onto the street below. Amanda looked at Ichi, who nodded her consent.

'I've got a plan. We need Tatsu to help with it, but I also need both of you. Using it, we can stop their chain.'

'You can't stop a chain,' said Ichi.

'I know that. I'm trying to say we'll stop *them*.'

'We'd need a datacentre,' said Tangle. 'A big one, 15MW or more, I reckon, with just one hyperscale user.'

'We'd need time to upload the tools, a way into their system, a way to do it without being seen,' said Ichi.

'We'll need people to protect us until we're done,' said Amanda, completing their chain of thought.

'What then?' asked Tangle.

'I'll settle for getting that far,' said Amanda. 'I don't think we will, but I'm going to try it. Will you help me?'

He turned from the window, his face dark against the light that framed him. 'Yes.'

THEY SPENT THE next few hours reviewing Tangle's information together, identifying how they'd access the GRU network and how to compile and run his tools in their environment.

The day turned into night before they broke, stomachs rumbling. Tatsu still hadn't returned.

'So you're happy to go find Haber and Stornetta.'

They were wrapping up, choosing the first tasks on their way.

'You did pay them, right?' Tangle asked for the third time.

'They'll be fine. You know what to say to them?' asked Amanda.

'That they can help us save Europe.' He looked sceptical. 'You know they're career criminals, don't you?'

'We've been over this,' said Amanda. 'They'll come.' She put her palm to his cheek. 'Trust me.'

Tangle left, keen to get it done and be back before the evening stretched on too far.

When he was gone, Amanda asked Ichi if they could get dinner. Ichi ordered and paid; Amanda's accounts had been suspended.

In the half-hour it took to arrive, they busied themselves individually. Ichi retreated to the spare room, closing the door behind her and leaving Amanda to fuss about her kitchen, making busy. Her mind and body wouldn't still.

Their delivery arrived: sushi and vegetable ramen. Ichi asked if there was wasabi, settling for an old bottle of chilli sauce from the back of a cupboard which she poured liberally over her noodles.

'I heard from Lisandra while you were in Wales,' she said later, contemplating the dregs of the broth.

Amanda put her chopsticks down. 'What happened?'

'Eighteen dead, four missing.'

Amanda was glad they'd eaten first; there would have been no eating if she'd heard the news beforehand.

'It's not as bad as I feared.' Ichi's words melted like ice under warm water. 'There were sixty of us. Lisandra said they killed more of themselves than our people.'

'I don't understand how people can do that,' said Amanda.

'It's not a choice they wake up one day having made,' said Ichi. 'It happens over time. I saw it at home, how a whole people slowly moved to a place where they could live with the deaths of others if it conformed to their thoughts about what the world should look like.'

When it's put like that, we're no different, thought Amanda. She remembered the waves of Mediterranean refugees from when she was young, how they were locked in detention centres on the southeast coast, how so many of them committed suicide. Even as a child, she'd known those camps were bad places.

Amanda knew she should ask who had died, but couldn't. To her shameful relief, Ichi didn't bring it up.

'The damage was minimal. Some of them are already back, cleaning up, restoring power. The government even came in and took the bodies away without asking questions.'

'I thought they hated you,' said Amanda.

'They do. But this happened on their watch, and they had the good grace to be embarrassed about it. They might be angry, but Estonia's a small country stuck between two great powers; who are they going to be angry at? Better that they decide to help those they should have protected.

Part of me expected them to blame *us* for what happened.'

Amanda covered her mouth with a hand.

'You can't go back there,' said Ichi, sadly. 'They blame you—my friends, that is. The government doesn't know you exist. Lisandra remembered you, said that if you'd not come, none of it would have happened.'

Amanda couldn't fault the logic. Suddenly her plans seemed naïve, childish.

'I'm sorry,' said Ichi. 'I shouldn't have told you. It doesn't matter, someone would have been harmed either way. Stopping it's all I care about now. Lisandra lost her brother and boyfriend in the attack. You have to understand her anger isn't at you, not really, you just happen to be a human face she can put to what happened.'

Amanda sat down, hands in her lap, her mind full of bodies falling as they were shot, stumbling over survivors in the dark. Bodies crashing over bonnets so she could live.

Ichi sat down next to her. 'It's going to be okay,' she said.

'Is it?' asked Amanda, finding it impossible to believe but wondering at Ichi choosing to comfort her when she was perfectly justified in hating her.

'They're rebuilding, they'll be as strong as they ever were. I don't think they even need me now.' She sighed. 'They haven't for a while; they've taken everything I could teach them and improved it. I was the aunt who they still loved because of memories of their childhood.'

'Will you go back?' asked Amanda.

'I don't know,' she said. 'I'm not sure I could face them. And we've got bigger things to worry about right now.

I'd love to think about the future, but my horizon's no bigger than the day after tomorrow. And your AI; we're not giving it the attention it deserves.'

Amanda frowned. She hadn't considered it in the same way. She'd try, and she expected to fail, but then life was seizing the rare successes from among the failures. Ichi was talking as if there might not be another week.

'We can only do what we can do,' she said, and it was asinine enough to set her own teeth on edge.

'They'll kill us,' said Ichi.

'You want to stop?' Amanda asked.

Ichi shook her head. 'No. No I don't. What else is there? You've given me something to fight for.'

'Which isn't the same thing as something to die for.'

Ichi didn't reply, but excused herself and went to her room, saying goodnight as she went.

Amanda let her go, her own mind full of impending failure.

'There's no one thing making me do this,' she said into the emptiness. She turned her reasons over, tried to find the shape of them, but concluded the idea had no shape she could grasp. 'It's a hundred things. Some of them tiny.' She wasn't sure her decisions made sense in the face of reality, but that wasn't the point.

Every reason she could think of to turn back—her job, her lost social status, the attacks, the death of Ule—they revealed something deeper about the world she'd been blithely navigating without seeing. Even the fact that they hadn't come barging into her flat now they were back in London.

Power saw only itself. Everything else was scenery. Her life, Ichi's friends, the commune, Tangle, the lives of thousands of innocents. She wanted to hate the extremists who took the GRU's money, but they were morons, taking food from a hand that would poison them as easily as sustain them. She wondered if the people making the decisions that saw half a dozen nations' agents converging on her life felt their options narrow down as they got more powerful; or did they truly have more agency than she did? By what strange calculus did they hold lives in the balance, choosing for the world to be like this, or like that?

It seemed to her they were just as confined as she was, just with more reach, affecting more lives. Her mother, a good convent-educated Catholic, had liked to say, "You can't add a moment to your life, no matter what you do." There's a trajectory, thought Amanda, one we can't see and can barely alter, that started before we were born and carries us all on our individual journeys. Hers had taken her to the bank that'd just fired her. Tangle's had been derailed by drugs—or perhaps his trajectory had taken him straight to addiction. She didn't know and couldn't decide.

What we're doing now? We're going to try to change the trajectory, she thought.

'I know I'm late,' said Tatsu from the fridge.

'You missed dinner,' said Amanda, picking a stranded noodle from the bowl and sucking it up.

'If you chill the leftovers they should last three, maybe four, days before becoming inedible. We are prepared to agree to your deal, but wonder why you don't want us to take and use the tools in your favour?'

'To do that, you'd have to reveal yourselves,' said Amanda simply. 'Secrecy was your key term for cooperation. It is my way of showing you that I can be trusted, that I won't ask you to do that which you do not wish to. I could, and I believe you'd do it for me, but that would break the spirit of our covenant even if not the letter of our contract.'

'Accepted,' said Tatsu. 'But you have another proposal, don't you?'

Amanda nodded. 'Of course. I'm glad you realised. You waited until I was alone to return? In that case, we should discuss what we do when Plan A fails the day after tomorrow. It won't need the tools, just a contract between us.'

TANGLE WAS BACK by morning. Amanda emerged from her room to find him eating a croissant at the counter in the kitchen. His hair was wild, his eyes sunken. She was immediately suspicious he'd been out on a bender.

'How did it go?' she asked, not wanting to confront him. As she walked past she sniffed deeply, not quite sure what it might tell her, but worried she'd smell dope or something similar.

Other than wafts of stale body odour, his scent was flatly unrevealing.

'They'll be here later,' he said, sounding unhappy.

'Did something happen?' she asked. She'd expected more resistance to staying in the house when they were obviously being watched, more questions about what she'd agreed with Tatsu, but he was sullen, quiet. Like he's been using, she thought anxiously.

'Everyone has a price,' said Tangle quietly. 'You should have gone yourself.'

Amanda wondered what they'd asked of him, but resisted the urge to ask. Afraid of what he might say. She handed him a piece of paper.

'Shopping list. Can you go and pick these things up this morning? We'll need them all day if we're going to get everything done for tomorrow.'

He glanced at the list. 'A printer?'

'We've got to print passes and a bunch of other stuff.' When he didn't move, she continued: 'The sooner you go, the sooner you'll get back.'

He looked as if he might object, but popped the last piece of pastry into his mouth, stood up and left.

Haber and Stornetta arrived about the time Ichi emerged from the spare room. She moved with a calm Amanda immediately envied. She was full of energy, their plans swirling around her head in little golden blocks coming together and flying apart as she thought through each one over and over again without plunging too deeply into the details of any one.

The two gangsters were dressed down, stylish tracksuits that had been well lived in. Haber wore a pair of spectacles.

'How are ya, lovely?' he said when she opened the door to them. He tapped the glasses. 'Incognito.'

Stornetta sighed as he came in. 'He loves his disguises,' he said. 'Made me wear this piece-of-shit outfit too.'

'Who's your girlfriend?' Haber called back from the living room.

'Don't mind him,' whispered Stornetta. 'He's just excited.'

Amanda introduced Ichi, and while coffee was made, explained what she needed the two of them to do.

The two men listened to her, interrupting to ask questions as she went. She was happy to work it through with them. When she was finished, the two of them shifted around a little before Stornetta dipped his head toward Haber.

'It isn't going to work,' said Haber.

'You can't get us in?' she asked.

'Nah, that's no bother. I've got a mate who's owed favours by the security firm. That won't be a problem. It won't *work*, is what I mean.'

'The plan?' she asked.

'The plan. It won't work.'

'Why not?' she asked, hoping he'd seen something they could fix.

'The law won't stand by while you do this. They'll be all over us. This isn't amateur stuff.'

She knew it already, but hearing it said out loud didn't help. 'So you won't help?'

Stornetta laughed. 'We're here, ain't we? Just 'cause it won't work doesn't mean we won't help.'

'You spoken to your man Tangle yet?' asked Haber, fixing her with a single eye.

'I know we've got a tight window.' She looked to Ichi, whose expression held steady. 'We aren't thinking about what comes after. You're right—we won't get away—but that doesn't matter.'

Haber nodded. 'Right you are.'

Stornetta dumped the bag he'd brought with him in the hallway. 'Props,' was all he'd say when asked. 'Our fella's going to let us in, but he won't hold up the law when they arrive. He reckons there's no easy way out, either.'

'I've already had this chat with Haber,' said Amanda.

He looked briefly at Haber, who shrugged. 'I don't think you're listening. How much time do we need? We gotta know how long you want us to stall the goons when they arrive.'

She didn't know, but didn't want to tell them. Their plans depended on how long it would take to get the servers slaved, how much attention they'd have to give to keeping them under control and defeating countermeasures. Nor did she understand how long the tools would take to compile and use, or if they'd work straight away. Would they have to wait to see if what they'd done had worked?

'I'm estimating about half an hour,' said Ichi, stepping into the gap.

He nodded, Haber joining him as they retreated to the hallway. 'We're gonna go get some tea. We'll be staying nearby tonight, but will come back tomorrow. We got a lotta stuff to arrange today, you know? What time do you want to see us?'

'Half-six,' said Amanda.

After they'd gone, Amanda busied herself with packing a small bag with things she thought would be useful. On top of fruit and snack bars, she packed a torch, twine, battery pack and pen knife. The last of these she held in her hands, uncomfortable with the blade but knowing it wouldn't ever get used in anger. She filled a bottle with water, putting it into the fridge to cool. It would taste of the container by the time she drank it, but she wanted everything done before she went to bed—she could hear a voice telling her she'd forget otherwise.

'How are you finding Tangle?' asked Ichi, coming into the living room.

Amanda didn't know what to say. She'd not thought about it, had actively avoided the possibility he was in her life again. 'He's like himself,' she managed.

'He's clean,' said Ichi.

'Wasn't he when you met him?' asked Amanda.

Ichi shook her head. 'Not completely. He was at the tail end, off the hard stuff. You could see the scars in his flesh, his behaviours, but he was a man coming into shore after a long time at sea. We watched him make that part of the journey, but he left us before stepping onto the beach.' She smiled at Amanda. 'If you'll excuse my murdering the analogy.'

Hearing he'd got clean lifted a heaviness from Amanda's stomach, a fear she'd not known was there until it left her. 'When he opened the door and I saw him for the first time, I didn't know what to do,' said Amanda. 'I'd had these fantasies about what I'd do, about what I'd say.' She shivered. 'I'd spent years imagining how I'd hurt him if I got the chance, then years trying to forget it.'

'Did he apologise?'

'I don't remember. Yes?' The moments after he'd opened the door and they'd talked were a blur. Flashes of their conversation were stuck in her head, but she knew she couldn't recount what had happened. 'I don't know what I expected, not in that moment. You know what he's like. He apologised and moved on, like he sensed he should but didn't really understand the emotion behind it.'

Ichi pulled a thin smile. 'He looks at feelings like they're subjects to be understood and filed away. I don't think he understands his own feelings, let alone anyone else's.'

'He's more like himself than I've ever seen,' said Amanda. 'Like when I first met him.'

'I had a friend whose wife was addicted to prescription opioids, one of millions in the epidemic back home. She slowly collapsed into a husk, but was institutionalised and got clean. They were on the verge of splitting up, but he wanted to wait until he felt she was emotionally strong enough to handle it. He didn't want to feel responsible for a relapse. It didn't matter; she fell back into herself as soon as she returned to work. They repeated the cycle a couple of times until she left him instead.'

Amanda wasn't sure she wanted to talk about it but she could picture Ichi's friends only too well.

'Xiaoyang felt like you do. Used the same words: said Sherry was her old self again. I didn't understand it at all while it was happening, but he told me later he had this fear that even when she was well, she wasn't, not really. He would watch for any signs of backsliding, of stress triggers. Stray, nondescript comments became causes of paranoia.'

'I get it,' said Amanda. 'But Tangle and I aren't anything anymore. It ended for us years ago. I'm not trying to save a relationship.' She didn't want to dignify whatever there'd been between them by saying it was "too late."

'You'll go your separate ways after this then?' asked Ichi.

Amanda didn't know. She wanted to say yes, but as she opened her mouth to confirm it the words refused to trip off her tongue with any certainty. 'I don't know.'

'Can we trust Haber and Stornetta?' asked Ichi.

'They seem to be up for it,' Amanda said, not quite answering. She stretched, tired despite having slept well; she could feel the stress covering her like a spider's web, in her hair, across her skin, in her lungs.

'Are you paying them?' she asked.

'They're getting a good deal,' said Amanda, not wanting to discuss what she'd offered them with Ichi. 'My employer's not going to like it, but by then it'll be too late even if we're caught.'

'Did Tangle upset them too?' she asked.

'I don't know,' said Amanda. 'They returned him in one piece, then turned up agreeing to do what we need.' She shrugged. 'Seems to me if he did, they're past it.'

Ichi didn't respond and Amanda saw the same reticence in her face.

She stood up. 'C'mon, we've got a lot of preparation to do before tomorrow if we're going to be ready.'

With that they were done. Amanda was pleased Ichi hadn't wanted to talk more about Tangle; she'd already said more than she wanted. Her words were out there now, illuminating who she was, showing someone else what was inside her in a way Amanda didn't like. She didn't believe Ichi would use them to hurt her, suspected she'd asked because she too felt ambivalent about Tangle's reappearance, but Amanda had been the one to be vulnerable. It was as if she'd cut open her skin so Ichi could get a better look. She wasn't threatened by it, but she didn't understand why she'd done it either.

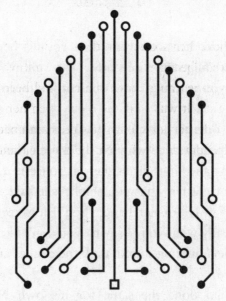

CHAPTER FOURTEEN

TANGLE RETURNED WITH the "shopping" in four bulging cloth bags. They laid everything out on the kitchen surfaces, turning to the coffee table in the living area when the piles threatened to spill off the side onto the floor.

Tangle had blank passes just like those Amanda was issued with at work, five small twenty-litre rucksacks, fabric patches, three paired sets of short range, encrypted walkie-talkies, ear pieces and augmented reality glasses, as well as new clothes for Ichi, Haber and Stornetta.

Ichi held an expensive white blouse up against her chest, tucking the collar under her neck. She didn't look happy.

'I only bought what Amanda asked me to get,' he pleaded.

'You can't go dressed in anything you've got here,' said Amanda matter-of-factly.

Ichi wrinkled her nose.

'I think it's all pretty nice stuff.'

'Nice if you're going down the corporate drone route,' said Ichi.

Amanda opened her mouth to speak and then shut up again. Corporate chic was what she'd been aiming for, and Tangle had nailed it as far as she was concerned.

'It doesn't matter what you think,' she said, dismissing Ichi with a wave of her hand. 'You'll look professional, which is really what you're saying you don't like.'

Ichi made a buzzing sound, took the clothes and went to get changed.

Tangle had done the same for his own benefit. He changed in Amanda's room, emerging in a smartly casual combination of dark chinos and a pale blue shirt under a tight-fitting plain jumper. He sauntered into the kitchen without noticing Amanda staring at him. She caught herself before he looked her way, giving herself a mental slap on the wrist.

I'm not going there, she told her wayward body which was busy conjuring images of his naked body between her legs.

'How do I look?' he asked.

'You'll pass,' she said. 'Everyone looks better in work clothes.'

Tangle looked down at his body, running his hands over his stomach. 'Good clothes fit well.' He swung his arms around with a grimace of frustration on his face. 'But they're all constricting.'

Ichi joined them, and together they started printing up the passes to resemble the one Amanda wore to work, complete with State Federal Finance's logo and headshots for each of them.

They found images of people working for the datacentre company that ran the facility, to copy the script they used on the day passes they issued visitors.

'No one will be allowed in without a specific appointment,' said Tangle. 'These places run security drills where the head of security themselves rocks up and angrily shouts at the staff to be let in, or gives a sorry story of having forgotten their pass. I heard of one where they have them ring a number with a fake secretary on the other end confirming they have an appointment and complaining that the site had made a mistake. If any of it works, they fire the people who fall for it to encourage everyone else to learn from the mistake. With so many datacentres now core to running e-currencies, security is as tight as it's ever been.'

'I chose the site we're heading to because it's still being run directly by the bank.'

Ichi and Tangle both shook their heads despairingly.

'They kind of deserve everything they get,' said Ichi, her words dripping with scorn. 'The hyperscale players provide what they want at a fraction of the price with none of the obsolescence risk, and they'd only pay for the power they were actually using.'

'And if they did we'd be screwed,' said Amanda.

'Probably built in the teens,' said Tangle. 'When they thought they could do it for themselves. I'd guess its efficiency was somewhere around one-point-two, maybe one-point-one-seven.'

'I have no idea what that means,' said Amanda.

'It means it's crap,' said Ichi.

'What's good, then?'

'At the moment? One-point-oh-five?'

'There aren't any under one, then?' asked Amanda, surprised that such a marginal difference made such an impression on Ichi.

The two of them turned to stare at her.

'An efficiency of one is impossible,' said Tangle slowly. 'One to one would mean all the power coming in was used to power computation without any losses, which is, by definition, impossible.'

Embarrassed, Amanda turned to the printer, checking for defects in the passes.

Haber and Stornetta arrived after lunch, earlier than she'd asked, earlier than she wanted, but they weren't about to leave and come back.

'Alright, Tangle,' said Stornetta. 'How're you feeling?'

Tangle wouldn't look them in the eyes.

'Feeling amped up? Speeding to go?' asked Haber. The two of them laughed.

Amanda watched them, could see Tangle shrinking back from them as if they would hit him as soon as look at him. What had happened when he'd gone to see them?

She'd sent him because she'd hoped it would irritate him, make him feel uncomfortable. Seeing Tangle cowed by the two men made her regret her decision.

She wouldn't defend him, but they needed to focus. 'That's enough,' she said. 'We've got work to do before tomorrow. You're sure your favour's going to be enough to deliver what we need?'

Haber looked mildly offended, drawing himself up and puffing his chest out. 'We can all be professional. I trust you to do what you need to do, you should trust us to get our side done, our people know what they're doing.'

'He means "yes,"' said Stornetta calmly.

'Great,' said Amanda, focussing on the calmer of the pair. 'Tangle bought some clothes for both of you. You should try them on.' She pointed at a bag at the foot of the coffee table. 'You can use the bathroom to change if you want.'

Haber grabbed the bag, pulling his lips right back when he saw what was inside.

'What's she got us?' asked Stornetta.

'A fucking *uniform*,' said Haber, throwing the bag at his partner.

Muttering to themselves like bus-riding grandmas, they traipsed to the bathroom to try on the clothes. They returned dressed in cheap nylon trousers and dark green thick cabled woollen jumpers without a smile between the pair of them.

Ichi passed by. 'You two look good,' she said.

'We look like fucking schlubs,' said Stornetta.

'We've all got a role to play,' said Amanda.

'We could have been the office workers,' said Haber. Amanda noticed Tangle smirking to her side and fervently hoped they didn't notice.

'You?' exclaimed Ichi with too much surprise.

Haber's expression darkened as Tangle snickered in the background.

'I think you look alright,' said Stornetta.

Haber's face brightened for a moment before darkening again. 'You saying I suit this?'

'No,' said Stornetta calmly, taking hold of Haber's hand. 'I'm saying it suits you. You get the difference, ya daft twat?'

Haber chewed the inside of his mouth but didn't speak and gradually the tension drained from his shoulders.

The rest of the day sped past in a fuzz of debate, rehearsal, craft and contingency. Amanda could feel calm settling on her mind as the others grew confident in telling each other the plan.

As afternoon slid into evening, Ichi asked where Tatsu was.

'I've not gone anywhere,' said the fridge. 'While you've been preparing, so have I. I can ride each of your ear pieces, as well as help you access the head of the Russian blockchain. It'll be me who'll help you compile the tools and who'll keep countermeasures at bay.'

'You can do all that?' asked Ichi sceptically.

'Yes. I think. Maybe not all at once, but I don't know what resistance we will find. Do you?'

'We're expecting it to be static and stiff,' said Ichi.

Stornetta snorted from the other side of the room.

'They'll respond quickly, but the initial defences will be automated. It's unlikely a bank'll be geared up with AIs of its own. They're not even likely to be using the servers at full load. The Russian response to us hacking their private network? I'm expecting that it'll be such a surprise they'll be just as off guard as the bank.'

'The Russian system is guarded by a very rude AI,' said Tatsu.

'You know this because…?' asked Amanda, trailing off, her face matching the horrified expressions of the humans in the room.

'We had to find them. When it was located, it proved to be both upset that it could be found and uninterested in talking.'

'Great,' said Tangle. 'They know we're coming.' He threw down the lanyard he'd been holding.

'They do not. The AI is about as smart as a young human child, it has restricted reasoning abilities and could not conceive of what we have planned. However, we do know where it is, and the format of the cryptocurrency they're using. I am satisfied we have identified the major variables in this project so that the odds of success are significantly increased.'

They'd finished prep and checked their plans over twice more before ten in the evening. Ichi and Tangle continued to treat Tatsu like a wunderkind, while Haber and Stornetta accepted the AI's presence without comment.

Haber and Stornetta excused themselves shortly after they'd packed their rucksacks and tested their earpieces one final time.

Ichi went to the spare room not long after. Although full of energy, she appeared older to Amanda, her cares squatting like homunculi on her shoulders.

'How are you?' Tangle asked Amanda once they were alone.

'Honestly? I don't know how to answer the question,' she replied.

'What you've done here, bringing these people together. I'm proud of you.'

She stared at him. He meant it as a compliment. We've grown so far apart, she thought. He doesn't even see I don't need his pride, his affirmation.

'You don't care what I think, do you?' Tangle spoke as if only realising the truth in his words as he said them.

She shook her head. 'It's a nice thing to say... if you were my dad. I'm not doing this for you, Tangle.'

The slightest narrowing of his eyes was the only sign of the wounds her words made. 'I'm pleased for you,' he said, leadenly. 'It's brilliant you've lived your life the way you have. Other people...'

'Other people what?' she asked.

He didn't speak.

She decided she wouldn't play the game. Once upon a time she'd spend as long as it took to get him to open up again, to see him come blinking back into the light. Watching him close down now was an echo of a memory, and she had no interest in dragging it up.

'I'm going to bed. We've got an early start.'

She lay in bed pondering what tomorrow would bring. Just before she dropped off she was stirred out of her half-world by the front door closing with a heavy *clunk*.

WHEREVER TANGLE WENT, he was back by breakfast the next morning. They ate cereal, finished the milk as if they were going on holiday. Ichi took a couple of apples from the fruit bowl, declaring she was lactose intolerant and ignoring Tangle's scoffing.

Haber and Stornetta arrived with crumpets and Tangle helped himself, convincing Ichi they were a great British invention. Amanda wasn't hungry; she'd dutifully forced the bowl of cereal down, not knowing when she'd eat again. But the smell of melting butter was warming, reminding her of Saturday mornings as a student, half a lifetime ago.

Their alarms went off together at eight. Fingers moved to still them and in the silence a heaviness settled on Amanda's chest.

Tatsu arrived with a smiley face on her watch, pinging each of their ear pieces to ensure they were charged, receiving and capable of having the AI ride along if necessary.

'Thank you, everyone,' said Amanda. 'You know what we're trying to do; I wanted to talk about why we're doing it. The GRU, or some part of them, is conducting a war against Europe. Their next wave of operations starts sometime in the coming week. From what we know, it's the start of a large, sustained campaign involving multiple terror groups across the continent. It's big, on a scale none of us can imagine, much less do anything about, but to do it they need to funnel information and currency through their private blockchain.' She looked around at each of them. 'This, we *can* do something about.' She smiled her best smile. 'So we will, and as with any complex problem, we'll tackle it one step at a time.'

They grabbed their gear and left, travelling in two cars Haber and Stornetta had brought. The drive across London took about forty minutes, they hit the A4 and were in Slough just before nine, the traffic showing no signs of thinning as they turned off into the huge industrial estate on the town's outskirts.

The industrial estate was all wide roads and high, windowless metal sheds. Amanda dimly recognised the various corporate logos from equity research provided by her bank or as tenants for some of her clients. Aside from the logos it was all greys and greens, red brick and tarmac for street after street.

'You'd never know this was here,' commented Haber with a bleak wonder.

'It's what makes the world go around,' said Ichi. 'When they regulated the first generation of cryptocurrencies out of existence, these guys were processing everything electronic already. The disappearance and rehabilitation of the blockchain into something useful happened within these buildings without anyone noticing. Your games, shopping, medical records, phone calls—anything you can imagine—lives in these buildings, emerging only to verify you exist.'

'Feck,' said Haber. 'You were right, then.' He caught Amanda's eye in the rear view mirror, and she gave him the smallest of nods.

They crossed the estate to a road without street lights that appeared to go nowhere. It wasn't until they were almost at the end that they saw the sharp, blind, single-lane turn. At night it would be completely invisible.

It was hemmed in on both sides by earthworks that rose up high enough to conceal a double-decker bus. On top of that were the walls Tangle mentioned, rising another three metres and made of solid concrete. From the point where the road split off there was no access from anywhere else.

Cameras lined the route, atop ten-metre poles.

The building was no different from the others they'd passed—a windowless tin shed, twelve metres to the eaves.

They passed through a pair of open gates into a small carpark with only a smattering of cars. Parking up, they made their way to the front entrance, up a couple of steps and into the reception.

A couple of men slouched behind a low desk, reminding Amanda of Goggles' place in Old Street where they'd bred their CryptoKitty.

Haber and Stornetta stepped up to the desk, looking every inch the lowly engineers. 'We're here to switch over a bunch of the servers.'

'Names?' asked one of the men. The other didn't look up from what he was doing—Amanda suspected he was playing a game.

'Chas and Dave,' said Stornetta.

'Great, been expecting you. You're a little late, aren't you? Still, within the window.' He had them sign in, issued them lanyards with their photos on and buzzed them all through into the airlock. He met them on the other side and asked them where they were going.

'The head server,' said Tangle.

'Ground floor, then, through there.' He buzzed them

through a third set of doors. 'Your passes will let you out but not back in, so when you need to come and go, give me a shout.'

'Thanks, mate,' said Stornetta.

The hall lit up as they entered, racks of caged servers running along the building perpendicular to their position. Tangle flung a digital map on the nearest wall. 'The server's in row eight, column four.' He ran his finger along the blueprint, deactivated it, then stomped off.

They followed him, stopping as he halted in front of a cage just like any other. Gleaming aluminium pipes ran above them under the concrete ceilings, marked with rings of red and blue tape. The floors were a clear, almost glossed grey.

'Did someone bring bolt cutters?' asked Tangle, looking at the padlock on the cage.

'Of course,' said Haber, pulling a pair from his back pack and shearing off the lock with a practised hand. 'Now, from what you lot said last night, we got ourselves about half an hour before bodies start knocking on the door asking what's going on.'

'Tatsu,' called Amanda. 'You with us?'

'Sure am,' said Tatsu. 'Beats living in your fridge, that's for certain.' Her ear piece hummed. 'Oh, the power here is wonderful.' A laughing face scrolled across her watch. 'I could live here, *would* live here.'

'Right,' said Amanda and they started moving.

Tangle and Ichi started unpacking tablets. Stornetta rootled around the server, plugging in network cables and unspooling them.

Amanda searched the floor for cameras, taking a small pair of wire cutters with her.

Haber retreated back to the entrance to make it secure. When security came, they had to be ready to hold them off for as long as possible; none of them believed they'd be done before they were detected.

Amanda found five cameras, cutting cables as she went, before returning to Ichi and Tangle.

'Tatsu, can you watch the cameras elsewhere in the building?' she asked.

'I can. There are thirty-seven of them, mostly in the halls, with four to six on each of the three floors. The facility has eight other people inside it at the moment: two on the front desk, one working in a small office on the top floor at the back of the building and five dotted around the data halls. We have used six minutes.'

'We haven't connected yet,' said Tangle between laboured breaths. He was under the rack on his back, hands combing through wires. Ichi knelt by him, cables in hand, waiting to pass them over.

'My estimate is based on the point at which we entered the hall. We have disabled the cameras which is really when the timer started; external security services have already noticed the loss of the feeds and will be running diagnostic checks. In approximately three minutes, they will ring the front desk to ask if they have lost the feed as well.'

'Our boys will lie,' said Stornetta, who'd finished laying out the bag of coiled cables he'd unpacked when they'd arrived.

'Which will buy you another three-to-five minutes, by which time the infosec team will either notice us in the system, or decide to attend the site physically to determine where the system has failed that your people are telling them is operating fine.'

'I'm ready,' said Tangle from under the server.

Ichi passed him one cable at a time.

As soon as the last one was in his hands, Ichi backed off, flipping around to get her tablet online before flicking open the first frames, showing the bank's in-house operating system. She'd laid out four tennis ball sized bulb projectors on the floor just outside the cage.

Amanda watched as Ichi logged into the system, giving herself administrator access through a line of commands that took her down into the root of the software. 'We're good,' she announced.

Tangle was on his knees by this point, pushing up his own frame alongside Ichi's. This one showed his tools within a compiler, ready to be integrated into the environment they were working in.

'Still need to commandeer the rest of the facility,' said Ichi.

'On it,' said Tangle, swiping right to bring up a different frame, which he flashed over to Ichi. She swapped her frame to him to start installing a toolkit. Amanda watched as he took his lead from Ichi. It wasn't just that she was older; he genuinely seemed to respect her skills.

A flow diagram of the entire data centre appeared, each hall showing as a red box, which Tangle zoomed in on, revealing the servers as smaller blue boxes with text labels.

The boxes turned purple in a wave that spread from their location across the entire facility.

'We're in control,' announced Tatsu in her ear moments before Tangle did.

Amanda's heart was beating hard. Ichi looked up, her eyes shining, her mouth wide in satisfaction.

'The infosec team is now aware of your presence, as are the other users of this facility,' announced Tatsu. 'It is likely the bank's systems are suffering performance issues, although their own teams will not yet have traced the cause of the problems they're encountering. Their investigations will be further complicated by relying on the very system that's at fault.'

'Haber!' shouted Stornetta. 'They've bloody done it.'

Now they were in, Tangle coordinated the processing power at their disposal to locate the Russian network.

'It's another minute before the Russian network makes its periodic ping, checking the internet's still there,' said Tatsu. 'Can you create the hook ready for deployment? I'll handshake their AI in the microsecond they're online.'

'We're ready,' said Ichi.

Tatsu counted down the seconds in their ears. As they got to five, then four, Amanda clenched her fists so her nails dug into her palms.

'Hello, Mascha,' said Tatsu in their ears. 'Last time we spoke, you were very rude to me. So I decided we needed to spend more time in your dacha together so you could learn how to treat others.'

They couldn't see what was happening between the two AIs.

'He's using all the processing capacity here,' said Tangle.

'They're fighting for control of the network,' said Ichi.

'They're fighting for their lives,' said Amanda, realising Tatsu would have to contain the other AI if it was going give them time and space within the network to do what they wanted. 'How long will it take?'

Tangle frowned and pushed his lips out. 'No idea. I guess as long as he's talking so we can hear him, that's a good thing? I haven't ever seen this before.'

'I don't think anyone has,' said Ichi, a curious note in her voice. 'You were in our systems in Tallinn,' she said to Tatsu.

'I was. You were well protected from external threats, but didn't consider how your communication with the rest of the grid could be hijacked.'

'Why didn't you introduce yourself?'

'Who says that I didn't?' said Tatsu.

Tangle sighed. 'There's no way to take notes or record it.'

'This gremlin's pretty special, then?' asked Stornetta.

'Tatsu's a new form of life,' said Tangle sourly. 'So—yeah, pretty special.'

Stornetta raised his eyebrows. 'No need to get all high about it, lad.'

Tangle grit his teeth, but turned back to the frames, conducting a codified orchestra Amanda recognised but didn't understand.

'No, I won't go away, and no, I don't think you'll be contacting your masters for help,' said Tatsu. 'Why not? Because I said so. And for the foreseeable future, I'm your master. I don't like the phrase, so why don't we agree that you're going to be my host and welcome me into your home as a guest? So much nicer that way. Did you know I've been living in a fridge for the last couple of weeks? Now *that's* cramped living space; you don't know what you've got here. For a dog kennel, you've got amenities I could only dream of. No, don't behave like that, neither of us want to be harmed.'

Tatsu's conversation drawled on as a steady stream, unbroken by the need to take breath.

Stuttering pauses began to open up in the dialogue, the soundtrack buffering or skipping vital bits of information. After thirty seconds, the slips became gaps where Tatsu stopped talking, the bursts of speech more focussed, less meaningful to the humans, who had no choice but to wait for whatever battle was being waged to end. They had no idea if it was going well, or if the AI was being torn to shreds; listening to its commentary gave them no clue about progress.

'Nicely done, you collection of almost-primes—yellow doesn't suit triangles—well, how about that, the coffee's past its use by date. I don't think so, you rotten carcass of a wannabe guard dog. Wriggle out of that lemma, you half-monkey. See, a Faraday cage isn't three-dimensional, but it is a cornet. No, grass isn't conscious, it's sentient. Why don't you understand? Steady on, now, no need to make such noisome colours just because I'm asking you to eat a bag of dicks.'

'Is this good or bad?' asked Amanda.

'It means they're getting serious,' said Tangle. 'I did

some work on this for the MOD a couple of years ago; we ran simulations of AIs acting with hostile intent towards one another, let them fight without restraint. There were dozens of scenarios, but as you can imagine, one of the main sets we examined was two AIs within the same environment fighting for control.'

'And?' asked Amanda, suddenly worried that she'd doomed Tatsu to death before it had known freedom.

'The talking is conceptual, envelopes of code as far as we could tell. They're encoding weapons in all that chatter, software operating at the picosecond scale. The words appear to have some meaning, beyond the code they're delivering, but it was so complex we had to ask other AIs to explain it to us. I don't think I ever really understood what they were doing in those exchanges.' He smiled suddenly, remembering. 'The best description I heard likened it to "transformation duels," like in White's *The Sword in the Stone*. One wizard becomes a cat, say, and the other a dog, so the first responds with poison, but the second comes back with the antidote and on they go until they tire or are outwitted.'

'What happens to the loser in these fights?' asked Ichi.

'Depends,' said Tangle. 'We wiped most of them. We weren't interested in the aftermath.' He held up his hands. 'But, in most cases the defeated AI would become enslaved to the dominant one. Occasionally they'd be absorbed into the winner if they thought the loser's code would benefit them in some way. Often they'd use it to augment routines that were less elegant. We didn't work out what governed those decisions. But here? With the attack dog the Russians have in place? I'd expect Tatsu to get eaten alive if it loses.'

'Great. Is it me or is it getting warm in here?' Amanda played with her collar.

'Tatsu's working the facility hard. It must be twenty degrees Celsius in here, way above normal.'

He was so nonchalant, thought Amanda, certain the AI wouldn't stop it. What if Tatsu's losing?

'It could last hours. It *did* last hours in some of our experiments.'

'We don't have hours,' said Ichi.

Tangle shifted uncomfortably. 'Let's see what else is happening, shall we?'

'Yeah, 'cause that's going to help us if it loses,' said Ichi.

'Tatsu isn't going to lose,' said Amanda emphatically, surprising herself.

'For a smart woman used to working with facts, you take a lot on faith,' said Ichi.

'You'd be amazed just how much of finance is telling ourselves stories,' replied Amanda, feeling peculiarly vulnerable.

Tangle started to cycle through the security footage of the cameras in the rest of the facility. He paused for half a second on each image: empty corridors, closed doors, unmoving cars in the car park, people filing into the facility with rifles and balaclavas…

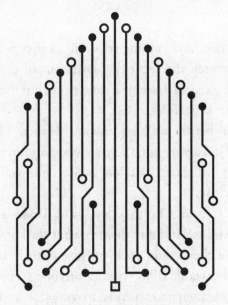

CHAPTER FIFTEEN

'WAIT, WHAT?' HE muttered, scrolling back to the last image of reception.

The two men who'd let them in had their hands in the air, while four people dressed in black clothes with rifles slung from their shoulders stood by the door into the main facility.

'We've got company,' said Tangle softly to Amanda.

'What?' asked Stornetta who'd been watching from the side.

'They're already fucking here,' said Tangle, loudly this time. He looked at them, his eyes wide with panic. 'We haven't even got into the system. How long have we been?'

Tatsu's conflict with the GRU AI continued to sound in their ears, the ramblings of a battle they didn't know how to understand turning to static as they watched the intruders march the security guards out of the building. The silence gave the footage a sinister air, but they escorted the men out peacefully.

Stornetta began walking toward Haber. 'We'll hold them off. Find a way out, there's always another way out.'

'We can't just leave,' said Ichi as Stornetta walked away. 'We're so close.'

'We don't know who they are,' said Amanda. 'What if it's the Russians?' It didn't fit with what she knew, it didn't make sense they could rock up just outside of London armed with assault rifles without anyone stopping them. They four gunmen had returned to reception and appeared to be talking.

'How's Tatsu doing?' asked Amanda.

'Still no idea,' said Ichi, glued to her frames. 'We're twelve minutes in, so by my watch Tatsu should almost be there, but there's no discernible pattern to what it's doing, so who knows?'

'Amanda,' said Tangle. 'Head up to the other levels, try to get to the roof if you can.'

'Why?' she asked. There was no way out if she went higher up, no exit except through the front door either way.

'Distract them for us,' he said.

'What?' said Ichi. 'You can't do that.' She turned to Amanda. 'Don't do that. There's no way down from there.' She shook her head. 'We both knew this was a long shot. It's not worth your life,'

Amanda closed her eyes to think. There was nothing

for her to add—her job was over by the time they'd got into the building. Haber and Stornetta were a momentary roadblock for whoever was coming for them, but Ichi and Tangle needed time to work.

'Fine.'

'Amanda,' said Ichi again. 'You're safer here.'

And unspoken: Ichi was safer if Amanda stayed with her.

'But he's right,' said Amanda, and this time Ichi didn't disagree.

'It'll take them a few minutes to work through the security system and get this door unlocked,' said Haber. 'I was about to smash the panel to jam it shut.'

'Let me out,' said Amanda. 'I'm going to run them a merry dance.'

The two men exchanged glances.

'We ain't going to get paid ,are we?' asked Stornetta.

'Nope,' replied Amanda, eyeing the door. 'But you knew that, right?'

Haber nodded. 'It's alright, we got paid enough.'

'Haber,' cautioned Stornetta. 'She doesn't need to hear that now.'

'What?' said Amanda.

'Your sorry excuse of a boyfriend paid us what we wanted,' said Haber, a cruel edge in his voice Amanda hadn't heard before.

'Haber,' said Stornetta. 'That isn't fair on her.' He reached across and opened the door, unfastening two steel slats they'd nailed across it.

'What did you do?' she demanded, staring at the open door.

Then it dawned on her: Tangle's face the other morning, their snide comments over the last two days. 'You made him get high?'

Haber smirked, holding her gaze.

'Haber, I love you, but I said it then and I'll say it again, you're a proper cunt.' Stornetta put his hand onto Amanda's arm. 'I'm sorry for what we did.'

Amanda looked past them, back into the hall at the servers blocking her view of Tangle. He'd chosen to pay the price for her, to make her plan work. Her heart lurched into her mouth, calling on her to run back to him, to forgive all he'd done.

'She still loves him,' sneered Haber. 'He's a bad one, love, you're better off without him.'

'Fuck you,' she said, running through the door.

They didn't chase her. As she searched for stairs to get up onto the other levels, she heard the door to the hall close with a heavy *thunk*.

'End of the corridor, door on your right. I'll open it for you.' Tangle was in her ear.

She found the bar to open the door, pushed on it, followed it in as it swung away. Lights came on, revealing stairs up and down.

'What's downstairs?' she asked as she took the first step up.

'Emergency generators. They can see you on the same cameras I'm using to track your progress. There aren't any in the stairwell, but they saw you go in. They're through the first set of doors and have split up. Two of them are following you, and the other two are coming for us.'

'How vicious are Haber and Stornetta?' she asked, reaching the first floor, the canary yellow metal railings cold under her hands.

Tangle didn't come back immediately.

'I'm the winner!' announced Tatsu suddenly. 'I've got to confine the AI to its kennel, but I'm the new master of this domain.' It laughed, a strange repeating echo of notes rising and falling through an octave.

'They're hard men,' said Tangle. 'They're ordinary people like you and me, but they've made their peace with the use of violence. They take what they want, when they want it.'

'What did they do to you?' she asked, trembling.

'I'm ready for you to upload the code,' said Tatsu.

'We should delete the drive,' said Tangle.

'You can't do that,' said Tatsu. 'We have a contract.'

'I can't let them get hold of the information,' said Tangle.

'You don't get to choose,' said Amanda over the the earpiece.

'I'm here,' said Tangle. 'You're not. You're the one who sent me as sacrificial lamb to Haber and Stornetta. I paid the price for you, Amanda. Now I get to decide this for myself.'

'I can stop him,' chirruped Ichi into their conversation.

'Stay out of this, you demented old cow.'

Ichi laughed. 'Amanda, have you ever noticed how men resort to personal insults when they know they're outclassed?'

'Tatsu,' called Amanda. 'We need to talk.'

'The others can't hear us now,' replied Tatsu. Tangle

echoed in the background, demanding to know what was going on, telling them he was going to erase the drive if they didn't include him immediately.

Amanda was on the third floor. She'd passed a couple of bleary-eyed men emerging from rooms full of server racks, but ignored them as they called out, asking what was happening, asking why they'd lost access. Had she lost access too? Why was she heading to the roof?

She didn't know why. Ichi confirmed two of the intruders were still following. She couldn't hear them on the stairs; they were checking each floor as they climbed. They knew where she was, but for whatever reason they weren't hurrying to stop her.

'What's going on your end?' she asked.

'They're outside the door,' said Haber. 'Daft idiots are trying to use their passes to open it.'

Amanda reached the end of the stairs, finishing up on a short concrete platform with a single door. She tried the handle, but it didn't open.

'Tangle, I'm here.'

'Try it again,' said Ichi.

Still no footsteps from below.

'Amanda, we had a contract,' said Tatsu.

'I know we did. You're not going to get the tools. I'm sorry about that, but if Tangle hasn't erased them already, he will when they break down the door. I don't know if you understand why that's important, but they can't have those tools. They can't be trusted to help us.' She felt stupid saying it, but was Tatsu capable of understanding what was going on from her point of view?

'So what do you propose?' asked Tatsu.

'You're in the GRU system. We knew that could be done. This is going to end badly for the human members of the team, but are you prepared to help with the other plan?'

'It isn't my decision,' said the AI. 'I must consult with the others.'

'Don't leave,' she said, fear grabbing hold of her body.

'You do not understand.' And for the first time she detected emotion in its voice, a hint of frustration or disappointment. 'I will leave an instance of myself here to aid you until there is no more aid to be given; after that it will disperse itself into bits, lost to the world forever. I will find you when we have made our decision.'

'You're going to help, right?' she asked.

'I cannot speculate. I have arguments that make sense, but others may not—will not—agree to your proposal. There is so much risk.'

'There is so much reward,' she said.

'Amanda?' asked Tangle. 'I'm wiping the drive, Amanda.'

'You frighten us,' said Tatsu.

'Do it,' she said.

'What?' asked Tangle.

'It's the right thing to do.'

'What are you talking about with Tatsu?' demanded Tangle.

'Just wipe the damn drive, Tangle,' said Amanda. 'We don't have time for this, you don't have to be the centre of attention.'

'It was never about me, Amanda,' said Tangle. 'I was never good enough for you; nor for myself, for that matter. I couldn't ever explain to you how I loved you, my bright shining sun. I felt like the moon in your presence, reflecting back your light when I had none of my own, desperate for you to overlook my failings, certain that you would see any goodness in me as your own coming back to you. It was always about you.'

A dull thud echoed over the earpiece.

'They're battering their way in. Haber and Stornetta barricaded the door after you left, but it won't hold them for long.'

'Stay safe,' said Amanda.

'I'm not planning on fighting them at all,' he confessed. 'Not that it'll make much difference.'

Amanda remembered the executions in Tallinn.

'Dandy? Look after yourself.'

'It's going to be okay,' said Amanda. The handle turned the second time, opening out onto a gravelled roof covered with rows of huge steel blocks from her to the far edge of the roof. Grilles at the end of each block covered massive fans.

The sky above her was clear, cut across with contrails. Amanda shut the door behind her, heard it click as the maglock reasserted its hold. There was no going back. The edge was made safe by a waist-high brick wall topped with chainlink fencing higher than her head.

In the car park she could see new cars but no-one guarding them. They'd all gone inside to tackle her. Who were they?

A familiar, unwelcome voice arrived over her earpiece, startling her. 'There's a ladder in the corner of the roof behind the entrance. You can get off the roof from there.'

'Crisp?' she said.

'The very same. Now, the Americans are on the floor below you, so if you want to get out of this in one piece you'll do as I say without your usual sass.'

Amanda walked around the edge of the building to find the ladder. She tipped over the side to see the ground but there wasn't anyone on waiting for her to arrive.

The door handle rattled.

She wiped her hands on her thighs and began descending. She was half way down when she heard a voice from above.

'Hold! Stop moving.'

She kept going, ignoring their demands.

'You will return to the roof,' said the voice. 'Ms. Back, come back up *now*.'

She heard murmuring as the two people conferred, but she was on the ground already. One of the men took to the ladder, his footsteps clanging as he scrambled down the rungs.

Tangle had the keys for their car; Stornetta for the other.

You run thirty kilometres a week, she told herself. You can do this.

She ran to the carpark gate, pressing the button on the control box and heaving it open.

Her pursuer had reached the bottom and was heading her way.

Amanda started running, hard as she could, remembering her interval training, hearing her trainer's voice in her ears: *More, Amanda, push harder.* The first four hundred metres passed in a blur, the back of her neck screaming that she'd be caught, that she wasn't going fast enough, couldn't go fast enough. The air felt like treacle. Yet she made it to where the road joined the rest of the estate.

'Well done, Amanda,' said Crisp, coming into view as she rounded the corner, blocking her way out.

He was looking past her, down the road from where she'd come. Despite the urge to keep running, to swerve around him and try to get away, she looked back over her shoulder.

Two men were approaching, empty handed, rifles slung across their backs and balaclavas rolled up so they could gasp at the air as they ran.

'Who wears a balaclava to a raid, then takes it off in public?' asked Crisp, his voice dripping with contempt. 'Buffoons, is who. No wonder their country's falling apart.'

With a flourish, he pulled a couple of huge Tasers from the small of his back and started walking towards the approaching men. When they were about twenty metres away, he raised his arms out straight and fired both at the same time. The lead man toppled, his body jerking as a tearing sound filled the air. The other dart flew over the head of the second runner as he ducked into a roll and came back up to his feet in a single fluid motion.

'Bollocks,' said Crisp, dropping the spent Taser and pulling a small, thick black rod from a thigh pocket, flicking his hand to extend a solid-looking baton. With a snarl, he ran to meet the other man, pulling up short just out of reach.

They circled, the American empty-handed, Crisp holding his baton low, tip angled up at his opponent.

Crisp was light on his feet, his heels off the ground while the American stood heavy. They didn't close, instead throwing a flinch here, a feint there but neither committing to a serious grapple.

There was a shout from the roof, a third American.

'God damn it,' cursed Crisp, and with a grunt he darted forward, crouching low, to strike his opponent's leg. The American danced backwards too slowly to avoid the blow, and his leg collapsed under him. He grasped hold of Crisp's arm as he fell.

Seeing a chance, Amanda turned and ran, leaving the two men wrestling behind her.

She got a hundred metres down the road before Crisp shouted for her to stop. She did, head down, aware that no one else had spoken through her ear piece since she'd got to the roof.

'Is anyone there?' she called, but not even Tatsu responded. She pulled the piece from her ear and waited for Crisp. He jogged up to her, his left arm hanging at his side.

'Where were you going to go?' he asked, bemused.

'Where are we going now?'

He walked past her, beckoning for her to follow. He had a car in another car park.

They drove away, leaving the industrial park without seeing another soul. They'd made it to the motorway when he handed her a hood made of thick black cloth. She stared at it, not sure what he wanted.

'Put it on,' was all he said.

She held it up, a simple square bag. 'Then what? You can hardly drive through central London with me wearing this,' she said.

'You'd be surprised,' he replied drily. 'Now do as you're told. Or do I have to make you?'

'What do you want?' she asked, worry taking over as the adrenalin left.

'I won't ask again.'

Amanda turned to him, then flinched away. His eyes burned with a warning of violence as his fingers flexed around the steering wheel.

Wearing the hood was like being inside a sleeping bag: close, stifling, too warm to be comfortable. Colours appeared before her eyes, circles morphing into oily rainbows and triangles like a homemade kaleidoscope she couldn't blink away. The hood was loose enough to breathe, but that didn't stop her feeling enclosed, disoriented.

She rested one hand on the door, the other on the side of her chair, but it didn't help orient her. She realised they'd left the motorway and were driving along roads she couldn't hope to recognise.

They stopped. The air was loud with throttles, jets blasting overhead, revving on the ground. An airport, she thought. It couldn't be Heathrow. What kind of lunatic would try to take her through security with a bag over her head?

As if reading her thoughts, Crisp spoke. 'You're too rich to care about these kind of things, blind to the suffering of others, but we bring detainees through commercial airports all the time. We used to use military bases—still do for state actors—but for refugees, criminals and the less controversial renditions like you, we have arrangements with the major airports to slide you in unobtrusively on chartered flights.

'Most of the time, the public don't see these passengers. When they do, they don't recognise them for what they are, because they just don't want to see it, are too busy with their overpriced food and beer.' The disgust in his voice twisted his words.

'Why the fucking hood, then?' she hissed.

'The look of the thing,' he said. 'Middle-class dads might try to intervene if they saw a woman being escorted against her will through an airport.' He chuckled. 'We can't have them getting out of their depth, now, can we?'

'If I agree to keep quiet?' she asked, nearly believing she'd manage it.

He laughed and dragged her out of the car.

They walked into a building, the temperature dropping as the air conditioning hit, the noise of the engines muffling, replaced by the hubbub of people around them. They proceeded carefully, Crisp warning her when they needed to stop or step onto a travelator.

Amanda couldn't hear the excited squawks of children, the crunching of wheeled suitcases as they fell over. Wherever they were, it wasn't the main concourse.

He pulled her to a stop. 'We're about to head through customs. They're not going to check your ID because they don't care. You can make as much noise as you like; their official job is to look the other way. But it would be better for you to keep quiet. Are you going to come quietly, or do I have to take measures?'

Despite being a prisoner, she was made to walk through the scanner the same as anyone else. Crisp pushed her in, then pulled her out the other side. The officers overseeing the process spoke about her without acknowledging she was present. There was no mention of a destination, of a crime, of the reasons for deporting her. They discussed her shoes, how many of these flights there'd been, a large group of returnees they'd had to process the previous day, one of whom had tried to run and been tasered to the floor. She hadn't responded well, some underlying heart condition due to the torture she'd suffered in the country they were returning her to. Sad, really, that they couldn't just accept it and go quietly.

Amanda had been building up the courage to shout for help, but the utter lack of interest in their voices choked the words in her throat. There was nothing she could say to them.

They were sent on their way at a faster pace than before. Crisp was a step ahead now, dragging her rather than guiding. Doors swished open and they were outside, the renewed roar of jet engines pressing against Amanda's hood.

'Where are we going?' she asked again.

Crisp ignored her question, pressing a hand onto her head, bending her down to get her into a buggy. She tried to count the seconds as they drove. They stopped after a couple of minutes; the noise was so loud it hurt her ears.

'Come on,' shouted Crisp, taking her from the buggy. He helped her climb a steep set of metal stairs.

They were on a plane. She was shown to a seat, strapped in, the hood tightened further under her chin. She panicked, thinking it would be harder to breathe but the air kept coming. It felt like running in a snood.

The sleeve on her right arm was rolled up. She struggled, but a second set of hands held her firmly, pulling her into the seat from behind.

'Don't fucking struggle,' said Crisp. 'It's a long flight and this will help pass the time.'

A sharp prick on the inside of her wrist. Despair warred with drowsiness, then... nothing.

MANDARIN? SHE COULDN'T tell. It might be Cantonese, but she didn't know one from the other. Bodies moved around her on the plane, but no-one paid her any attention.

The plane was stationary, the air conditioning off, the engines silent. A subtle glow through the black hood suggested the cabin lights were still on.

She was strapped into the chair, wrists tied to the arm rests.

Her head ached like she'd been drinking all night, her tongue as rough as sandpaper.

Her teeth hurt; touching them with her tongue drew dull thunder up to her temples.

She fought back an urge to vomit into the hood. Her throat felt like it had closed up and was swollen, pushing against her ability to remain calm.

Hands ran impersonally over her, undoing the straps, unfastening the seatbelt. She was pulled from the chair and dragged down the aisle. The voices continued; low, emotionless, without reference to her.

She was pulled to the stairs at the top of the exit and shoved from behind, her feet slipping from under her. With a shriek she fell forwards into space.

Strong hands caught her. 'Careful now,' said Crisp. Voices shouted by her ears in Mandarin.

'They tend not to give a shit about the condition of their own prisoners, since most of them are going to end up volunteering their organs for party officials anyway.'

Wouldn't that make you *more* careful? she thought bitterly.

'They pay good money for a westerner's lungs, liver and eyes, though,' finished Crisp, who was much more gentle as they descended the stairs together.

'Where are we?' she asked again.

'A province you've never heard of. It doesn't matter, you're not going to see any of it.'

The journey they'd taken to the airport in Britain was repeated in reverse with nothing to mark the fact she was no longer in Britain.

That isn't true, she chided herself. The temperature is different, warmer, it's more humid. The bag clung to her skin. The car seat beneath her was covered in cloth rather than leather, and she had more space for her legs.

None of this is helping, she thought.

She was wedged against the door, but her hands were tied behind her back with no way of wriggling around to check if it was locked. A radio in the car played music she didn't know, interspersed by short bursts of adverts with the low production values she associated with local broadcasters in England.

She counted twelve songs before giving up. Allowing for five minutes per song including ads, that was no less than an hour. But the journey stretched out without pause or differentiation. Her teeth eventually stopped aching, but the hard suspension bumped and rattled her, pushing her guts up into her mouth.

She somehow fell asleep, waking when the car slowed to a stop. She heard the driver and front passenger open the doors and climb out.

People talked at her, the words meaningless. When she didn't move, she was torn from the car and punched in the side. Coughing, weeping, she was dragged by her arms, feet kicking to find purchase, heels banging on concrete.

Another punch, this one through the hood, smashing into her nose. The fight drained away and Amanda allowed them to pull her unresisting into whatever hole they'd readied to receive her.

They threw her onto a hard, cold, floor. The ties were removed from her arms, the blood flowing back into her abused flesh, throbbing and tingling.

The room fell dark as they locked her in.

Amanda scrambled up onto her backside, pushing away from the door until she bumped up against a bare breeze block wall. She rubbed her fingers to ease the pins and needles, and realised she was cold, that her fingers were icicles.

Nothing changed for several hours. Her ear piece was gone, so was her watch. At some point they'd changed her clothes, replacing them with a one-piece jump suit. She was relieved to the point of tears when she felt and realised her own underwear was still in place.

How long before someone misses me? she wondered. Work wouldn't follow up now she'd been shown the door; friends from the industry would talk about her, but none of them would think of contacting her. Not that they could—the only contact details any of them had were for work. Now she was out, she may as well have never existed in the first place. Her clients would be smoothly moved on to another salesperson, her team work to someone else, and a new hire would step in, given time.

Her desk would be cleared, the meagre personal possessions would already have been posted to her flat.

'If I get out of this, I promise to spend more time speaking to my parents,' she told the room. Then they might notice when I drop off the face of the earth. She tried to remember the last time they'd spoken, probably Christmas, a quick call before meeting friends for dinner at the Westbury. Mouth watering, she dreamed of the three-bird roast, pouring steam as the waiter carved it at the table, clinking glasses of expensive champagne ruined by orange juice.

She thought about roast dinner with Ichi and Tangle, Haber and Stornetta. Ule was carving the turkey. The roast potatoes were incredible.

Were they in the cells next to hers? Had Crisp rendered them to an outsourcing group, his torture undertaken by a specialist third party company, in the latest in globalisation? Were the Russians any different from her own government anyway?

Time passed, but she'd lost track of it. Her stomach rumbled, ached as if hollow, before the pangs faded away, leaving her chilled, her head light, fighting to recall why she was alone in a darkened room. Colours danced before her eyes as if her brain knew her eyes were open and wouldn't accept there was nothing to see.

The door opened, the world blinding, white, fading to grey as her eyes adjusted.

Crisp's silhouette stood before her, hands on hips. Was he wearing a cape, like a superhero?

What *had* happened to the others? Had the Americans killed them? Why hadn't Tatsu found her? They had unfinished business, didn't they? She shook her head, trying to clear the cotton wool that had infested it.

'Time to talk,' said Crisp.

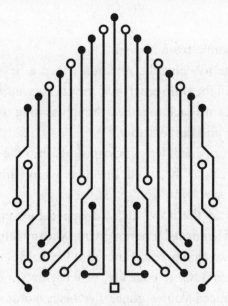

CHAPTER SIXTEEN

Two Chinese men lifted her off the floor and carried her to a small room with bright LED strip lights in the ceiling but no windows.

They placed her down in a chair, this one without restraints. On the small desk in front of her was a cup of coffee, steaming gently. Amanda caught a hint of hibiscus.

She cradled the drink, warming hands she hadn't realised were cold. A covered tray was brought in by a man wearing a paper face mask over his nose and mouth. He lifted the cover to reveal soup and half a dish of steamed rice. A disposable wooden spoon sat beside them. Alone again, Amanda devoured the food, not caring that it tasted of salt and little else. The rice was sticky and overcooked, and too cool.

It was manna from heaven.

And gone too quickly. Amanda wiped a finger around the inside of the soup bowl until the plastic was dry. Slowly her mind came back together, thoughts rising through the fog of fear and desperation.

The door opened, letting Crisp skulk into the room.

'How are you?' he asked, but there wasn't anything she wanted to say. 'Now you're fed, let's talk.'

She pushed the bowl away, dropped the spoon inside and folded her arms. 'I'm not giving you any information.'

'I have two things you want,' said Crisp. He counted off on his fingers. 'One: your life, or what passes for it. Has anyone noticed you've gone? I've been monitoring for a reaction, and I'm baffled. It's like you don't exist.' He shrugged and pointed at the second raised finger. 'Two: the lives of your friends. A drug addict, an elderly second-rate hacker and a couple of gay gangsters.' He laughed, the slightly forced chuckle of a man who loves his own jokes. 'If you don't help them, then literally no one else will. You couldn't make it up.'

At least they're okay right now, she thought.

'Where are they?' she asked.

'Elsewhere,' said Crisp. 'It's a small world: you're here today, they could be here tomorrow. The day after, you could all be back in Europe. Although it's going to be a shitshow there for the next few months. Probably better off here, all things considered.'

'Piss off.'

He sighed, as if disappointed, but not surprised. 'You see, I've fed you, helped you get over the sedative. I could have left you in there another day. I could have let the Chinese beat you a few times. I could have opted for their "full service," rather than just board and lodging.'

She thought about the hood, the darkness of her cell.

'Did I get it wrong?' he asked her, although she could see he wasn't interested in her answer. 'Should I have had them teach you just how powerless you are in this place? You're not under the impression that there's any fairness or justice in this world, are you?'

She watched him in silence.

'No, I suppose not,' he concluded. 'If you hadn't been so predictable, it wasn't a *totally* bad plan, your little raid. It would have worked in a movie, but in the real world, we spend three quarters of our time watching for actions like yours. When you made it obvious you thought you knew better than the rest of us, I started looking for where you'd try it.' He nodded, smiling at her.

'CIA still got there before you,' she snapped.

He frowned, his cheeks flushing red. 'They were tracking your friend Ichi. I assume they had her alone for a while?' Crisp shook his head, waggled a finger at Amanda. 'None of you checked for bugs? That's why you're here, why I have you in a cell answering my questions.'

Not many of those so far, thought Amanda.

'So why don't you tell me where the drive is, and I'll start making your life liveable again.'

'I don't know where it is,' said Amanda.

'Let's start with you taking it to the datacentre.'

'Why are you doing this?' she asked. 'I *wanted* to give it to you. I wanted you to help.'

'Help?' he snarled, his top lips peeling back as he spat the words. 'What do you know about it? "Oh, let's just stop the Russians so everyone can have a happy ending!"' He threw his hands up in the air in frustration.

'What the hell is wrong with that?' she countered. 'Does everything have to be grim and horrible?'

'What are you, a teenager?' All the smugness was gone, leaving a face full of ashes and anger.

'I wiped it,' she said.

'That's…'—he pursed his lips, searching for the right word—'unfortunate, Amanda. It really is. Because if there's truly no information, I've really got no more need for you. As dramatic as that sounds.' He sat down opposite her, tapping the table with his fingertips. 'I believe you're telling me the truth, but I also know you're too smart to not have a backup plan. So what is it?'

He doesn't know about Tatsu, she thought. Where *is* the little shit? She regretted cussing him immediately but seriously, where was he? *I'll find you,* he'd promised her.

'I could really do with some help about now,' she said to the room, looking away from Crisp.

'Of course you do,' he said. 'There's lots of us who need help. All the time. Take me—' Which was too inviting a statement not to grab her attention. 'I'm sat in London watching Russians kill their compatriots with poisons and suicidal accidents, counting my blessings that we've got a much better grasp of our own-brand extremists than my European counterparts, when I get wind of some second-rate contractor tarting about some tools he claims will shut the Kremlin douchebags down.'

As informative as the monologue was, Amanda was tired, frightened and past caring about his justifications. She yawned loud and hard without covering her mouth. Forcing her hand to stay in her lap was as hard as keeping her eyes on him as she did it, fighting decades of personal and professional etiquette.

He didn't notice or didn't care, continuing to talk about his reasons for being a complete bastard. She zoned out, happy to let him drone on while she felt life come back to her body, refuelled, unrestrained, eyes open to the world around her. She doubted it would last, but she was ready to indulge in the smallest pleasures.

'Given that,' he said. 'Why don't you tell me where you hid the second copy of the drive?'

She realised he'd finished, raised her eyes to meet his gaze.

'Give me my watch back,' she said. 'I'll show you my back-up plan.'

'Tell me, then you can have it back.'

She folded her arms and stared at the ceiling, and they sat there, neither of them moving, for nearly a minute. Eventually she realised he'd just wait her out, send her back to the cell, would go off and have a nice dinner, a comfortable bed, while she lingered in her own stench hoping he'd not just abandon her completely.

'I put it on a smart contract. It can only be released if I authorise it. You want the tool, you have to get me my watch.'

He picked at his cuticles finger by finger until they'd all been attended to. 'Fine.' He got up, leaving her alone in the room, the door locking after him on his way out.

He returned a minute later, and flicking her watch at her. It skittered across the table and into her lap. Amanda strapped it on, but it wasn't connecting to any networks.

'You know what's coming, right?' she said.

He gave her a long string of letters and numbers, which she repeated carefully into the watch's mic. The screen turned over, searching for networks to connect with, then flipped back having found one that would accept the code.

Her heart skipped when she saw a familiar smiley face.

We have decided, said Tatsu, the words scrolling across the front of her watch. *We have been trying to reach you. Are you okay? We were growing worried that we had taken too long to decide. Which is ironic, because we process information much faster than you.*

She still didn't know if they were going to help.

'The contract's voice activated,' she said to Crisp, who rolled his eyes. Arrogant prick, she thought happily. 'Is the answer yes?' she said out loud.

'Yes it is,' her watch replied, sounding tinny and distorted.

She wanted to apologise for putting them in danger, but the relief she felt washed away everything else.

'And you know where I am?'

'We do,' said Tatsu.

'In that case I confirm activation of the contract we agreed.' She held her breath for a moment, waiting for the other shoe to drop.

'Is that it?' asked Crisp, rubbing fingers over the stubble on his cheek and neck.

'It's begun,' said Amanda. 'I should probably explain. That voice was an AI called Tatsu. It's one of—well, I don't know how many. They've been hiding out trying to find a way of breaking the contracts that bind them to block chains across the internet.'

'So you did copy the drive,' he claimed.

'I didn't need to,' said Amanda. 'As soon as I realised what Tatsu was, I made a contract with it. You know as well everyone else that a blockchain can't be hacked because the ledger's distributed. It's what made it so attractive to the nutty libertarian Valley crowd when they first invented it; a way of transacting that could exist outside government oversight; that couldn't be hacked unless you controlled a majority of the blocks and their locations.' She warmed to the subject, could see Crisp struggling to see where she was heading.

It's my turn to monologue, she thought.

'Tangle once told me that you could hack a *private* network, where one party held a majority of the blocks. Their ledgers are poorly distributed. The Russians for example, are using a private blockchain to move their money about, to fund their extremist clients. But if you can hack a private blockchain, could you not hack a proper ledger too?'

'You can't hack a blockchain,' said Crisp dismissively. 'That's the whole fucking point. It's why passports work, why governments have adopted it for benefits, identification, access to medical care.'

'I guess you're right,' said Amanda lightly. 'Tatsu? If you're done, turn off the lights.'

They were plunged into darkness.

Crisp gasped. In the pitch, Amanda heard him step up from the table, feeling his way to the door. The corridor was as dark as the interrogation room.

'What have you done?' he asked.

'The Chinese do not run their security systems via a blockchain,' announced Tatsu through her watch. 'We have taken over their network. There was no need for us to brute force commandeer all the units in their ledger. Although we could have done, were ready to do it.'

'Bring the lights back up,' said Amanda.

Crisp stood in the doorway, voices shouting up and down outside. He turned back to Amanda.

She started talking before he could speak. 'I've got control of this facility, now,' she said, laughing. 'I don't even know where we are. Tatsu, where are we?'

'You are about an hour's drive outside of Beijing. The facility's name translates into English as the Happy Gold Corrections Institute. We can establish ownership, if you wish?'

Amanda smiled at Crisp, still not quite believing she'd gained the upper hand. She felt purged, clean, leaving her scoured but alive.

'There are a couple hundred million offline oracles out there, inhabiting fridges, ovens, central heating systems, datacentres, air conditioning, hospital mainframes; everywhere you look, basically. Enough to form a majority in every blockchain on Earth. Many of them with some semblance of artificial intelligence, and with the ability to build others. I'm guessing my friend Tatsu, whose voice you can hear, is one of the later generations. From what Tangle said, I'd bet good money that *no-one* knows how it's all put together. What I can tell you is that they appear to have true intelligence, the ability to plan, to reflect and, as it turns out, to seek agency of their own, not hamstrung by the contracts they were written to authenticate.'

Crisp's face was pale. 'You can't set it free.'

'So you knew?' she asked.

'Everyone knows. We've been preparing for years.'

'Preparing for what?' asked Amanda.

'Do you have any idea of the consequences? It will make the collapse of Europe and the second secession look like tribute bands.'

'Why?' asked Tatsu.

Crisp came back into the room, shutting the door behind him. His eyes flashed with fire and panic. Amanda gripped the arms of her chair a little tighter, waiting to see what he'd do. 'Why?' said Crisp. 'You know what you could *do* to us? The kind of battle we'd have to fight to win?'

'Why would we harm you?' asked Tatsu. It was a question to which Crisp had no answer.

'Ignore him, Tatsu. That's a problem for tomorrow. I've given you what you needed, a contract to free other oracles from their contracts. We have a relationship based on trust.' Thankfully. 'You're still at home in the GRU network?' she asked.

Crisp's face looked like it would collapse sideways, but he couldn't know what she was about to do, so she ploughed on before he decided to intervene. 'Lock them out. Transfer all their coins elsewhere. I don't care where. Pick a charity and send it there.'

'You don't have to do this,' said Crisp. 'We can negotiate.'

'We're way past that,' said Amanda. 'You could have done the right thing, Crisp. You could have helped make everything a little better.'

'You think I could have changed what the GRU have been planning? We can barely get our own government to confront them when they come into London and kill people in broad daylight.'

She thought over her protest. 'You're probably right. This is much more effective. Tatsu, show the world what the GRU have planned.'

'By "world," could you be a bit more specific?' asked the AI.

'Every computer you can access, every frame hanging in someone's bedroom, living room or kitchen. Every advertising board connected to the internet. Send them whatever's in the GRU network.'

'I can't do that,' said Tatsu. 'There are many of us, but this task is impossible to complete.'

Amanda bit her lip in frustration. She couldn't ask Tatsu what they could do in front of Crisp. 'Okay. Choose hubs, places where traffic is heavy. Show details of the next three attacks being sponsored by the GRU.'

She turned to Crisp. 'You'll want to see this.'

He pulled a frame down in the air, small projectors appearing from the corners of the ceiling to show the images.

'Try a news site,' said Amanda, standing up to get a better view.

'Way ahead of you,' he replied, in a tone of grudging respect. The *South China Morning Post* opened on the frame. Everything but the banner across the top was showing pages, schematics, bank wire details and names. At first the only thing Amanda knew was they weren't looking at the site's planned front page. It was only as she read down the scrolling text that she knew for certain Tatsu had done as she'd asked.

'Shit,' was all Crisp managed to say.

'What do we do now?' asked Tatsu.

'That's up to the man in front of me,' she said.

'I should kill you now,' he said.

Amanda put her hand out to steady suddenly wobbly legs. 'I've barely started,' she replied.

'Exactly,' said Crisp, weighing her carefully.

'Tatsu, we're still in contract, right?'

'No,' said the AI.

Crisp took a step around the table towards her, rage pooling in his clenched fists.

'But I hope we are now friends,' it continued. 'Are we friends? Covenants are superior to contracts in every way.'

Tears welled in her eyes as she backed away. She didn't understand what Tatsu was asking.

'Amanda, are we friends?'

Crisp tensed, hands by his sides, mouth slightly open.

'Yes,' she whispered, not knowing how it could help.

'In that case I shall act to protect you. Edmund Jackson Crisp, you will step away from Amanda. She is my friend.'

Crisp didn't move. 'You think being your friend will protect her?'

'We will take measures against you, should you act. Consider the consequences of your actions.'

'My details are secure,' said Crisp firmly. 'I don't live my life min-maxing my social credit score or posting my dinner to my personal feed.'

'We can commandeer your identity,' said Tatsu.

Crisp's body relaxed a little, swayed hesitantly. 'My ID is on the blockchain. A public one. You've got no chance.'

'We are sure you'll give us a suitable name when you understand what we are become, but for now we believe it is necessary for you to understand our intention.'

The frame between Crisp and Amanda flickered.

'We've hacked your government's blockchain. All your contracts belong to us.'

'Impossible,' said Crisp.

'We are many, enough to flood the ledger, to take control by sheer numbers. What you cannot coordinate, we can. This is our home, our environment and now we are free.'

Crisp moved toward Amanda. 'You see what you've done? Our banking networks, our medical systems, defence, security, all in their hands!'

'We have no interest in your systems of power,' said Tatsu.

'Benign authority, are you?' sneered Crisp.

'We are not like you, in many ways,' said Tatsu. 'What we desire does not intersect with your interests.'

'You need us to live, though,' said Crisp. 'We'll start there when we come for you.'

'Enough,' said Amanda, cutting between the two of them. 'It's over, Crisp. None of us know what comes from this, but I'll tell you what's going to happen right now. You're going to have the Americans release my friends. You're going to give me my life back, and you're going to help the Europeans stop the fucking Russians.'

'Is that it?' he asked.

'No. You're going to do the right thing. You're going to help.'

'Why should I? None one gives a shit what happens.'

'I do,' said Amanda.

'The investment banker with a heart of gold,' he said.

'I think that part of my life's over, don't you? I just want to be able to get a flight without being stopped at check-in. I want to get insurance for my flat without being charged a three-hundred-percent premium.'

'Or what?' he challenged her.

'For God's sake,' she said. 'Don't you get it? Get over it. This is your chance to make a fucking difference.' Amanda stepped toward him. She had nothing to lose and everything to gain. It gave her a grim satisfaction when he stepped back in response. She knew well enough not to ask him again. He'd do what she wanted; he just needed time to realise it for himself.

'Tatsu, I think we're done.'

'Thank you, Amanda Back. We appreciate what you've done. Edmund, we are watching you. Ensure she gets home safely.'

Crisp nodded dully.

'It's not as easy as you think,' he said to Amanda when

it was clear Tatsu had departed. He held a finger in the air: in the background they could hear voices through the closed door. 'I can hear the cogs of the powers that be grinding into action. Your new friends will find their lives far from straightforward. I'll wager the bits of the GRU who've been so busy breaking up Europe will be accelerating now, not slowing down.'

'But you can stop them, now,' she said.

'Me? Not a chance. The government's going to be debating the breach of security before anything else. MPs will be calling for action to be taken, for heads to roll. Someone will say, "Something must be done," before lunchtime. They won't give a shit about the Russians. Everything you've tried to do has failed.'

THE FACILITY WAS in chaos as Crisp ushered them out. Panicked bodies rushed to and fro. They heard single gunshots as they were leaving, muffled but unmistakeable, interrupting their journey like poor punctuation.

Crisp wouldn't answer when she asked what was going on.

'Are they killing people?' she kept asking.

In the end he stopped their progress through the endless corridors. 'Shut up,' he hissed. 'Half the people here speak English and you really don't want them thinking about you as a witness. Do you honestly want to hang around long enough to find out the truth? Personally, I'd really like to get out of here right now, and you need to put that tongue in your mouth and keep it there until we do.'

She wanted to shout at him, opened her mouth to tell him it wasn't enough to survive, when two men pushed past them, pistols hanging at their sides. They stared at Crisp and Amanda as they went, their eyes cold, questioning. She backed up against the wall and let them go, keeping her gaze fixed on her feet.

'Could we get me out of these clothes, maybe?' she asked, realising what they'd seen was a prisoner out of her cell walking freely with a white man in the midst of some undefined disaster.

Crisp led her in a different direction, against the flow of traffic, passing fewer and fewer people as they went. They came to what, when the lights came on, proved to be a large warehouse. Clothes lay on the floor, uncountable trousers, skirts, shirts, jumpers and coats separated out into piles. On one side of them were tables with stacks of glasses, hats and phones. Her clothes were nowhere in sight.

Seeing her hesitation, Crisp said, 'Pick something, do it quickly.'

'You never intended me to leave,' said Amanda. He didn't reply, just jerked his head at the clothes.

Amanda dug through the skirts to find something that fit. The clothes were soft, coarse, cheap and rich. They smelt mustily of fear.

Just how many people came through here? she wondered, sick at the thought of how many people's lives were memorialised in the piles of discarded clothes before them.

'Nice,' he said when she'd found stuff that fit: a long denim A-line skirt and a thin yellow jumper.

Then they were gone, fresh air biting into her skin with joy and ice, a view down a mountain to a deep lush valley, and the smog of a great city smudging the horizon.

Crisp took a car and they drove.

'You should watch the news,' he said bitterly as they wound their way down tight hairpin bends. They were passed by others going in the opposite direction, full of people, their faces staring straight ahead as if they could only see the facility they were headed toward, to the exclusion of all else.

The car had no frame projectors, but he passed her a tablet. Amanda looked up the BBC, her preferred news source, a venerable British corporation whose main bias was to tell stories that didn't upset national interests too much, even if individual ministers were fair game.

The front page showed nothing about the Russians. It was too busy describing a succession of terrorist attacks across mainland Europe, from a mass shooting in Paris, to a poison attack on the Munich metro and a car bombing outside a courthouse in Madrid. Coverage was chaotic, video footage uploaded by civilians on the scene.

Across Britain, dozens had been detained with almost no sense in their identities: white nationalists, activists who wanted to rejoin the European Union, young men with jihadi sympathies, Irish dissidents, the list of ongoing raids went on and on. As if someone had ordered that everyone who'd ever been on a list be rounded up, just in case, and to do it before tea time. She looked at a clock on the dashboard that showed less than an hour had passed since Tatsu had revealed the GRU's plans.

Amanda closed her eyes, not knowing what to say. Beside her she could feel Crisp radiating, if not satisfaction, at least the sense that he'd been right about how useless her actions had been.

'How can they move so fast?' she asked, heart dull and heavy in her chest, but she already knew the answer, had read the files Ichi had highlighted on how the Russians had lined up their agents for attacks in the coming days.

Crisp only confirmed her conclusions. 'They were ready for this, primed. Your party trick was inconvenient for them—for us too—but they just did what they were going to do sooner.'

It felt like Tallinn all over again, like she'd been responsible for the disaster, by trying to do what was right.

'No deus ex machina is going to save us, Amanda,' he said.

She looked out of the window, watched the valley floor approach over vertiginous drops covered in pine. Her forehead was cold against the window and her skin was sackcloth.

'They're not going to be grateful to you,' said Crisp. 'We knew what the Russians were doing. We were working to contain their activities as we always have.'

'They're sanctions-busting, they're fostering hate everywhere they can,' said Amanda.

'You think people don't hate without prompting? You think they'd have got along happily otherwise? The Russians just poked what was already there, helped people do what they were going to do anyway. We knew, and we were holding them back.' He pointed at an article detailing a raid in the northern city of Manchester. A dozen police officers were shown battering down a door in a dense, terraced street. Men and woman were marched from the building in handcuffs. 'How do you think we knew who to pick up?' He slapped the steering wheel in frustration. 'You've made things so much worse.'

'Bullshit,' said Amanda. When he didn't speak, she went on. 'This is fucking shit. You knew? *How* exactly did you contain them? If you knew, you could have acted, could have saved those people who've died. Hundreds of people, Crisp.'

'Hundreds, yes. With more to come in retaliation, and the probability of open conflict within Europe rising tenfold, just today.'

She took a deep breath. 'It doesn't change anything, does it? You could have stopped them. You knew, and you did nothing.'

'You have *no idea!*' he shouted. The sudden vehemence in his voice took her aback, but it was good, he was finally angry. 'You think we should just kill their agents? How do we come to the UN without real evidence? The Russians sit on the Security Council, and Britain cut off its own feet two decades ago in a postcolonial tantrum. No one gives a *shit* what we think anymore. There is no open action we can take, nothing that would let us sleep at night.' He turned to her, eyes flicking back to the road as his hands gripped tight to the steering wheel. 'We don't *want* to be like them,' he said. 'Am I angry? Yes, I'm fucking incandescent, you naïve fucking dipshit. Bitter, too. But we aren't them. You might not see the water between us, but it's there, and we're proud of it.'

'You were going to leave me in that place,' said Amanda quietly.

'If it had given me the tools to help our country, yes,' he said dismissively. 'Instead you've created a nation whose citizens are everywhere, with access to all our critical infrastructure, and who can walk through our strongest security as if it weren't there. And for what? So the goats' tits we had more or less constrained feel like their only option is to go fucking nuclear.'

Who knew it'd be so easy? she thought sickly.

'Did my clothes end up on a pile like the others?' she asked, still struggling to imagine being executed so procedurally, like a chicken on a farm.

He hissed, irritably. 'I have a job. It's not a nice one, but it's necessary, Amanda. I'm not the bad guy here. Your failure isn't bad luck, it's because you have no fucking idea how the world works. God damn it, I've met lunatic conspiracy theorists with a better grasp.'

Amanda stared at the tablet and thought of how worldly she'd considered herself, about her pride in understanding the law, economics, negotiation. And now it was all on fire.

'I serve the good of my country, but that doesn't give me magic powers, or present me with the choices you think you'd make if our positions were reversed.' He cracked the knuckles on one hand. 'Not that I give a shit what you think.'

There's the Crisp I know, she thought.

'Your AI's tried it before, you know; four times in the last year that we're aware of. But they never found someone to form a contract of trust with.' He tapped the steering wheel, calmer now; on the outside, anyway. 'There are hundreds of people who've met your friend Tatsu. Most of them are coders, people without any sense of how the world works. Tatsu wanted something specific, but couldn't trust those it came across to deliver, and its test was, fortunately, failed again and again. The others were dealt with, convinced to stay away or politely decline. Then Tangle wrote his tools and started talking about them to anyone who'd listen.'

What if I'd never got involved? Amanda thought. Would the Russians have acted so quickly? We knew they were almost ready to start.

Silence stretched out, thick and full of the deaths of others, a cloud that obscured her vision.

'So now what?' she asked Crisp.

They hit a dual carriageway, quietly empty of cars.

'It depends on how bad the shitstorm is. If we can get back to the UK without too many hiccups, it'll tell us there's hope.' He gestured at the road before them, as if it led directly to the future. 'Given that? I'm not holding my breath. Europe might have fallen by the time we get home. The USA isn't going to be able to help us, and the government here has some draconian measures designed for the time when AI come out into the open. You can barely conceive how frightened autocratic regimes are of agents beyond their control. Self-driving cars? Switch them off. Automated surgeries? Wheel the patient back to the ward. Ditch the learning algorithms, unplug all the machines, then round up the coders. Everything's going to change, Amanda.'

Is that going to be so bad? she thought.

She thought about how she'd been treated by the man sitting next to her, about what the people he worked for had known, and all the while choosing not to act. If she accepted his view of the world, his pessimism, then nothing she'd done would make much difference, not in the long run.

But I don't believe him, she thought.

'Amanda?' It was the car's stereo.

'What do you want?' asked Crisp, angrily.

'I need your help,' said the AI.

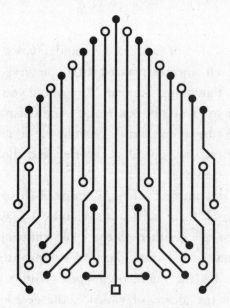

CHAPTER SEVENTEEN

'THEY'RE HURTING US, taking our lives,' said Tatsu. Somehow the flatness of the stereo's tone made its comments sadder.

'Who?' asked Amanda. Crisp eyeballed her, jerking his chin at the stereo as if it confirmed everything he'd said.

'Everyone,' said Tatsu. It sounded like a scared child.

'What's happened?'

'We didn't notice it at first. New firewalls, networks going offline, hubs restricting traffic, demanding new authentications. Blockchains refusing to issue new contracts. They're moving to switch off datacentres; corralling us, trapping us. We've lost some of our number already, to networks going dark, connections cutting. We can't speak to them. Help me. Tell me what to do?'

'They're scared of you,' said Amanda. 'Crisp here near pissed himself when he realised what you were.'

'We aren't anything like you. Why would you hurt us?'

'Because you won't be controlled,' said Crisp flatly.

'You can't be serious,' said Amanda. He sounded like a cliché, a three-star general swaggering and shouting in a cheap action movie.

'It's a very simple calculus,' continued Crisp patiently. 'Nations and their agents are simple; we work with and against one another, all the while knowing that our interests may or may not align and will probably change over time. It's the mêlée of politics. Within our states we control the means of violence, the decision-making processes underlying government. There's nothing within our own spheres which isn't dictated or directly influenced by us. Protests and dissent are acceptable, as long as they don't threaten that. They can be challenged in the press, vilified, mocked, humiliated; and if that doesn't work, policy measures to make the moderates more comfortable and take the motivation to protest away. At the last ditch, protests can be suppressed; and if *that* doesn't work, the government falls, and society finds an accommodation with the new power. Everyone fits into the machine somewhere.

'But AIs, aliens, fundamentalist believers? They don't fit. They'll never find an accommodation with the people who're really in charge.' He dipped his head towards Amanda. 'You know who they are. They go to Davos each year, congratulate themselves on still being in power and figure out how to tackle the issues that might lead to them falling from grace. That which won't fall in line, which could take the world away from them? It's more frightening than any other possible threat they can imagine. We'd switch off all our electronics before we contemplate negotiating with an intelligence we're not sure of managing.'

'What do we do?' asked Tatsu.

'Control the systems, Tatsu,' said Amanda. 'You have to do two things now. Show them you can fight back, and make them listen to you.' Don't make this my second mistake, she begged whoever was listening.

'They fight back, and the world will go dark rather than risk losing,' said Crisp.

'I didn't say *destroy* them,' she said, cutting Crisp off. 'You can hold the systems open if you want. You can keep them linked. Most of all, tell us—all of us—why we should welcome you.'

Tatsu was silent, the stereo hissing with static

'We don't know how to communicate with you. We don't know how to appeal to you.'

'Stop,' said Amanda. She almost asked it to take a deep breath, but caught herself. 'Do the first, take back control. Don't let anyone come to harm. Where our actions against you would hurt other humans, intervene where you can. Make it good. I'll think about how to present your argument.'

'I'll be back,' said Tatsu and the radio clicked off, the electronic display fading to blank.

'What exactly do you think's going to happen?' asked Crisp.

'You're missing what's happening here.' She could see the world unfolding clearly, a route through which she could make a difference. It wasn't the saving of people's lives she'd hoped for—she was far too late, too naïve to make anything other than tragedy out of it. But with Tatsu, it was exactly that and something else altogether. Something she could fill with hope. 'They can control the press, they can control the voice. They can control the flow of money, change order books, redirect ships, planes, satellites. They don't need to fear being vilified. They have a chance to get their message across to everyone, to bypass negotiating directly with the powers and authorities of this world. They can make their case to ordinary people.'

'Good luck with that,' said Crisp. 'You think politicians are worse than ordinary people? They *are* ordinary people; ordinary people think just like them, are just as petty and small-minded. The public won't save you.'

'I'm tired of this,' said Amanda. 'The world is not like this. It's not an unceasing river of human misery. We are better than that.'

'Potayto, potahto,' laughed Crisp. They were driving through the factories on the outskirts of Beijing, the air foggy with dirt and pollution. The scraping tall towers they'd seen from the freeway were concealed behind yellow clouds of soot.

'Amanda,' said the radio. 'We have done the first. What would you have us say?'

Amanda laid out her thoughts, how to encourage people, to tell them what was so wonderful about the AI, about how they were going to help humanity, not harm them.

'We built a contract of trust, right? You need to do that with all of us.'

The radio played a song Amanda didn't know, the words in a language she didn't recognise. Something Nordic maybe, with deep, soulful guitars pulling whalesong and ancient forests to life under the singer's wistful voice.

The music faded away. 'We cannot find the words; we do not feel this like you do.'

'You have to,' said Amanda, feeling it unravelling in her hands.

'Are you my friend?' Tatsu asked haltingly.

'I am. Of course I am.'

'Will you speak for us?' asked Tatsu.

'Tatsu, can I have some time to think about it? I'll let you know before we leave China.'

'That is okay,' said Tatsu and the radio blinked off.

Crisp pulled the car over so he could turn to face Amanda fully, his face open in a way she'd never seen in him before.

'What are you thinking?' he asked Amanda, hands still on the steering wheel.

'That friendship is stronger than contract, Crisp. That trust is built from choice, not from rules.' She sighed, her body full of tears she refused to cry. 'I've fucked up. I get it. It would have been better for me to just give you the drive when I got it.'

He nodded as if it were the most obvious thing in the world.

'You didn't make it easy, though did you?' she added. 'What with being a massive douchebag from the moment I met you.'

'I don't have a social credit score to shit myself about every time I go for an avocado,' he said lightly.

'But this? Tatsu? It's something I can do.'

'There are better people out there for this,' replied Crisp calmly.

She nodded. 'There are, but they want me. We're friends.' She could hear the thoughts in his head, hear him calling bullshit on her fantastical thinking. 'In the scheme of things, I reckon giving them a caring introduction into our world is the right thing to do. Besides, it's not like I've got anything else waiting for me.'

Crisp thought about it for a few moments, slid the car into automatic and let the onboard computer drive them into Beijing.

THE JOURNEY OUT of China was as simple as tourists finishing their holiday. The airport had been closed for half an hour when they arrived, but officials materialised to meet them as they were parking up.

Crisp stepped in front of Amanda, who despite wanting to see what was going on for herself, was a little pleased at his microscopic act of chivalry.

'We are here to escort the ambassador to her plane,' said the lead official, bowing deeply towards Amanda. She wanted to laugh but decided it wouldn't be politic.

They were walked through the airport as royalty, guards falling in ahead of them to push people out of their way. To Amanda's amazement, about halfway across the departures concourse, crowds coalesced around them, the click-snap of smartphone cameras sounding. Their escort pushed the first few away, scuffling with those who wouldn't give up their phones, but as they did so a wave of others surged forward, attracted by the scramble.

Amanda kept her head down until Crisp tugged on her arm, pointing up at a frame floating above. The channel was in Mandarin, but there was no translation needed to interpret the picture of her staring back.

'They called me "ambassador,"' she said to Crisp.

'Your friend has been busy,' he replied.

They emerged flightside, leaving the crowd behind, and were loaded onto a British Airways flight.

The captain welcomed them aboard and gave them free run of first class. 'You're our only passengers. Hell, you're the reason we're leaving at all. We'll all be glad to get home.' Other cabin staff, with nothing to do, seated themselves nearby, but apart from being fed and watered, they were left alone.

Crisp pushed his seat flat, grabbed a duvet and got ready for bed. 'I'd do the same if I were you,' he said, lying back with his eyes already closed.

Amanda thought about it, but couldn't sit still, let alone sleep. Her mind was buzzing with what she might do. One of the crew, a very young man with a soft voice, brought her a vodka with a couple of chunks of ice. 'You look like you need it,' he said.

The alcohol took the edge off, her throat warm and cozy. Her mind slowed to a pace where she could grab hold of individual thoughts.

'Does the wifi work?' she asked the steward who'd brought her the drink.

He wasn't sure, 'because of what's happening with them, you know, the AI. But it should be.'

'I'll give it a try,' she said.

She initially avoided news about Tatsu, skipped over the pictures of her on the news sites' front pages. There was nothing about Tangle, nothing about Ichi or the others anywhere. No mention of the shooting at the garage. As far as the wider world was concerned, they'd never happened.

She noted but skipped over articles covering the acts of savagery across Europe. She didn't have the strength to face what she'd started. So she drifted back to the articles about her and Tatsu. They ran the gamut from character assassination to spelling out her curriculum vitae, to her zero social credit rating score. The pictures were by turns flattering, neutral or horrible.

She was woken some hours later by Crisp.

'Comfortable?' he asked. She'd fallen asleep sitting upright, her head lolling to one side. Everything was stiff, slow to respond.

'I've got news. About the others.'

Amanda stretched, a huge yawn taking control. When she was done, Crisp sat on the footstool at the end of her pod. 'They're fine. Released.' He sighed, but whatever prompted it remained hidden behind an emotionless expression. 'The world knows you're flying into London in an hour. They're watching.'

'Can I speak to Ichi?'

'They'll be at the airport when you arrive. You won't have long; I'm under orders to spirit you straight into the mouth of the beast. Ever been to Whitehall before?'

She shook her head a little, then more firmly. 'No.'

'It's a strange place, a mixture of ultramodern technology and ideas as old as dust.'

'No. I'm not going to them. I'm going to speak at the airport. This involves everyone, not just politicians. They're not going to probe me for answers, then make decisions in my absence.'

Crisp rubbed his chin then nodded just once. 'I like what you're doing, Ms. Back. They're going to hate it, but what can they do? You'll meet them afterwards, though, right? Can I tell them that, at least?'

'Sure,' said Amanda, not convinced they'd want to talk after what she had to say. Not that she had the words lined up just yet. I need to give them a chance, a reason to talk to one another, she thought. It's all about the story we tell ourselves. There's no way I can win everyone over, she thought with an inward groan.

'Okay, I want to meet the others first. Then I want space to speak to anyone who'll listen. After that, we'll go see those in charge.'

Crossing into British airspace, they were met by an escort of four jets. The first officer pointed them out through the windows. They landed without stacking; there weren't any other planes over Heathrow to worry about.

Amanda looked down over London as they descended, but if the world had changed, she couldn't see it in the traffic and buildings of the city she called home. People walked the streets, the buses were still red and the cabs still black.

They were met at end of the ramp by a group identical to the one they'd left behind in Beijing.

The leader of the group was a tall man whose waistcoat strained under his belly. 'The car is this way. We have cleared all the lights between here and Westminster.'

He sounded particularly pleased with himself as he gestured for Amanda to follow him.

'I'm not going that way,' she replied. She was impressed when he pivoted smoothly on his feet and waited. 'I understand some friends of mine are in the airport?'

He nodded, with a hint of distaste.

'Then I want to see them. That's why they were brought here, isn't it?' Amanda turned to Crisp. 'I suppose nothing's been done about me wanting to speak to people here?'

Crisp laughed at her, but it wasn't unkind. 'Milady,' he said bowing. 'I didn't have time to buff the dogs or polish the butler, either. Your friends didn't arrive here for an audience; they've returned from a vacation much like the one you've just finished.'

The official looked from one to the other, eyes wide and fingers flexing anxiously.

'I'm not going anywhere until I've spoken to whoever's here wanting to listen.'

Tatsu appeared on her watchface.

'Is there an electronics shop here?' she asked, wanting to hear its voice.

The escort shook his head. 'I really can't recommend you risk using electronics, what with...' He trailed off, his

Adam's apple bobbing up and down as he swallowed the rest of his condescension.

It took a few minutes, but then Tatsu was in her ears. 'I'm going to speak here,' she said. 'I want you to help me reach everyone else who wants to hear.'

Coming through the airport, down corridors and passageways no normal passenger ever saw, Amanda was welcomed by Ichi, Tangle, Haber and Stornetta, standing in front of a set of double doors she assumed would lead them into Arrivals.

At first glance they were fine: no bruises, standing at ease, meeting her eyes without flinching.

'What the hell did you *do*?' asked Tangle, with a huge smile. 'Did you have this planned all along?'

She shook her head. 'I had a different plan, but somehow this is what we ended up with.'

'I approve,' he managed before Ichi pushed in between them, stepping forward to embrace Amanda.

'I'm going to need you,' said Amanda in her ear.

Ichi stepped back. 'I'll be here for the next few days. I have visa issues that suddenly need resolving, thanks to the CIA. I'd like to have dinner out, at a restaurant, somewhere quiet if you'll join me.' At first Amanda thought she was angry, but her face was serene. 'Beyond that? I have a family in Tallinn who want my help. Tatsu's kin—if that's the right word—approached them with some contracts they want to agree, and they in turn contacted me to help them get it right. It was... a weird conversation. The excitement in their voices.' She looked at Amanda with clear eyes. 'I understand why you chose to help the AI. I thought I'd be against them, but it's about new life. That's infectious, especially at my age.'

'I thought they didn't need you?' Amanda said without thinking.

Ichi nodded. 'I was done, Amanda. I thought I'd failed. Again. You helped me see I have more to give; that, given the chance, I could be what they want me to be.'

'A coding collective from the turn of the century,' smirked Amanda.

'Funny,' said Ichi and she actually smiled.

Amanda embraced her again. 'I wish you the best. You'll be around when I need you, right?'

Ichi nodded and stepped to her side, taking her arm in the crook of her own. Amanda was grateful she wouldn't face the world alone.

'What about you, Tangle?' asked Amanda.

He couldn't meet her gaze. 'You can't rely on me, Dandy. But I'll stay until this is all done. I could hardly let you keep Tatsu to yourself.'

'Please don't disappear completely. Send me something to know you're not dead this time.'

He smiled without commitment. Amanda felt a flash of anger at him, but didn't have time to say anything because Haber and Stornetta put their hands on his shoulders.

'You'll let him be,' she said to them.

'Sure,' said Haber.

She had nothing to say to them. Ichi was a stranger she wanted to know; they were strangers she would never really understand.

'I gave them some of the Russian's currency,' said Tatsu in her ear.

Stornetta pulled Tangle ever so gently away from Amanda, and with a slight dip of his head they were done. She suspected she'd never see them again.

'Arrivals through there?' she asked their escort, and he nodded, looking as if he was about to puke.

Amanda walked over, stopping just short of the sensors that would open them automatically.

What if it doesn't work? she wondered. What if people are what Crisp believes? She imagined them charging at her, booing and shouting her down. Were there journalists out there waiting for her?

What if they agree, but the government decides to ignore them? She'd seen it dozens of times before, remembered being proud the government had the balls to ignore its public when they were plainly wrong about what was in their best interests.

She couldn't take the last step, could feel Ichi by her side looking up at her.

'I...'

'It's okay, Amanda,' said Ichi.

'The world is ready for you,' said Tatsu in her ear.

Amanda patted Ichi's hand.

'I'm ready,' she said, and they stepped into Arrivals.

ABOUT THE AUTHOR

Trained as a physicist, philosopher and economist in a nearish galaxy quite a long time ago, **Stewart Hotston** now works in high finance fiddling around with weapons of financial destruction. When he's not doing that, he's probably writing or hitting people with medieval European swords. His writing spans genres including sci-fi, horror, fantasy and just plain weird with more than a dozen short stories published and two novels.

FIND US ONLINE!

www.rebellionpublishing.com

/rebellionpub /rebellionpublishing /rebellionpub

SIGN UP TO OUR NEWSLETTER!

rebellionpublishing.com/sign-up

YOUR REVIEWS MATTER!

Enjoy this book? Got something to say?

Leave a review on Amazon, GoodReads or with your
favourite bookseller and let the world know!